D1260187

LEAVING TOMORROW

Also by David Bergen

The Age of Hope (2012)

The Matter with Morris (2010)

The Retreat (2008)

The Time in Between (2005)

The Case of Lena S. (2002)

See the Child (1999)

A Year of Lesser (1996)

Sitting Opposite My Brother (1993)

LEAVING TOMORROW

A Novel

DAVID BERGEN

HarperCollins*Publishers*Ltd

Leaving Tomorrow
Copyright © 2014 by David Bergen
All rights reserved.

Published by HarperCollins Publishers Ltd

First edition

HarperCollins books may be purchased for educational, business,
or sales promotional use through our Special Markets Department.

HarperCollins Publishers Ltd
2 Bloor Street East, 20th Floor
Toronto, Ontario, Canada
M4W 1A8

www.harpercollins.ca

Library and Archives Canada Cataloguing in Publication
information is available upon request

ISBN 978-1-44341-138-7

Printed and bound in the United States of America
RRD 9 8 7 6 5 4 3 2 1

To L

But beyond this, my son, be warned: the writing of many books is endless, and excessive devotion to books is wearying to the body.

—ECCLESIASTES 12:12

LEAVING TOMORROW

I.

....

I Am Telling You This

To be an individual, to make one's way, to shape and form oneself in a unique manner, to live forever, to love and be loved, to know what I want, to rise and fall and then rise again, to speak the truth. This is essential.

I was born on a seiner off the coast of northern British Columbia at 3 p.m. on Wednesday, January 23, 1955. We lived in a small fishing village, Port Edward, and on that day a squall had to pass before we followed the coastline to the local hospital in Prince Rupert. By the time the boat set sail, my mother was down in the hold shamelessly baring herself. The rain fell sideways, dark clouds toiled above the boat, and she, who never used the Lord's name in vain, cried out once to God. The imprint of her fingernails on the arm of my father. She vomited beside the small bed, onto his shoes, and he wiped the vomit from her mouth with a dirty towel. She babbled and moaned and then announced that it was time.

She reached down with a sure hand to feel my crown, touching the soft spot of the skull, anointing my brain. I leaped at her touch. And leaped again. She sat up and crouched and panted and took hold of my head with both hands and her biceps bulged and she said *Ohhh* and I slid out onto the sheet between her legs. She gathered me up, placed her mouth over my nose and sucked up the fluid. Spit on the floor. With her right hand she cleaned my eyes and mouth. I did not speak. She held my feet between her fingers and capsized me over her lap. She touched the tiny walnut that was my scrotum.

"A boy," she said. I cried out.

And so I arrived, surrounded by the fish moving within the darkness of the Pacific Ocean. My mother, a nurse, told my father how to cut the cord with the scissors from her medical kit. Her voice was low and soft and I turned my large head to seek out the source. The boat rose and fell with the high waves, like the waves I had felt in her belly as she walked every day from the house to the small clinic where she vaccin-ated the Indian and Japanese children. She lined the fright-ened things up and then called them one by one, saying softly that this won't hurt, just a little prick, and then, as a reward for their stoicism, she handed out licorice candies, individually wrapped.

My mother's father was a former missionary turned dairy farmer who liked to dress up in fine clothes for supper, just as his own father had back in Russia before his furniture factory was taken by the Reds and his uncle was shot by the bandit Makhno, which is a story I would hear, and hear again, as a testament to faith and strength and forgiveness in the face of lost wealth. My grandfather was a consummate reader of both Tolstoy and the Old Testament, and he announced that I should be named Jonah, or Noah, or Ishmael, or if none of those, then Leo, after the greatest writer that ever lived. My father said that I should be Moses. My mother, who deferred to no one, called me Arthur Jacob.

I had an older brother and sister, Bev and Em. Em carried me in her arms and named to me the fish of the sea that lay in the holds of the boats and were then spilled out onto the wooden docks. She was five at the time, but her arms were strong and her chest was warm and I was her baby brother and I was something important to protect and hold. She saw me as her living breathing doll, and she dressed me in clothes that were girlish and dainty, and dandling me, she sang rhymes that still come to me unbidden, as if from a dim place in the corner of my brain that has gone unused for a long while, and then is brightly lit.

> *Two years old*
> *Going on three.*
> *I wear my dress*
> *Above my knee.*
>
> *I walk in the rain.*
> *I walk in the snow.*

It's nobody's business
If I got a beau.

We walked the streets of that small fishing village. She pushed me in a wheelbarrow and up the hill we climbed, and down the hill we ran, me bouncing, my mouth agape, Em calling out, "Whoosh, whoosh, whoosh."

At eight months I took sick. My breathing faltered and my temperature rose. One afternoon I turned blue as I sucked ragged breaths, my mouth moving like one of those fish that has been thrown up onto land. My mother bundled me in a wool blanket and carried me down to the docks, where she hired a boat to take me to the hospital in Prince Rupert. Before the boat left, my father, certain that I would die on the voyage, took a photograph of me in my mother's arms. The camera was a Miranda T 35mm SLR, and it looked at me with its one eye that opened and closed with a soft click. That photograph no longer exists. That is to say, I have never seen it.

The doctor at the hospital insisted that I remain there for two weeks. My mother, bereft but practical, returned home. I was placed on a ward with seven other babies of varying sizes and temperaments, two of whom died from meningitis before I was discharged. Apparently they suffered the same fever I did, only I conquered mine, though in later years the effects of that fever would follow me and haunt me and feed me. At night, all alone, I tossed and turned and cried and cried, which was a good thing according to the doctor, who said that my lungs could only improve with all that howling.

The night nurse, a young Métis woman named Hildegaard, whose skin carried the scent of citrus and tobacco, took pity on me, and when she had finished her duties, she came to me and picked me up and rocked me through the night. Her hair was dark, her eyes were dark, her mouth when she spoke to me was a dark hole into which I stared, and yet for all the darkness, she was a light that shone down and warmed me. She was a new mother herself and she discovered early on that though I liked my bottle, I was quietest when she unbuttoned the top of her uniform and offered me her full breast, which I happily took. She whispered and sang and told me I was a big boy and a handsome boy and that the girls, well, they would flock to me. As she suckled me I opened and closed my little hands and I studied her crooked eyetooth until I fell into a sleep and dreamed of fish with orange bellies that had travelled thousands of miles to fight their way up a river to the place where they would lay their eggs and then die.

On our last night together she cooed into my ear as she changed my cloth diaper, and I got so wound up I peed all over her crisp uniform. She laughed and sucked my pudgy hand and said, "*Bahbahbah*, you naughty boy."

After I was discharged, I missed Hildegaard dearly. My small heart was broken into pieces, a suffering so acute and painful that for the rest of my life I have been aware of how a lover can pierce the soul and then take flight.

At home again, I cried and cried in the hope that my mother would offer me her breast. At night when she picked me up and I burrowed into her chest looking for a nipple, she laughed and pushed me away and said, "Oh, you just stop that right there." And so I played with my own ear and stroked my own jaw, and my loins moved. They still move to this day when I hear the name *Hildegaard*, or I smell the zest from a lemon, or I pass by a young dark-eyed woman smoking on the street, or sometimes, in the early morning when shaving, I lean towards the mirror and touch my own chin.

WHEN I TURNED ONE, MY MOTHER CARED FOR TAMIKO, a Japanese girl my age whose parents worked in the canning factory. Tamiko and I sat together on the living room floor, fighting over the toy tractors in my playbox and eating "mother-and-child"—made with chicken and egg—that Em spooned up for us, one for Tamiko, two for Arthur. Tamiko's eyes were dark and her face was flat and she smelled of fried fish, and sometimes, in the late afternoon, worn out, we slept side by side, our arms touching. We were both early walkers, and as I wandered the house she followed me, clutching and grasping. Her father, Haruki, owned his own fishing boat, the same purse seiner on which I had been born that wet January morning. And so we had much in common, and if our family had stayed in that small fishing village, I am certain I would have married her and lived the life of a man who heads out to sea in the morning and returns in the evening to hold his woman with hands that smell of Chinook salmon and black cod.

However, a child's fate is decided by adults and by circumstance and by contingency. The contingency in this case was the death of my sister Em.

It was summer and we were on holiday near Tofino, camping close to a beach where Em and Bev played in the waves while I sat naked in the sand between my mother's legs. My mother read. She held the book before her so that I too could see the words and lines and page numbers and her fingers at the edges of the pages. While we were reading, and while I scanned the pages and felt my mother's chest rise and fall behind me, my sister Em was drowning. She was caught by a large wave and thrown down with the surf and she broke her neck and the sea water entered her lungs and she died. My brother Bev saw her disappear and then waited and he waited some more, and when she did not reappear, he ran up to where my mother and I sat reading. He said that he couldn't find Em.

My mother dropped her book in the sand and she threw me aside and ran towards the water's edge. Her long brown legs, her red bathing suit, her arms reaching up to hold her hair from her face. She plunged into the surf up to her waist and then back out again, all the while calling, "Em. Em. Oh my God, Em." Several other people on the beach approached and helped her with her search. My father, who had been back at the campsite, appeared and ran into the water, diving and returning to the surface and diving again. Bev stood with his chin in the air, his eyes wide open, a frightened and reluctant witness, and then he ran, up the beach and behind some grey and forbidding rocks, where he was found an hour later, huddled and sniffling.

I, on the other hand, was curious and so I stood and moved down to the shore. A breeze passed over my skin and gave me goose bumps. The waves fell around my feet and as they returned to the ocean I felt the pull outwards. It was a lovely feeling and so I stepped deeper into the water, which now swirled around my bare bottom. I sat down from the force of a wave and rolled onto my back, drinking the salt water. My eyes burned. I coughed and sputtered. I rolled into deeper water, moving my arms. My feet were in the air, my head under water. Perhaps I was looking for Em. Perhaps I was simply another drowning child. The water was cold. And then I was lifted high into the air by my mother, who was screaming my name and God's name and Em's name. She laid me down on the sand and her frantic and beautiful face descended and her mouth went over mine and she breathed into me. I sputtered. I spit out the sea water. She held me to her chest and wept.

For a period of time after Em's death, my mother went away. She was certainly there physically, but she became colder. And more pitiless. Not immediately, and certainly she would deny my assertions, but after Em died, she talked to me in a different way, as if from behind a thick veil, and when she held me she did so as if I were an odd child, not hers, but someone else's, or perhaps she wished that I were someone else's and then she would be free from distractions. I am telling you this.

A MONTH AFTER EM DIED, AFTER THE FUNERAL AND with my parents still deeply grieving, my family moved to a ranch near Tomorrow, south of Calgary. My father was a restless man who couldn't abide working for others, but in this case he found an amicable rancher named Chester Dewey who had several thousand acres and eight hundred head of cattle and who needed a man to break horses. Dewey came from an American family out of Montana that had bought land in southern Alberta in the late 1860s. They built up a large ranch and then when oil was discovered, they received the mineral rights. And so Dewey was a wealthy man who approached ranching as a hobby. He had a wrangler's cabin set far back from his ranch house, and it was there that our family lived. We caught glimpses of the regal life the Deweys lived, the parties, the fundraisers for the local politicians, the servants, the large library organized by Dewey's wife Anna. She would give me access to all those books—until I became too close to her daughter Alice, and then the library would be closed to my comings and goings.

We had moved for various reasons. The Alberta climate was drier, which was good for my lungs, my mother was bereft and longed to run away from the ocean, and my father, who had grown up in Montana, wanted to have a go at something he understood and loved. His blond hair was long and shaggy and he favoured a goatee. He wore a Sheplers 20X cowboy hat and Justin Full-Quill Ostrich boots. His jeans were tight, his hands were rough. My parents had met when my father was a bull rider. He had come up to the Stampede in Calgary and was kicked in the gut and ended up on the hospital ward where my mother was working. The first thing she said to him was, "There are only two things you'll see on the back of a bull. A fly and a fool." She was cleaning a wound at his right hip and in doing so she had to work near his groin. He closed his eyes. She didn't.

He said, "Maybe a male nurse would suit me better."

She looked at him. "I've seen men before." She tossed her head in the direction of his crotch. "This one's nothing special."

"Doreen," he said.

"That's me."

"I'm just a little embarrassed."

"Because the bull beat you up?"

He grinned. "When I'm up and about again, you might want to see me."

"See you?"

"Yeah. Maybe go out on a date. Grab a drink."

"I don't drink."

"That's fine. A soda, a milk shake."

"I don't go out with men who drink."

"I just quit."

"I'm not loose, or easily pleased."

"I didn't think so."

"Neither am I sentimental, so don't bring me flowers."

"I understand."

"I'm not sure you do."

"How's that?"

"I'm not interested in being wooed."

"Okay."

"We'll go out for a soda, we'll talk, and if I like what I see, we might meet again."

"How about so far? How do you like it?"

She shrugged and walked away.

My mother was the fifth daughter of Mennonite Brethren missionaries who did church planting in Tanzania and Ecuador. She grew up running barefoot in villages near the Serengeti, and listening to her father preach the gospel on the radio in Guayaquil. She was sent away for her education, boarding at international schools in Nairobi and Quito. She spoke Spanish and Swahili and she carried in her the seed of pining that my father recognized as independence and forcefulness. Perhaps he saw my mother as a wild mustang that he would tame. It was not to be. She was religious in a straightforward and simple manner, and after she ascertained that he was a Christian, the first thing she asked of him was that he be baptized as an adult. No sprinkling or pouring, but complete immersion, which was the right way.

He was baptized by her father one cool spring day in the Bow River, just after the ice had broken up. It was a Friday morning and the family gathered along the bank. The sun was pale and weak, and there were geese floating amongst the chunks of blue ice. My father went under and rose from the river with a sharp cry. My mother's sisters clapped and sang. My mother wrapped my father in a wool blanket as he stumbled from the river and she kissed him on the forehead and whispered his name, James.

They were married that same week, on a Sunday, back in Abbotsford, where my mother's parents had settled and her father had purchased a dairy farm. My mother was not terribly pleased to be taking my father's name, Walker. Her family name was Wohlgemuht and she bristled at the fact that she would lose the solidity and meaning of her Russian-German-Mennonite heritage.

"Walker is a strong name," my father said. "It means 'to walk or tread.'" He grinned.

"Does nothing for me," my mother said.

My father, believing he could not lose, suggested that she set up some form of competition between the two families. "Not a quilting bee, with four sisters you're a shoo-in, but maybe something more physical, like calf roping, or a horse race." He grinned again. My mother said she would think about it. The next day she suggested a milking contest. But not just any old cow. It would be a contest involving wild cows that had just calved. One cow per group and the first to produce a quart would win. Winner would keep the family name. My father had two brothers, Alistair and John. They too had been raised on a ranch and they knew animals, but none of the brothers had spent much time milking. Even so, my father thought that there couldn't be much difficulty in milking a cow, even if it was wild. The brothers were strong of hand and hardy, with forearms like forged iron. And so he agreed.

The thing about wild cows is they have no interest in being milked. The cow will be outraged and ornery and have no truck with having its teats touched by human hands. Typically, one person will rope and hold the head while another pulls at the tail, so the image is that of two wranglers playing at tug of war. A third person will do the milking, trying to avoid being kicked by a stray hoof. The sisters, with their soft voices and soft hands, wrestled a gunnysack over the cow's head, and while one sister held the roped head in place, two of them stretched the tail, and another talked nonsense into the cow's ear, while the fifth, my mother, did the milking. They won easily. The men's cow was tearing around the pen with my father dragging behind, holding its tail, when the women held up their quart of milk, declaring victory. The brothers were astounded, and utterly impressed. So impressed that Alistair and John went on to marry two of my mother's sisters, Beth and Cathleen. And so it turned out that at family gatherings there were numerous double cousins running around, which became confusing because two of us had the last name of Wohlgemuht.

My brother Bev was born nine months after the wedding, and my sister Em a year after that. I made my entrance four years further on, a bit of a surprise, unplanned, ten pounds of sinew and heart and blood and desire. Arthur, Art, Arturo. My mother called me all of these.

I took to lying between my parents at night. It had been a long battle to get there, but my mother, who drove into Calgary every day before the sun rose to work the twelve-hour shift at the Foothills Hospital, couldn't sleep when I banged the wall or shook my crib, and so she broke down and took me into bed with her. I found that the best position was to lie on my back with arms outstretched so that I could touch both of my parents. My mother allowed me to grasp her cotton nightgown, or to curl a fist near the furrow of her breasts, or to touch her neck, but my father, who slept naked, had no clothing to hold. The three of us purred through the night as the wind howled up the valley and rattled the windows and a hard sleet poured over the roof.

In the morning, when it was still dark, we talked. First about the Dodge that mother drove to the city. It was faltering and needed to be replaced. There was no money. My father said that he would look into it. This usually meant that nothing would be done, because my father, a dreamer, had other fish to fry. Then we talked about Em, and these conversations were usually interrupted by tears and then silence, and then the three of us holding each other. What we did not talk about was my mother's warm-weather lunch ritual, when she left the hospital and drove to a nearby girls' school where she parked the car on the street, rolled down her windows, and listened to the music of girls at play, the slap of the rope on the pavement, the chant of *Two little dickie birds*, and in her bravest moments, she lifted her head and caught sight of seven-year-old Theresa hanging from the monkey bars by her legs, dark hair tumbling down down down, and then, released by the sound of the headmistress's voice calling out, "Time, girls," and the bright shrill whistle that followed, Theresa performed a neat somersault, completed a perfect two-point landing in the sand, and with a happy cry, her rail-like arms flailing, she disappeared. Oh my. About this, in bed together, we did not speak. Then, when the sadness threatened to overwhelm us, we talked about Bev, who was obstreperous and had run away one morning because he hated school and wanted to help on the ranch. My father chuckled at this. He was pleased.

My father said that Chester Dewey was asking him to break horses that were too young. "He's impatient. Ride a two-year-old and you'll end up with a swayback. I told him that."

"These aren't your horses, James."

"Two and a half at the earliest is what I said. I can't do my job with Dewey snorting orders."

My father had a hard time keeping jobs. He usually ended up arguing with the boss and walking away. My mother worried that this was another one of those situations, and she said that the boys didn't need another change in their lives.

"Too much," she said.

My father said, "Fine, Dewey'll end up with a stable of horses with weak vertebrae that all go lame. Some folks are always in a hurry to get what they want, and then when they get it they end up sorry."

My mother said that he worried too much about the animals.

When she was quiet, he talked of the wolves that were hungry after the long winter and had descended from the north, or come down from the foothills to seek food. A heifer had been killed along the fenceline near the Granger place. He'd found the carcass in the coulee near the Texas gate. "I'll take Bev up with me and we'll check it out. I'll ride him in the bow of the saddle and belt him to the horn. He loves that."

"Wait till Saturday and I'll ride with you. Arthur too."

I thought this was a fine idea.

"You won't shoot a wolf, Reenie."

"If I have to. If he's eating our livelihood I will."

A long arm reached across my vision and I saw the pores on my father's biceps. "Hey," he said.

My mother's breathing was noisy. She said my name, but I knew that she wasn't calling me.

My father got to his knees and slid me to the edge of the bed. I turned my head and watched him lie down on top of my mother. I breathed through my nose and saw my father

kiss my mother's breasts. She let him. She said, "Oh, James."
I climbed on top of my father's back. He sighed and rolled
me off and picked me up and carried me to my room. It was
cold and there was ice at the edges of the windows. My father
left and shut my door. I shook the crib, which was my cage,
but no one came. I squatted and shit into my diaper and then
scooped up the shit and spread it on the walls.

My mother, when she found me later, said that I would
be cleaning up my own poop, filthy boy. My father fetched
his Miranda and took a photo of my work. "An artist, Reenie.
That's what he is. A real *Manit*."

WE RODE UP THAT SATURDAY TO THE COULEE NEAR
the Granger spread where the Texas gate separates the prop-
erties. I was tied to my father's waist and he carried a lever-
action Winchester Yellow Boy in a scabbard. Rose, his bay,
was frisky and keen. My father had wrapped his coat around
me and buttoned it so that I could not see. It was dark and
then light as his body moved and the cracks of his coat opened
and allowed the spring sun into my cave. When he talked his
voice vibrated into my skull. Bev rode with my mother, on a
horse my father had named Emily, a small Appaloosa that my
father claimed was so tame you could eat a six-course meal off
her hindquarters. We rode single file, with me leading. The
horses snorted, the saddle leather creaked, and I slept against
the belly of my father.

Late in the day we found a cow lying in a gully, bawling horribly, its calf breeched. My father handed me to my mother, who slipped me under her coat. Father dismounted. He fished around in the cow and located the rear legs of the calf and pulled the fetlock joints over the pelvic brim. Then he fetched a rope and using a bowline knot he tied it to the feet. He looped the other end of the rope to the horn of his saddle and slowly backed Rose up. The calf slid out blue and steaming, and the cow scrambled to its feet. She stood wavering, and then went down on her knees and rolled onto her side.

"Go on," my father said.

We rode away and heard the shot of the Winchester, and when Bev turned around to look, Mother said, "Keep riding."

Over the next week the calf slept next to the electric heater in the kitchen, on a wool blanket, and every morning Bev fed it warm milk from a bottle. He named the calf Blue.

I HAD BEEN AN EARLY, BRILLIANT TALKER, USING LANGUAGE from the age of one, but about half a year after Em died, I stopped speaking for a time. I didn't plan it, it just so happened that I couldn't find the words. For one year, up until the age of three, this would persist, and various doctors, from my general practitioner to my neurologist, were mystified. One surmises that it might have been a form of infant aphasia, brought on by my ten-day fever and reinitiated by the trauma of my sister's death. My neurologist, a squat man with small glasses through which he squinted at my eyes and head and ears, ruled out aphasia because I appeared to understand everything that was said to me. "Lift your arm. Blink. Touch your finger to your nose, stick out your tongue." I have since learned that the request to stick out one's tongue is one of the first a neurologist will make when assessing a patient who has lost the ability to speak or understand. In one case a patient will wet his lips, and in another, he will use his hand to help stick out the tongue. The inability to put out the tongue is a neurological disorder of the same order as the inability to speak. This was not my problem. My tongue moved when my brain told it to. I was able to chew, salivate, and swallow. I recognized shapes. When told to pick up the ball, I did so, and repeated it for the triangle, the square, the trapezoid, and the pentagon. To all of this I responded correctly. Odd for a three-year-old to recognize a trapezoid, but then I was a strange and assured child. I was alert and aware and full of knowledge (translated mutely) when I was read to, and if this was so, if I was capable of comprehension, then I must have been suffering dumbness brought on by shock. Or, my doctor said, it might be *attitude*.

And so my mother worried, though I did not. At that time, worry was not my predilection, and hence I was found to lean towards *a casual acceptance of life*. I had everything at my fingertips: love, food, clothing, music. My mother, when she was in the house, listened to the radio, and when she was not listening to the *Back to the Bible* broadcast, which was heard every day from Nebraska in the morning hours, she found classical music. I was particularly fond of anything by Mozart, which the doctor said indicated that I was attuned to structure and pattern. I was tested for acuity regarding numbers, but at that I did poorly. I was too young. At that age, at that time, speech was unnecessary. All my other senses were alerted and I vacuumed up the aural, the visual, the tactile, and stored it away for later. I became a sort of mnemonist.

When I began to speak again, my doctor announced that this was consistent with the clinical evidence that, in childhood, if the speech area is destroyed, normal speech returns after a year or more of aphasia, and a speech area is formed in the previously non-dominant hemisphere. I had lost my ability to speak, and then regained it because I was a child. My brain was still developing.

MY FATHER, TACITURN AND BROODING, WAS CONstantly looking out from under the brim of his Sheplers to someplace in the distance, as if the possibility of pleasure and release might be found beyond the foothills, in the mountains that rose to the west. He was self-taught, with a hunger for knowledge, honest in his actions, wary of emotions, happiest when driving down to Montana to buy horses for his boss, or when he was in the corral breaking those same horses.

The spring I was five, I sat on a crate beside him inside the corral and together we broke horses. The method was pure.

He had a book and a bag of apples. He read the book out loud so that I could hear the story and so that the horses could hear his voice. The first few days we were alone, reading together. The book was *Moby Dick*. I had known fish, been born among them, and so it was fitting that we read together a book that described the biggest fish of all. We began with the prelude, reading the words for whale in various languages: *cetus, hvalt, wal, hwal, baleine, ballena*. We then passed on to the quotations from various Great Works that included descriptions of whales. We genuflected to Montaigne, The Psalms, and to Milton, who wrote, *That sea-beast / Leviathan, which God of all his works / Created hugest that swim the ocean-stream*. My father, never one to pass up an opportunity to educate, explained to me the silver tongue of Lucifer, the fallen angel, a beautiful favourite who had tried to overthrow God.

By the end of the second day we were well into the first chapter and the brood mare stood nearby, listening to the story. The following day the American quarter horse stallion joined her. The stallion sniffed my father's legs. The mare nuzzled my ear. My father, using the same reading tone, said to me, "Don't look at her. She's curious, and she wants you to notice her, and she's surprised that you don't see her. Best to pretend she isn't there and she'll keep coming back." He reached into the bag, pulled out an apple, broke it in half with his hands, and without looking at either horse, he held out half for each.

The next morning, when we walked out to the corral, both horses were waiting beside my crate. My father said in a low soft voice, "Who's a big boy?" and he stroked the stallion's neck. The horse shivered and moved sideways. My father picked up several lead ropes and tied them together. He took the rope and threw it over the stallion's back. The stallion danced sideways, throwing its head in the air. Its eyes were wild. My father pulled the rope away and, all the while talking tender nonsense to the horse, continued to lay the rope on the stallion's back, around the legs, under the belly, and over the ears and eyes and nose. Gentle and easy. My father did this every day for a week until the stallion allowed my father to wrap the rope around all four legs and then pull it free. The mare and I watched.

Bev of course had caught wind of all of this and kicked up such a fuss that my father promised him that on Saturdays and evenings after school they would break the mare. "She's got spirit, that one." Bev accepted the offer, though he was discontented. Walking out to the stable that evening, me trailing behind, he turned and said, "Ain't you a sweet pile of shit."

In the weeks that followed, my father would run his hand down the stallion's leg and say "up," and soon the horse obeyed, lifting his leg on command.

Whenever the stallion did something well, without balking, it was my job to feed him half an apple. My father broke the apple and gave me a piece and I stood beneath the horse and held my palm flat, and the horse's head went down and its lips lifted the apple ever so softly. My father had warned me not to extend a finger. "He'll think it's edible and he'll bite your finger off. I've seen it happen."

Before placing a blanket or saddle or bridle on the horse, my father let the horse smell and feel the tack. He rubbed the saddle against the horse's back and then walked around to the front of the horse and let him sniff at it. The horse was quiet. The first time my father got up into the saddle, talking all the while to the horse, he was thrown off. I was watching from the other side of the fence. My father got up off the ground and talked to the horse and said, "Just doin' what you hafta do, eh, boy? Not to worry. Ain't gonna hurt you." He called out to me that he was okay. "When you fall, you climb back on right away. Don't let him think he's victor." I did not know that word, *victor*, but I stored it in my small brain, as I did all unfamiliar words, to be used in the future, and of course it would come to pass, in my later years, that words such as this would enlarge and inform me.

My father stroked the stallion's neck and his withers. He talked to him. He said, "Just you and me, bud." He put his foot in the left stirrup and swung his other leg up and over. The horse stood shivering slightly for several seconds. My father had fitted the stallion with a martingale, a strap that ran from the bridle to the front cinch, so that the horse couldn't throw its head and rear. Still, it bucked, but my father stayed on and the stallion took off, running for the far fence, stopping abruptly, and then charging back. My father pulled him in near to where I was sitting. He'd lost his hat and his hair was a pale yellow and his forehead was marked from where his hat had lain. The sun was behind his head and I couldn't see his eyes, but I knew that he was happy because he kept saying, "How 'bout that? How 'bout that?"

We named the horse Moby. Two months later, on a day when Bev was at school, my mother sat the railing of the corral wearing her outdoor clothes, jeans and shirt and cowboy hat, and she watched me sit Moby and ride a full circle, stop, back up, and canter, and all the while I clucked low and soft just like my father had taught me. I was a small bundle on the back of twelve hundred pounds of muscle and heart and meat. I was grinning as my father said to my mother, "He's a beautiful one, ain't he?"

MY MOTHER WAS NOT AS BIG A READER AS MY FATHER. She preferred listening to the radio as she cleaned the kitchen after supper. I took my bath then, sitting in the steaming water that she had poured into the metal tub that sat on the kitchen floor. At some point she would wash my ears and hair and then hand me the soap and tell me to scrub my bum. I dutifully did this and then stood, and she wrapped me in a towel and dried me off and handed me my pyjamas. "Can we read?" I would ask, anticipating the couch and her warmth and the sound of her voice. She was usually tired by that time and she acquiesced and so we curled up together and she opened a book of my choice and began to read. And she fell asleep. I did not mind. She was close at hand, and by that age I had learned to read, and so I turned the pages until she woke with a jump and looked down at me and said with a smile, "Just catching a wink." This was my domain. Bev had no interest in reading or being read to, though there were evenings when mother would force him to sit with us. Within a few minutes he would slide off the green couch and crawl after Peter, the cat, who was chasing mice. And once again, my mother and I were alone together.

The year I turned six, in the darkness of the winter evenings, my mother read the expurgated version of *The Pilgrim's Progress* to me, and one night, lulled by her voice and trembling from the danger held within the story and then desiring, like Little Christian, the utter freedom from that terrible burden, I whispered in her ear that I too wanted my trouble to be gone.

"What do you mean, Arthur? What trouble?"

Indeed, what did I mean?

"I want to be like Little Christian."

And so we prayed, and when we were done praying, she was crying. She rarely cried, had not cried since Em's funeral. But now she was, and my meek wish had produced those tears. It pleased me so, and it saddened me, because I was aware that this might never happen again, and I marvelled at the pleasure my meagre request had brought her. She held my hand. She kissed the top of my head and her tears dropped onto my crown. She pulled away. Her hair was drawn up in the disarray of a sort of bun, a barely controlled affair, but I noticed the back of her neck and the wisps of stray hair there, and what I did not know then was that forever after I would be attracted to women who wore their hair up and whose necks were laid vulnerable and bare.

THOSE EARLY YEARS ON THE RANCH WERE FULL OF freedom and exploration, and it turned out that much of my time was spent with Alice Dewey, the daughter of my father's boss. She was a year younger than me, but she had already discovered the sense of entitlement that comes with having money and land and a mother who reads Latin and teaches her how to lay out flatware just so and how to hold a fork and puts her in dresses and stockings and plans for her a life that is off the ranch, perhaps in New York or London, certainly not Calgary, and definitely not a life on the plains where the buffalo used to roam. Despite all that, it was quite natural that Alice and I were together. There were no other children within ten miles, and she didn't have siblings. A Blackfoot woman named Tessa Firstrider cared for her, and so, on the days when my mother had driven off to work and my father had arranged it thus, there were three of us, Alice, Tessa, and I, and much of our time together was spent in the big Dewey house, because why on earth would Alice come visit me at my small abode. Though, on the few occasions when she did come, especially when we were older and she was back for the summer and we wanted to get away from her mother's prying ears and eyes, she said she liked my house because it was small and safe and it smelled good. In those early years I didn't know she was a girl. She was a body, like mine, with ears and mouth and arms and legs that wrapped around my belly when we wrestled. Tessa used to let us bathe together, until Anna Dewey put a stop to it.

Alice was my first true love. When I was seven, and she was six and being sent off to ballet school in Winnipeg, I kissed her on the cheek and gave her a desiccated frog that we had dismembered that summer. I'd stitched it back together and mounted it and placed it in a glass box, and I thought that she would be pleased. She was, though she seemed more pleased by the kiss. She was wearing flat black shoes and white knee-highs and a pleated blue dress that belted at the waist. She stood with her heels together and her hands clasped in front of her stomach. Her hair was quite long by then and her mother, or perhaps Tessa, had pulled it up into a perfect ballerina bun, as if she were already a dancer and about to warm up, lowering her face to the thigh of the leg that rests on the barre. When I had heard that Alice would be spending the winters in Winnipeg, where one of the best ballet schools was located, my heart went immediately sad, and then it brightened as I imagined all she might teach me about ballet. I asked my mother if we could go to the library. I found a few easy-to-read books on ballet and I studied these and wondered if I too might be able to go to boarding school to take dance. I asked my mother. She said we couldn't afford it. Alice's life was not my life and I might as well get used to it.

My mother was the talker in our family. She was curious, and she humoured me, listening to my stories, answering my questions. My father and Bev spoke only when spoken to, as if words were like special diamonds. Or perhaps they did not know how to move their thoughts from their brains to their mouths, or it might have been that they did not have thoughts. And so it was that my mother and I were the ones who conversed.

On that day she was standing at the counter making butter soup and her hair was pulled back from her face and her hands were flitting here and there and she was humming some song and she wore a light green dress printed with small white butterflies. Her legs were bare and her calves were similar to those of the dancers I had found in my books. I was sitting at the kitchen table so as to be in close proximity to her, for this is what pleased me most, and I showed her the images. Elongated lithe women and muscular men with inevitable strong jaws.

She came over and touched my head with her free hand. The other held the paring knife.

"You're impossible, Arthur. Obviously you were born in the wrong place, at the wrong time."

This was shocking, to think that this might be true. I said, "When? Where then?"

"Long ago maybe, during the time of Beethoven. Into an aristocratic family, with servants and perfumed and fancy dogs." Her voice was now weary. "But you got us. And we got you." She moved back to the counter and continued peeling potatoes.

"What's 'aristocratic'?"

"What I said. Fancy perfumed dogs and servants. Laziness. Privilege."

The word *privilege* went into my brain storage. I said, "Alice has a servant. Tessa."

"She's not a servant. Don't even think of her as a servant."

"Did you ever dance?" I asked.

"We weren't allowed. It was a sin."

"So Alice is sinning?" I said.

"She comes from a different place. Her family doesn't think that way. Could be they don't believe in sin."

Though I was now a Christian, and had experienced the *feeling* of salvation, I still had very little sense of how that made me any different than Alice, who didn't even know who Little Christian was. I had many more questions for my mother. I wanted to know how she thought. Where her feelings came from. Why she could be humming happily and then all of a sudden be talking about sin. But I saw that she was weary of me, and I had used up my quota of goodwill. As the butter soup boiled, I paged through my books, studying the various fantastic poses. I looked into the dancers' eyes and tried to imagine what it must feel like to be a sinner. Nothing changed of course, the dancers remained as they were, vigorous, with beautiful legs and arms and necks.

In August, before Alice left, she celebrated her birthday. I was invited, along with several daughters of wealthier ranchers in the area. There was one other boy, a weak red-headed son of a local politician. His name was Gerald and he was petulant and spoiled and all the girls paid close attention to him. A gift was necessary for this party and my mother and I had discussed what I might find for Alice. My mother said that Alice had everything a girl could need, even if she managed to live to the age of eighty. I said that wasn't the point. I wanted to buy her something beautiful and memorable. Perhaps a bracelet, or a blank book that might serve as a journal, or a pair of earrings. I had no money, our family did not have any extra cash, and so on the day of the party I dressed in jeans and a button-down shirt and a bolo tie, and I walked over to Alice's grand house holding a bag of popcorn that my mother had freshly made. It was salted and buttered and by the time I handed my miserable gift to Alice, the butter had leaked through the brown paper. Gerald laughed. The other girls were mortified, but they remained silent. Alice took the bag and placed it on the pool table beside her. She said thank you, very sweetly, and then she said my name.

Years later, when Alice would come home for Christmas holidays and together we played pool beneath the three green lamps that hung above that five-by-ten slate table, the grease spot from the bag of popcorn was still there, a cruel reminder of a childhood governed by poverty and want. At that party though, in that moment of handing over my gift, I was aware of my hatred for my father, a man who couldn't make enough money to allow his youngest boy the small pleasure of buying Alice Dewey something beautiful. But even more so I despised my mother, who didn't think that a girl like Alice deserved better than what I had given her, and whose pride overruled any humiliation that I felt.

HAD MY FATHER READ ROUSSEAU HE WOULD HAVE claimed that at least one of his children should be raised as an Emile amidst the foothills of the Rockies. He was not impressed by formal educators and said more than once that a family of badgers might do a better job of teaching his children. "Foraging and storing and waiting out the winter, the rudiments of survival, keeping your nose close to the ground, sniffing danger, understanding predator and prey, eating raw food, sporting warm fur, independence, an abundance of rutting. You can't learn that in a history book. Bah." Still, he kept a library of books that he dipped into late at night, sitting by the fire. Sometimes, in the morning when I woke, he was where he had been the night before, bent over a tome near the dead fire, still wearing his Sheplers 20X because his back hurt less when he wore his hat.

But my mother, sensible woman, insisted that I attend school. At the supper table during that first week of school she said that Bev was my older brother and I was lucky to have him looking out for me. She touched my arm as she said this and looked straight at Bev, whose eyes were on his plate.

"Isn't that right, Bev?" she said.

He grunted.

"Use words," my father said.

Bev looked right at me and said, "Yeah. He's lucky."

Bev and I rode the bus to town in the morning and returned in the late afternoon. He made it clear that I was to sit in the front of the bus while he headed for the back. "Don't talk to me," he said. During those first rides, I kneeled on my seat and looked backwards, as if he might disappear if I didn't keep my eye on him.

The bus was like a prison, with its own rules and mysteries. Certain seats were unavailable, and if you sat down in one of them you were likely to get your ear twisted or to be sworn at and pulled down into the dirty aisle where the mud and snow lay. Fights often broke out, with the weaker preyed upon by the stronger. Bev was one of the stronger, because he was older and tougher, though he didn't pick fights simply for the sake of fighting. And so I sat at the front of the bus, surrounded by the girls, who seemed to understand that decorum and good manners diminished in proportion to the distance from the driver. I found comfort with the girls and discovered that because I was not one of them I was treated better, and in fact was coddled and favoured. They found my brush cut to be cute, and my black horn-rimmed glasses made me look intelligent, and they were surprised at how tall I was for my age, and when I used my large vocabulary they called out to each other, "Did you hear that? Say it again, Arthur." And so I said the word again, perhaps it was *aristocratic*, or *veritable*, a word my father had used once to describe the supper feast my mother laid out, and the girls went *awww* as if I were a circus freak. I didn't mind it though.

Annalie was a girl my brother's age who often sat beside me because, I discovered in hindsight, she liked Bev, and inevitably she saw me as that small path through the bush that would lead to the larger pasture that was my brother.

That fall she always wore pants that were called knee knockers, a different colour for each day of the week, and her blond hair was cut in bangs, and she sometimes wore a cashmere sweater that was soft to the touch, which I discovered one afternoon when she sat down beside me and said in her breathy voice, "Arthur," and put her arm around my neck. I blinked and swallowed.

"Tell your brother I have something special for him."

"Bev?"

She laughed. Her teeth flashed white and I saw the inside of her mouth. "You have other brothers?"

I shook my head.

She removed her soft arm and touched the top of my head. "Okay? You'll tell him?"

I agreed.

"Watcha always lookin' at?" Bev said that evening as we walked down the driveway to the ranch to do our chores: feeding the chickens, mucking the barn, laying out fresh straw for the beef calves. "Don't go thinking I'm your friend."

I was quiet, running to keep pace with him, my large book bag banging against my leg. Both his arms were empty and swinging. He despised homework and school in general.

"Annalie has something special for you," I said.

"Who told you?"

"She did."

"You workin' for Pony Express now?"

I did not understand.

"Sucking the hind tit, that one," he said. "She's a runt."

"She just said."

"Said what?"

"She has something for you. Special."

"You didn't ask what?"

I shook my head.

"You roping the girls?" He hit my shoulder. Not hard, more a hit of recognition, maybe even affection.

This was unusual. I glowed inside.

By the end of that week Annalie was sitting beside Bev in the back seat of the bus, sharing her gum. Annalie would blow a bubble and Bev would pop it with his teeth and then suck it into his own mouth. And then they'd repeat the process, going the other way. I watched this from my vantage point in the front of the bus.

IN THOSE EARLY YEARS I LOVED SCHOOL, ESPECIALLY the subject of art, which was introduced to us in grade three by a teacher named Miss Chou. She was a very small woman who wore her dark hair up in a high ponytail, and every day her small ears held a different pair of earrings that dangled and sparkled against her pale cheeks. Perhaps she reminded me of Tamiko, the girl I first knew in Port Edward and would have married had we remained there. Or perhaps I loved the attention she paid to me as she leaned over my shoulder and breathed in my ear that *it should be like this, Arthur*, and she guided my hand, which held a pencil or a brush. I was nine. I was again in love. And of course I planned to marry her. The following year, when I was in grade four, and having perfected cursive writing, I wrote her letters and delivered them to her desk after school, quickly, before the bus came. The letters were addressed *Dear Miss Chou*, and in them I drew pictures of horses and labelled their parts, and I explained to her how to break horses and I described how the tides work, something I'd learned recently in Science. She wrote me back and said that she too loved horses, though she was afraid of them and had never ridden one. I went home that night and asked my mother if we could invite Miss Chou for supper, saying, "She's afraid of horses."

I pestered my mother for several weeks until she sighed and gave in and phoned Miss Chou, who lived in Tomorrow by herself in a small house. My mother asked if she would like to join the family for Sunday lunch. "Arthur has made up his mind. It would please us as well," she said. Miss Chou accepted, which surprised everyone but me.

On that day I wore clean trousers and a button-down shirt and a bow tie and suspenders. I stood in the living room with my hands in my pockets and attempted the air of a learned boy, someone who was used to salon talk, a world-wise fellow who could converse in various languages. I had placed on the turntable a symphony, one of the few classical records we had, handed down to us by my mother's father, a white-haired man I rarely saw, and though the record was mightily scratched from the cat, who liked to sharpen its claws on vinyl, the music was legible and pretty and I noticed that Miss Chou was aware of it. "Dvořák," I said, and she nodded.

My father paid close attention to her, in fact found her to be quite beautiful. She hadn't been ravaged by marriage or children and her stomach was flat and her arms were thin and she had no jowls to speak of. My father and I flanked her, and my brother Bev, indifferent and sullen, sat across the table. I had suffered a bout of diarrhea before she came and I kept smelling poop, on my fingers and around my body, and I was horrified to think that Miss Chou perhaps smelled it as well. She didn't pay enough attention to me, and was very taken with my mother, who said more than once how she admired Miss Chou's earrings.

We prayed before the meal. I was embarrassed, for I knew that Miss Chou did not go to church, and I snuck a look to find that she was staring down at her empty plate and smiling slightly, as if my family were amusing and backward.

Right off, because I didn't want my mother to talk about the kinds of food she had made, or my father to talk about the ranch, or Bev to make a fool of himself, and because I wanted

Miss Chou to see my family as cultured and elevated, I introduced the subject of Darwinism and natural selection.

Bev rolled his eyes and said, "Aw, lookee at the walking encyclopedia."

Miss Chou ignored Bev and addressed my deeper thoughts. She said that it was refreshing for a religious family to believe in evolution. Then she said, "Your son has a very good eye for drawing." She smiled at me.

I blushed.

Mother squinted. She was fonder of church and religion than she was of the finer things in life, like art, which was Miss Chou's realm. My mother's favourite artist was Norman Rockwell. My father liked paintings of horses. My brother didn't care. I held out for Picasso. Even at that young age I had an instinct for that bridge between doubt and belief, and as I would learn later in life, believers have no use for art and so the modern artist must descend into the camp of the doubter.

But now, I pursued my previous thought. I said, "Our cousin, Linda, she says that the dinosaurs in Drumheller are plastic and made from human hands, like sculptures."

"Not real," Bev said.

"Is that so?" Miss Chou said. And she said nothing more.

My head was brimming. It was a large head, but had a brain of average size. Not an intellectual brain but an intuitive and imaginative brain that made connections between flowers and women's underclothes, for example. When my mother took us up to see the dinosaurs in Drumheller with my cousin Linda, and Linda had scoffed at the plastic bones, I had become confused. I was a Christian, like Linda, but I didn't have her certainty, which, I realized later, came from ignorance and a lack of doubt. At the time, because it interested me, I had been reading about Darwin's voyage to the Galapagos, and trying to reconcile a universe that was billions of years old with a Mennonite God who was much younger. Linda's certainties, her arrogance, produced in me a strange feeling that I would later recognize as anger. She was a fool. And I was furious. I was aware of Linda's stockings, and her flat shoes, and the hole in her stockings just above her left heel.

But on this Sunday there would be no fury, for Miss Chou, our visitor, did not want to go against the wishes of my mother, who interrupted and said that the Lord works in mysterious ways, and who was to say how the five of us had come to be at this table, right now, eating and talking, though it appeared that none of us had the legs or teeth or skull of a dinosaur. How about that? She looked at Miss Chou. "More roast?" she asked, and Miss Chou graciously shook her head and said that the meal had been delicious, but she had had her fill.

I wanted to introduce Miss Chou to Moby, the stallion, and so after lunch my father and Miss Chou and I walked out to the pasture where Moby met us by the fence. He stuck his head between the railings and nosed my pockets.

"He thinks I might have an apple," I told Miss Chou.

She was nervous and stepped back. My father asked if she wanted to ride.

"Oh, no, I don't have the clothes for it."

She was wearing a mauve dress that accentuated her slimness. And there were her earrings of course, and a broach that matched the earrings.

"Doreen could lend you a pair of jeans and boots," my father said. He appraised her. "Though, you might swim in them."

She shook her head.

My father held Moby's mane and addressed his long neck with a stroke of his hand. "Come," he said. "Touch him."

He held out his free hand and beckoned Miss Chou to step forward. She did, hesitantly. She reached up and touched the place between Moby's eyes and then pulled away. I was on the fence, sitting on the top rung, and I felt at that moment that Miss Chou had touched me, had placed her perfect hand on my forehead, and then stepped back. Moby said something and stomped a foot.

In the late afternoon, my father and I drove Miss Chou back to her house in Tomorrow. I sat in the middle of the pickup, still wearing my fine clothes, and at some point Miss Chou, who had been conversing with my father about her origins and her love of teaching, looked down at me and said, "I like your tie, Arthur. Very classy."

We dropped her off on the street and she removed a glove to shake hands with my father, and I was aware of their hands meeting before my eyes and clasping near my chest. His wrist was thick and hairy and hers was olive coloured and unadorned, and I saw them both, quite unexpectedly, as naked. I did not see their private parts, but they were unclothed and standing before each other, just like the painting that Miss Chou had shown the class one fall day, a drawing of a man and woman facing each other with no clothes, and the woman's arms were raised and hid her bare breasts, and she was reaching up to touch the face of the man, who was looking away.

My father and I watched Miss Chou walk up her sidewalk and enter her house.

My father said, "She's an elegant woman." And then he said, "You have good taste, Arthur."

I did not know exactly what he meant, but I thought that this meant that he and I had the same taste, and I wasn't sure if that was what I wanted.

OUR FAMILY WAS NOT AS REFRESHING AS MISS CHOU might have believed. My mother had grown up believing in everlasting life, and she would make certain that her two boys would not end up in hell. We went to church every Sunday, and Bev and I attended Sunday School, and every evening after supper our family had devotions where we read the Bible and prayed. I loved the stories of the Pentateuch, but the favoured passages in our home were the Epistles of the Apostles, where lots of rules were set down and the early church was told to shape up. We memorized scripture. I was good at that, and it pleased my mother greatly when I could recite whole chapters, and her pleasure made me happy. My father was not especially keen on religion, but he went along because it was the easy thing to do. When Bev, at the age of fifteen, announced that he would no longer be attending church or Sunday School, my mother was resigned. She sighed. She said she would pray for him. I told her that I would still be coming to church with her, and she looked at me in her perfunctory manner and said, "Of course you will."

It was a world of contradiction. When Jesus would return, the dead in Christ would rise again and believers would live happily ever after in heaven. At the age of ten, around the time my brother denounced Church, our neighbour's wife, Bertha Doerksen, died of an embolism. She collapsed while wringing out the wash. We all went to the funeral. Her husband Harry wept. Three months later he married Gertie, Bertha's sister. My parents attended the wedding. I asked my mother one Saturday afternoon what would happen when Christ returned and Mr. Doerksen ended up in heaven with two wives who were also sisters. Which one would he sleep with? My mother looked at me in consternation. Then she sighed and said, "Arthur. What a question. In heaven we will all be happy and love each other. There will be no marriage." Even at that age I thought that her response was strangely dismissive.

In my later teens, when my brain was more developed and my capacity for uncertainty was heightened, I realized that adults did not have all the answers, and that Pastor Bock, grumpy and severe, might suffer the same desires I did. I saw him once, at a Christmas banquet, looking down the top of June Forsyth, a girl so beautiful that all the boys were afraid of her. I felt a certain power to know this about him, and a modicum of shame. As I grew older, I teetered between forgiveness and guilt, and then, faced with all that heaviness, I threw it aside and decided to enjoy myself. Only to repent the following day. God was a tyrant, and I was his servant.

A memory. I am fifteen and have joined the Friday night youth group for a winter hayride. Free from chores and the solitude of the ranch, I jostle with boys and girls my age. On the hay wagon, I find myself beside Glenda Peters. She leans into me and drags the tassels of her toque across my shoulder. She talks about God. She motions at the stars above us. She says that she is in love with Jesus.

"How about you, Arthur?" she asks.

"Yes," I say. "Yes."

This gives her permission to take my gloved hand in hers and hold it tightly as the John Deere pulls the wagon through the freshly fallen snow.

Up until the age of twelve I lived in that romantic world where women were a mystery—hidden and unknown, deliciously ambiguous, like a plant upon which one stumbles while wandering about in the desert, a flowering plant that is so surprising in its beauty that it defies being picked. I had, of course, had all manner of physical contact with females. Hildegaard breastfed me when I was sick, my mother held me and brushed up against me in many possible ways, Tamiko pummelled my head, Em mollycoddled and dressed me, and I had, from the age of three to seven, before she left for boarding school, spent hours with Alice Dewey. The summer I was thirteen, my aunt and uncle visited from Montana. They had five girls, one of which, Isobel, was adopted. She was the oldest and a year ahead of me in school. Isobel was taller than me, with short dark hair and eyes the colour of the river that ran through the land. I might use the word *flinty* to describe her eyes if it didn't suggest so readily a personality that was obdurate. She could certainly be a stubborn girl, something I would learn over the years to come, but I mean flinty in the sense of a whetstone, like the one my mother used to sharpen her knives. She had a strong and foul mouth, and was constantly being reprimanded by her mother, my aunt Beth. She was rough-and-tumble and careless, and she may have seen in me an openness that allowed her to be certain and aggressive.

I did not have friends that I hung out with after school or on weekends, or even in the summer when school was out. Most children living on ranches and farms made do with brothers and sisters, or spent their free time alone. In my case, I was even more a solitary figure, simply because I alienated my classmates with my aggressive knowledge and my disdain for their ignorance. And of course my brother would never be a friend. He was older and had other interests, and he didn't like me.

Isobel's family visited for two weeks. We'd spent time together in the summers throughout our younger years, but during this visit I found her to be suddenly grown, as if she'd been stretched both in mind and body. On the first day, a Sunday afternoon, Bev said we should ride a heifer, and so the seven kids traipsed out to the barn where Bev corralled a heifer called Riley. Riley was a good size, eight hundred pounds, and when Bev climbed onto her he was immediately bucked off. Isobel's sisters, lined up against the railing, their blond heads descending like a series of pale steps, giggled and cheered.

Isobel sat the top railing. She said, "She's in heat."

Bev climbed from the straw, slapped his hat clean, and said, "You think so?"

"I know so. Before you caught her she was bawling and pissing. Heifers in heat piss a lot."

She climbed down into the corral and approached the heifer, which skittered away. She grabbed the halter and danced sideways, reaching back to lift the heifer's tail. "Her bottom's sticky and wet. I could show you more but there are young ears here." She motioned at her sisters with her head.

Bev shrugged. I was standing inside the corral, hoping she would say more.

And then, with a quick swing of her right leg, Isobel was up on the heifer's back and the two of them were skittering about the corral, in a circle, the heifer's eyes wild, but for some reason she didn't buck. They came to a stop. Isobel slid off. I clapped slowly, aware of Bev kicking one of his boot toes into the straw. Isobel gave a little bow. She wore her hair in braids and they pointed at the ground as she dipped, and as she rose the braids landed on her chest against each of her shirt pockets. The girls cheered.

I liked Isobel, she liked me, and there was little time to waste. As she and I were both early risers, it often happened that we found ourselves outside, hanging around the stable, before the other children got up. The morning after she showed off her skills with the heifer, I asked if she didn't want to ride Moby. Moby wasn't truly mine, he was Chester Dewey's, but it was my job to stable and care for and ride him, and so I had taken to calling him mine. I said that I would take Tulip, my father's mare. And so we bridled and saddled the horses and rode out across the plain. Birds lifted and scattered as we passed them by, and then they settled again. Isobel rode just ahead of me, to my right, and I observed her straight back and the tilt of her hat and her long neck and the manner of her arms, bent at the elbow and held out slightly at her sides. She wore her hair in a ponytail that morning. Moby could be jumpy and difficult, but Isobel talked in a low voice to him and wasn't frightened as another person might be, and when we rode hard and raced, she was always before me.

We stopped near the river, dismounted, and watered the horses. We picked up stones and threw them, and then we found a rusted forty-eight-ounce tomato juice tin and we set that up and took shots at it with a slingshot.

At one point, after closing one eye to aim and then shooting a rock dead centre, she lowered her arms and asked, "You got any pubic hair yet?"

"What do you mean?" I asked. I knew what she meant, but I was embarrassed and unsure of her tone.

"Can you get erections? Have you ever had night emissions?"

"I'm not sure."

"Guess that's a no."

"What about you?" I asked.

"Erections?" She grinned.

"No. Puberty. Have you, you know?"

"I'm starting to grow breasts, but they're still quite invisible. I'm too skinny. Don't have my period yet either."

I nodded.

"When dogs fuck," she said, "the male has to ejaculate before it can withdraw. Its penis has this hook that won't let go until the semen releases. Which is why you got these attached dogs dragging each other around."

I said, "You a veterinarian?"

"I'm gonna kiss you," she said. She was standing really close.

"Okay," I said.

She leaned forward and our lips touched. She stayed there a while and I could feel her breathing through her nose onto my cheek. She pulled away.

"That was not bad," she said. We stood close to each other, almost touching. "Let's get naked."

We were far from home. The morning sun had warmed

the air. Out on the river a large bird floated, dipping its head and then lifting it to gaze about sharply. Isobel unbuttoned her top and let it drop. Her shoulders were bony and her skin was shockingly pale. I removed my shirt and took off my boots and jeans. She slid out of her jeans. Her underwear was white and too large for her. Our horses moved around us, grazing. We lay down on the bed of clothes that she had prepared for us. As she bent forward her spinal cord moved and her ribs were revealed as symmetrical, and I realized with the tenderest of emotions that here was the cage that held her heart. We kissed some more and then she touched my penis and I touched her vagina through the white underwear. She took the underwear off. I lay naked on top of her and tried to put my limp penis inside of her, but of course that didn't work. Still, I was moved, as was she. I could hear it in her quick breathing, and see it in the pink of her cheeks and the emphasis of her freckles. Though nothing was produced, no *double cousin fuck*, as she called it later when we lay side by side, fully clothed again, we acknowledged our complicity that day at the lunch table, when we sat beside each other and she reached out and held my hand.

We lay naked together every morning after that. We moved our hands over each other and asked how it felt. We had discovered that I was able to get erections, though not always. She kneeled to kiss me and then she lay back and I kissed her. There was a naïveté in our kisses. It made me feel small in a large way.

I ejaculated on our final morning together. I spilled onto her leg and she exclaimed and sat up and said, "I'm all sticky."

"It just happened," I said.

She touched my semen with her finger and studied it and then wiped her hand on the ground. She used bunches of prairie grass to wipe her leg.

"Was it nice?" she asked. "What did it feel like?"

"Strange. Weird. I didn't know what was happening."

"But it felt good?"

"Yeah. Good."

"I'm jealous," she said.

I was sheepish and slightly sad and I wondered why I would feel sad. I said that we should get dressed, but she wanted to just be still and look at the sky. And so we lay there, holding hands. We saw an eagle turning on high, right above us.

"Can it see us?" Isobel asked.

"Yeah. Though it doesn't care. It wants voles and gophers and mice."

"Here's a mouse," she said, and she touched my penis and laughed.

And then, for some reason, perhaps thinking she would be impressed, I quoted a verse from the Bible. On Friday evenings our family gathered around the dining room table and recited passages from the Bible that my mother had assigned us the previous week. And so it came to be that I had memorized large portions of the Old and New Testament, passages that spilled out of me verbatim. I had no sense of any deeper meaning, I was like a savant. Now, looking into Isobel's eyes, I quoted all of 1 Corinthians 13, which addresses love and prophecy and jealousy and arrogance, and concludes, "But now abide faith, hope, love, these three; but the greatest of these is love."

She sighed when I had finished, not out of admiration but in a self-reflexive manner, as if my voice had bored her. She said, "If I were a boy, my mother would want me to be a preacher. Lucky thing then, eh? Couldn't stand it." She got up and began to dress. She pulled on her underwear, and then her pants and socks and boots.

I remained on the ground, lifting my hips as I slid on my jeans.

She stood there, looking down at me, buttoning her shirt. "Will you write me?"

"And say what?"

"Anything. What you're doing, what you're feeling, what you're thinking. Especially what you're thinking."

"Yeah."

"I'd like that."

At that moment I thought that that sentence, *I'd like that*, was the most wonderful thing I'd ever heard. "Write me back," I said.

And it would come to pass that our letters to each other formed the backbone of a love that neither of us recognized or even talked about. Our lives were full of coincidences and affinities. After I left home and was living in Paris and she visited, we discovered that we were both reading the same story, *The Kreutzer Sonata*, and were in fact on the exact same page. Or, in one of her frequent letters to me, she wrote and underlined *vicissitudes*, a word I had recently discovered and begun to make use of. I perhaps took more pleasure than she in these little contiguities, for I was attuned to shape and patterns and structure. In any case, we were much more than parallel lines on the same plane continuing on to infinity.

AFTER CHURCH ON A SUNDAY AFTERNOON, THE DAY after Isobel and I had last lain naked together, Bev, Isobel, and I saddled horses and rode across the plains to the Little Bow, where we dismounted and let the horses step down into the water and drink. We sat on the bank. Isobel picked up stones and threw them out into the river. Her throwing arm was white and thin and I saw, watching from behind her, the sharpness of her elbow and the movement of her hips as she rotated.

My brother Bev joined her and of course threw stones much farther than she did, and she cursed with him and he with her, and at some point they were wrestling on the riverbank and then he was straddling her, his crotch at her face.

"Suck my dick," he said.

She hit his chest with a fist and turned her face away. She saw me squatting on the bank, watching the goings-on, and her eyes said, *There you are. And here I am.* She didn't want my help, and in any case I wasn't big enough to take on Bev, and in the end, I had no desire to help her.

In church that morning, during Sunday School, I had experienced an equal measure of guilt and giddiness, guilt because I believed that Isobel and I had sinned (consciousness of sin being the *condition sine qua non* of Christianity), and giddiness because we had been accomplices and seemed to have taken pleasure in the sin. Our teacher, Mr. Neufeld, had given a little talk on the omniscience of God, on his all-seeing eye. "He knows our thoughts, he sees our actions," Mr. Neufeld announced.

Isobel snorted, and then bowed her head, aware that she might be the only skeptic in the class. And being so aware, she raised her head suddenly and said, "How do you know that?"

Mr. Neufeld was not a theologian. He was an auctioneer known for his quick cattle rattle and witty repartee in the auction pen. Now he was at a loss for words. His naive confidence had been altered by the hard gaze of this strange girl from Montana. He fell back on his instinct. "It has to be true. God is God. He made us. Just as the builder of combustion engines knows all the parts, so God knows ours. Our thoughts, our desires, our pride, our wilfulness. Isabel."

"Is-o-bel."

He cleared his throat and repeated her name, emphasizing the *o*.

"I am an engine?" she asked.

"Of a sort. We all are."

The boys in the class tittered. Most of us had images of various kinds of motors—Hemis, a turbo-charged 357, double overhead cam. We were also enjoying ourselves. Sunday School had taken on a rodeo-like quality with Isobel present.

She said, "And when I blow up, or seize, or get old and die, what part of me goes to heaven? My pistons, the valves, the hoses, my fan belt?"

"Why, your soul."

"Where is the soul of an engine?"

It was a good question, we all knew this, and Mr. Neufeld knew it, and being good, it was also difficult. He didn't have an answer. And he moved on to other things. I watched Isobel. She wasn't proud of her display, she was simply speaking from despair, and I wanted to tell her that I knew she had a soul, I had seen it all that week as she pulled her shirt over her head and her grey eyes reappeared, whetstone clear.

But now, as I watched her on her back by the river, struggling with little effort against my brother's command, turning her head away from me, I saw that she did not suffer guilt as I did. She didn't truly care if God had witnessed our botched attempts at sex, simply because she did not believe in God. I had never met someone my age that did not believe in God. I was impressed and disquieted. My heart felt angry.

Minutes later we gathered our horses and began the ride back. I was riding Moby. He was fast, but tired quickly. Even so, I kicked him hard and rode low over his neck, talking to him. Moby and I were well ahead. I turned back to look for the others and in turning must have pulled Moby's rein slightly because he shied, stepped into a hole created by some prairie animal, and went down. And I went down with him, my right leg still caught in the stirrup. Moby got up immediately and stood on three legs, shivering and snorting, eyes wild, unable to move. I recall the blue sky and the angle of my broken leg and the strange look of Moby's right fetlock, which was pointing forwards as if indicating the direction home.

It was my brother who rode up first. He dismounted and looked down at me and then squatted and studied Moby's leg. "Stupid prick," he said. He plucked my foot from the stirrup and I cried out in pain. He was none too gentle, and he didn't seem to mind that fact. He rode on back to the house.

Isobel crouched by my side and held my hand and refused to look at my leg. It made her queasy. "Shit, Arthur," she said. There were tears in her eyes.

My brother returned with my father, who was carrying the Winchester. He crouched and inspected Moby's leg. Then he stood and shook his head. He looked down to where I was lying on the ground. He kneeled and touched my shoulder. "Don't move," he said. He took the saddle off Moby and laid it down for me to rest my head. I had begun to shake by this time and he covered me with the saddle blanket.

My brother would shoot Moby. He told my father that he could do it, he was fine, and the way he said it I thought that he was more than happy to kill my horse.

"Do we have to?" I asked. "Couldn't we reset the leg?"

My father shook his head. "He'll never run again. Not much use. Poor boy."

My father and Isobel rode back to get the pickup to drive me to the hospital. Bev stayed with me, and at some point he said, "Might as well get it over with." He looked at me and asked, "You wanna shoot him?"

I shook my head. And so I lay on the ground and watched Bev lever the rifle, aim at Moby's head, and fire. Moby let out a sigh and his big chest seemed to deflate, and he went down on his good front leg and then rolled onto his side. Bev put another bullet in his head.

I was crying.

Bev turned to me and said, "I should shoot you too."

"Don't be an ass."

"What's Mama gonna say? Be all blue and all. Maybe give you a titty to suck."

If I'd had the rifle in my own hands I would have shot my brother. As it was, I sought out a rock, found a clump of dirt, and heaved it at him. It hit his boot. "Asshole," I cried. I could not stop weeping and snot ran out of my nose and I tasted the salt of it. I was sorry that I hadn't hugged Moby before he died.

Bev squatted and studied the sky. He waited until I had finished crying and then he said, "Maybe you could read up on how to mend a leg. You know? Use some books as splints."

I closed my eyes. A hushed hatred lay between Bev and me. If some Ishmaelites had come along just then, he would gladly have sold me for a few pieces of gold.

He was quiet for a long while, and then he said, "I see that you fancy cousin Isobel."

"You don't know what you're talking about."

"I *do* know. Can hear it in your *vehement* denial. Thank you for that word, by the way." He picked a piece of grass and chewed it and looked at me, and I saw that he had a jaw like my mother, and the same colour of eyes, and at that moment I could not decipher the meaning in those eyes.

"You're a retard," he said. "And you'll have retards for kids."

"She's adopted."

"Yeah? Still your cousin, you perv."

"Fuck a cow." I began to cry, not for myself but once again for Moby.

And then I passed out, or I suppose I must have, because in the next moment my father was standing over me, and he was bending to grasp my arms and my mother and Bev were on either side of me and my mother said, "Oh, Arthur. Arthur, Arthur." Her voice inside my ear was beautiful to hear.

I HAD BROKEN MY FEMUR AND WAS PUT IN TRACTION for the next several months. Those were the months when the space inside my head opened up and I discovered love, though I did not yet know it was love. I cannot disguise what is true, even if the truth appears predictable and sentimental, as if life were orderly.

We had in our house an atlas and it was to this atlas that I turned during my convalescence, specifically to the pages of France. I would open the atlas and study the names of French cities, and the regions, and I imagined the lives of the people that lived in the small spaces on that map. Rouen, for example. I did not know how to pronounce the name of the city, but the spelling interested me, those three vowels set together, like nothing you would find in English. Each time I opened the page to France (I had no interest in the other countries that bordered France), my spirits both lifted and fell. I was excited once again to enter the gates of that country, and I ached for something that I might never have.

During those long days, with little sense of taste or judiciousness, I also read. I had always been a reader, but now, lying on my back with idle hands, I discovered that I was hungry for words and stories. I did not choose a book for the name of the author or its title or because it was famous or not famous. I would pick up a book, open it, read the first page, and if I liked the "feeling" it elicited, I kept reading. I can tell you now that I read much that mattered and a great deal that didn't.

The books came to me via Mrs. Emery, Tomorrow's town librarian. She had heard about my accident and took it upon herself to provide me with reading material during my restoration. This is what she called it, *restoration*. She was a round woman with fat arms that stuck out of the short sleeves of her dress, and she wore a green hat that sat on her head like a pin cushion, and from underneath that hat sprayed her red hair, and the combination of green and red reminded me of Christmas. At some point I began to call her Mrs. Christmas to her face, for she was a bearer of gifts. She liked her new name. She entered our house every week, huffing and puffing and calling out, "Ho ho ho, it's Mrs. Christmas," and she set down a box of books, and from that box I would choose my reading, willy-nilly, with little percipience. And so, by chance, I discovered a life outside of my own scanty existence. Mrs. Emery did not edit my reading. This was mighty unusual in my small town, where certain books would have been perceived as dangerous and influential, and where there were two sources for knowledge: the *King James Bible* and *Reader's Digest*. Mrs. Emery suffered no moral indignation when it came to stories. She was magnanimous in her offerings. The one-hundred-year birthday of Canada had come and gone, and this being so, as part of the celebration the library had received a large sum of money to buy books. Mrs. Emery had purchased many of these books. It was she who introduced me to Kierkegaard and Nietzsche, and though I had little comprehension of these two great men, it so happened that I too was interested in confession and spiritual anguish, and so my emotions were moved. When Mrs. Emery thought I had read too much of Zane Grey, she placed in my hands the collected works of Shakespeare and said, "If you're going to be a writer, you must start with this."

I did not know where she got this idea that I would be a writer. We had never discussed it, though we did have intimate conversations about how a certain story was told, or why a writer used a particular voice. For example, after reading *The Metamorphosis*, I said that I thought it was a funny story.

"You mean strange?" she asked.

"Yeah, strange. But funny too. A laughing kind of funny."

She had never thought of Kafka as funny, but she said she would reread it and let me know. She came back the following week and said that she saw some humour, but it was more physical, like when Samsa is on his back and can't turn himself over.

"His family's afraid of him," I said. "That's what I mean. Sad funny. And I couldn't figure out what the story was about. You know? But it didn't matter. Which was the weirdest thing."

"Exactly," she said.

I did not know how one became a writer. I had never met one personally, and authors' names, such as Austen and Kafka, meant nothing to me. Mrs. Emery and I never did discuss her bald statement about being a writer. It was like she had taken a handful of scrap paper that had once been a note with an important message on it, and she had thrown those scraps into the air, and it was up to me to put those scraps back together.

And so it came to pass that during one of Mrs. Emery's visits she announced that the library was holding a short story contest and perhaps I would like to submit a story. The judge would be Mr. Arndt, the high school English teacher. I immediately began to plan a story. It would be deep and dark and full of conflict and it would inevitably end in death. I took up my pen and began to write. I wrote a paragraph, reread it, and tore it up. I began again. I discovered that I had nothing to say, that my small world provided little material for a tale that might make the reader *feel* something. I lost hope. And then, as every beginning writer must do, I stole my story. I took one of the novels I had recently read. It was called *The Deep*, a story set on an Allied submarine during the Second World War, and I condensed three hundred pages into fifteen. I changed the characters' names, moved the submarine from the Pacific arena to the Atlantic, and concluded the story with the death of the main character after a depth charge from a German destroyer blows up the submarine. The thoughts of my captain, as he swims to the surface just before he dies, dwelled on mortality and the grasping for life. I called my story, "Beneath the Deep."

My story won first place in the contest. It was printed in the school newspaper. Mrs. Emery arrived the following week with the usual box of books and a bottle of Coke. She sat down and poured two glasses of Coke and we toasted my win.

"Wonderful, Arthur," she said. "I knew it was possible."

I grinned and thanked her. We drank to my success and to my winnings, which had arrived in the form of a one-dollar bill.

Throughout all of this I had worried that someone would discover my plagiarism. And in fact it was discovered. A boy at school, Donald Steingaart, had read the novel that formed the spine of my story, and it was Donald who announced to my brother that I had stolen my winning story.

Bev came home that day and sat down by my bed where I was convalescing. He grinned at me. "You son of a thievin' bitch," he said.

I stared at him.

"That story. You stole it."

"False," I cried.

"True. Steingaart told me."

"Told you what?"

"That you copied. This—" He set a book down on my lap. It had a green cover with gold embossed lettering. It was *The Deep*.

"You haven't even read that book," I said. "How would you know?"

"Donald knows. He reads."

I was quiet.

"Give me the dollar," he said. "Donald and I are gonna share it."

"Or what?"

He shrugged. "You'll be known as a liar and a cheat."

"It's my story to tell." I said that there were probably fifty books out there with that same plot line.

He laughed. Shook his head. "What do you know about telling? About war? About death? Arndt should have smelled a rat. Gimme." He held out his hand.

In despair, sensing yet not understanding that he was morally right but aesthetically wrong, I took the dollar from my pocket and handed it to him.

He snapped it with his two hands. "Thank you for that," he said, and slipped it into his own pocket.

Though I was afraid my mother would hear of my duplicity and be disappointed, nothing more was said of it, and so my first publishing venture ended in disgrace. It was a lesson in perfidy and in failure. I resolved from then on to be original.

At that time, my other source for books was Anna Dewey's library. When Mrs. Dewey learned of my accident and my slow recuperation, she sent over a handwritten note on handmade paper enclosed in a pale pink envelope. The note was addressed to *Arthur*. Me. It suggested that if I should be inclined, the Dewey library was available, and would I please respond to Tessa and let her know if I was interested. The note was so formal and so otherworldly in its evasion of stating the facts (simply put, she was asking did I want to borrow a few books) that at first I was horribly impressed by the wording and the evasiveness, and then I wondered if she was in fact genuine, and finally I understood where Alice had learned her subtlety with language, and the change of direction in her speech, which could so confuse, and I saw that the calf was a dead ringer for the cow. I sent a note back saying that it would be my pleasure to borrow some books. Thank you.

I had a cumbersome wheelchair that had been donated by the Red Cross, and my brother grudgingly wheeled me over to the big house. He pulled me backwards up the stairs, knocked on the door, and abandoned me on the wide porch. Tessa answered. She looked down at me and touched my arm and pushed me in. She said that she would get Mrs. Dewey. I sat in the grand foyer. The great chandelier hung over me. As a child when I looked up at that chandelier, I always imagined it falling. I moved my chair to the edge of the foyer. Tessa returned and asked if I would like some lemonade. "Please," I said. She disappeared. I knew that the lemonade would be freshly squeezed and there would be perfect cubes of ice that tinkled in the glass and the glass itself would be crystal and the whole experience, holding the crystal, seeing the perfect cubes, tasting the juice squeezed fresh from lemons, would be enough to make me happy for the rest of the day, forget about the books.

Mrs. Dewey appeared from nowhere. She had a way of doing this, and of course, later in my life when Alice was seducing me in the very library we were about to enter, Anna Dewey would walk in and discover the wrangler's son's dirty hands on her perfect daughter's perfect breasts. That would be later. Now, she was all grace and gentleness. "Welcome here, Arthur," she said, and she swept towards the library, ignoring the fact that I was unable to move in my wheelchair as long as I was holding one of her crystal glasses. I tried with one hand, but of course I spun in circles. Ineffectually, hesitantly, awkwardly, I managed to give myself two pushes with one hand and then to switch the glass to my other hand and give myself two pushes with my other hand. In this manner I zigzagged my way towards the library door.

When I finally appeared, slightly breathless, Mrs. Dewey turned to me and said, "I thought you were lost."

Mrs. Dewey showed me the areas of the library from which I was free to borrow. I had seen it before, when playing with Alice, but we had never been allowed to penetrate the premises. Over there, in that corner, those were collected first editions, hers—*would you please not touch them*. Here were the science books—*you are welcome*. This was theology—*perhaps you are interested*. Philosophy—*good for you*. And finally, a section that held an array of books that could not be classified: books on knots, butterflies, steam engines, and, much to my pleasure, trashy paperbacks replete with descriptions of sex and pills and affairs and more sex. And finally, novels. The fiction section was divided into countries, and so it was that I discovered England and Russia and, best of all, France. Camus and Sartre and de Beauvoir and of course Flaubert, who became a sort of lover. My favourite book of all was *The Red and the Black* by Stendhal, the story of Julien Sorel, a young peasant boy who has a mad admiration for Napoleon Bonaparte. Like Bonaparte, Julien is driven by passion and ambition. He educates himself and becomes a tutor to the children of Madame de Rênal, and then becomes her lover. Later, he makes his way to Paris, where he seduces Mathilde de la Mole, the daughter of his employer. Destiny awaits him. Failure is his fate. Upon reading this novel, I reread it and then gave it to Mrs. Emery, who, when she heard I had been given access to the Dewey library, made some joke about the Dewey decimal system. I suspected that she was jealous and covetous of the Dewey wealth, or perhaps disappointed that she had been usurped. In any case, she took Stendhal and came back to me with an assessment not nearly as enthusiastic as mine. "The poor boy," she said. "A little ambition is a dangerous thing." I realized then that she could be wrong about some things.

And so the library became my heaven. Once a week my brother trundled me between our small house and the Dewey palace, parked me at the entrance, and I entered quietly, gliding into the library, where I made my choice of reading material. I gathered up these books and placed them in my lap and waited patiently for Tessa, who would guide me back to my house.

Mrs. Emery was still bringing me books, and one day I discovered a *Vogue* magazine at the bottom of one of the boxes. When she saw me pick it up, she said, "How did that get in there?" and she reached to pluck it from my grasp, but I held onto it and put it beside my bed. When she was gone, after an hour-long discussion about science fiction, during which she said *goddamn* a lot (she was an atheist), I picked up the *Vogue*. The cover girl looked very much like Isobel. Same freckles, same short hair, but in this case the cover girl's eyes, where the tear ducts are located, were painted light blue like the colour of a robin's egg, and her eyelashes were dark and thick, and her lips were red. Isobel had no taste for makeup back then. The jaw was similar, slightly squared, and the cover girl had a dimple on her right cheek, just like Isobel. She was looking right at me. Inside the magazine there were more photographs. This unknown girl wore short dresses, and her legs were thin, and it appeared that she had a flat chest. I studied these photographs for a long time and then paged through the magazine, front to back. I felt an appetite for something, though I could not name it.

I still had the sketchbook that Miss Chou had given me back in grade school, and I asked my mother to find it. "Good," she said. "It's about time you did something useful." I see now that my mother might have been jealous of my freedom. She envied me, and because this was so, she wished to take away from me what she could not have for herself. She thought that I read too much, that my mind might be slipping dangerously into fantasy, and so to halt this she had been seeking ways to keep me busy. We lived on a farm, and a farm produced shit, and shit was a perfect place for flies to lay eggs, and the larvae then hatched and produced more flies—the inevitable cycle of nature. And so my mother wheeled me into the kitchen, where it was my job to swat the infinite number of flies that managed to escape the flypaper hanging near the door frame and breezed in each time the screen door opened. Or, my mother brought me potatoes and carrots to peel for supper, plopping the large pot in my lap. It became my job to polish the silverware, which I loved, especially for the initial hint of Silvo as I unscrewed the lid. As I worked, dark stains appeared on my fingers and hands, and the forks and knives were laid out in perfect gleaming symmetry on the table beside me. It was my grandmother's set, directly from Russia, brought over in 1926 when my grandmother's family escaped the clutches of the bandit Makhno, who tore through the Ukrainian countryside seeking out Mennonites to slaughter.

I had a natural ability for drawing, just as I had a natural sense for whatever I put my mind to: arc welding, breaking horses, creating the perfect béchamel sauce, architecture. At the age of fifteen, when I visited my neurologist, I had decided that this would be the career for me, the exploration of the brain and the temporal lobe and the middle cranial fossa, et cetera, et cetera—as it related to auditory and visual experience. Now, however, I would draw.

Other than Isobel, who was a girl, I had never seen a naked woman, though Miss Chou, in the innocence of grade three, had presented us with classical paintings, one by a French artist named Alexandre Cabanel, in which a woman, lounging on a wave in the ocean, exhibited her body and breasts, and there were infants that hovered above those breasts like overjoyed chubby birds. The women that I drew were girls like Isobel. They were lean and boyish, with no discernible chest. At some point I realized I might be drawing myself, without a penis.

Miss Chou had taught us that figures should be drawn in proportion, and the best way to do that was to measure the body in multiples of the head length: one body equals seven and a half head lengths. Weight distribution was achieved by using a vertical plumb line for all standing and walking poses. The line dropped from the pit of the neck to the centre of balance. Shoulders sloped in the opposite way to the hips. I understood all of this. I also understood the importance of not making too much of the hair, and that the mouth required three basic lines, and that hands were drawn by seeing each joint as a block form. Needless to say, I only drew women, for they moved elegantly, swaying their hips, hands almost at right angles.

From there I moved on to the clothes. At first I drew dresses, tops, culottes, and skirts. Then I filled the clothes with bodies, adding arms and legs and heads. Clothes made a woman beautiful. Clothes were the outside and if the outside was beautiful, so must be the inside.

After a time I grew tired of drawing simple clothes that a woman like my mother might wear, and so I began to draw the clothes that the women wore in my books. I drew, for example, the dressing gown that Emma Bovary wore. Her pleated shift with three gold buttons, the belt with heavy tassels, and her *little garnet-colored slippers* with *the broad ribbons that fell over the instep*. Or the dress that Anna Karenina wore to the ball when she danced with Vronsky. A low-cut black velvet dress all trimmed with Venetian guipure lace.

And then, because I cherished touching what was real, I took up sewing. Of course our family, being poor, had a sewing machine. It was a Husqvarna Viking. My mother had always sewn clothes for us. I had been taunted at school for wearing pants that were too short, or overly large shirts made of rough flannel. My brother Bev beat up anyone who teased him, whereas I slipped away and pictured myself in Vienna, wearing lederhosen and sitting down at grand tables to eat schnitzel with the aristocracy. My mother was surprised that I would want to sew, but she believed it was a good remedy for idle hands. My father went *Bah*, and said, "What nonsense. Give him a stick to whittle."

I used cast-off clothing and old curtains at first. But then Mrs. Emery, who had noticed my first rudimentary attempts at sewing, brought me pieces of cloth that she had purchased for a fair price at the fabric store in Tomorrow. I learned to work with nylon, denim, polyester, cotton, silk, and tweed. My mother had old patterns lying about and I used these to practise. I made a blouse using polyester the colour of blackened orange, and though it was quite ugly, my mother took to wearing it around the house. Bev, now eighteen and nearly finished school, was disgusted. He called me all manner of names and then, perhaps realizing that I was unaffected, stopped speaking to me. Calm fell upon the house.

THE THING TO DO, IF YOU WERE A BOY IN JUNIOR high, was to fight. Bev had a reputation as a solid fighter, he never lost, and because I was his brother I was expected to be a fighter like him. I wasn't. Fighting scared me. I sidestepped confrontation, and when it came I resorted to muteness or avoidance, and when I did finally speak, my words came out in a flurry, incomprehensible to those who had never learned to read and write properly. I was tall, which helped, and Bev was my brother, which proved a blessing at first, but eventually it was discovered by the tougher kids that, unlike my brother, I wasn't a willing fighter. Severn and Stu Turk were brothers at our school. They were tough and mean and for no explanation girls were attracted to them. Severn, the younger brother, had it in for me. Perhaps he didn't like my clothes, or the fact that I called him *scurrilous* or a *scallywag*, words he didn't understand. This would have been during the *s* stage of my close perusal of the *Concise Oxford English Dictionary*.

In any case, a confrontation with Severn loomed. This was the era when we still lined up before entering school, and Severn took to standing behind me in line and jeering. "Hey, Swiss Boy. Give us a yodel."

Severn thought that my family name, Wohlgemuht, was odd, and because he was just bright enough to know that the name was German, he took to calling me Adolf and Wohlkswagen and asking where my clogs were. The first time, I took him seriously and explained that it was the Dutch who in fact wore clogs, and then I tried to explain the origin of my name. "It's actually *wohl*, which means 'well,' and *gemüt* means 'mind.'" I went on to explain that the Volkswagen was simply the "people's wagon," and that as far as fine machinery and inventions and quality ideas go, the Germans were unsurpassed.

He sneered. His face looked concave like a spade, and his large nostrils were the two rivets that attached the tool to the handle, which was his tall lanky body. He pushed me and I stumbled backwards. "Still happy, Wohl?" he asked.

I felt despair. The kind of despair that just comes without warning and makes it hard to breathe. I sucked in some air and said that I would be much happier if I could be left alone.

He laughed. "Meet me after school. Behind the shitter."

"I have no desire to fight. Fighting is for baboons and male lions who seek a mate."

"No desire. Who do you think you are? Desire? What bullshit." He worked his hands in circles as his mouth sought out his words.

I wondered if this was finally my punishment for the sin of carnality. Perhaps I even wanted to be punished. Even so, I was still leaning towards self-protection.

"What do you want?" I asked.

He paused and his small eyes blinked, as if this were not a question to be considered. Then his body sank slightly and he said, "I want to fight you. I want to beat the shit out of you."

"Why?"

"Waddya mean, why?"

There is a scene near the beginning of *Madame Bovary* in which Charles Bovary arrives at a new school and enters the classroom and throws his hat against the wall like the other boys in the class, because *it was the thing to do*. Bovary is laughed at, and ridiculed, not least because he is awkward and slightly stupid and new to the school. I was a bit like Charles Bovary, though I knew that I was not stupid. I was far better read and more intelligent. But I was Bovary for other reasons. I was awkward, did not know all the rules, was unfamiliar with social cues, which made me prone to mockery and bullying, and like Bovary I was the opposite of cosmopolitan. If I had any intrigue or sophistication in me, it was gained through reading, which for me was the most dangerous form of learning because it was done with little complexity. I was a void sucking up all knowledge. And this being so, I was also a lover of *character* and I wanted to be someone other than myself. I wanted to be a character in a novel who elicited sympathy and pity and affection, and who would go on to marry a very beautiful woman, even if it was a woman who would destroy herself and her family. Even at my young age I understood that I could have been a better lover than Charles Bovary. One of the great pleasures of reading, especially reading done on a ranch in Alberta by a young boy who wants more, is the possibility of other lives, the possibility of extending one's arm and being pulled through the curtain onto a stage where Swann is in love, and Emma rides her carriage in circles through the city with the blinds drawn, and Joyce's hapless boy is infatuated with Mangan's sister, for whom he will buy a trinket at the market. I was that boy who rode the train to the bazaar, and I had failed to get the trinket.

That afternoon I had a presentation in Language Arts. I had chosen the topic of fish because of where I was born and because I knew a lot about Pacific Coast salmon. Unfortunately, I was unaware that the other students resented my "foreignness" and that they resented even more my constant references to the fact that I had been born on a boat. I liked to tell this story, thinking it was interesting, but at some point others usually became bored and said, "Aw shut up, Wohlgemuht," and walked away. But during the presentation on fish I once again mentioned my birth circumstances, and at this point Mr. Singleton, our teacher, stopped me and said, "Arthur, we've heard this story before. Perhaps you could save it for a special occasion. Maybe tell it once a year?"

I nodded and looked down at my notes. Severn was guffawing in the back. I realized that everything in my presentation hinged on the metaphor of birth and life and the struggle of the salmon upriver and their inevitable death, and this being so, and because I had been cut short on the birth part, I was lost. I managed to finish, but it was a poorly done talk, far too short, and very much lacking in clout. I basically offered up fish facts, and then sat down.

Mr. Singleton asked if there were any questions.

Sonia Rempel, who had passed me love notes in grade two, and had, since then, up through the years, dated most of the boys in our grade, including Severn Turk, and was therefore considered a bit fickle, raised her hand. "If you were born on a Japanese boat, wouldn't that mean you were Japanese?"

The class roared. Mr. Singleton smiled and then said, "Okay, enough."

I waited until the snickering had abated, and then I said that it was a brainless conclusion to make. It would be like saying if she, Sonia, had been born on a bed manufactured in Russia, then she was Russian.

"But I am almost Russian," Sonia said, swinging her shiny blond hair. "My mother was born there."

I was dealing with imbeciles. I sat down, pretending arrogance, yet I felt a deep humiliation, especially because Mr. Singleton, whom I hated at that moment, seemed to have enjoyed the repartee. Flaubert, in January 1837, wrote, *I felt very early a profound disgust with men from the moment I came into contact with them. From the age of twelve I was sent to school: there I saw a shortcut to the world, its vices in miniature, its origins of ridicule, its little passions, its little coteries, its little cruelty; I saw the triumph of force, mysterious emblem of the power of God; I saw faults that would later become vices, vices that would be crimes, and children who would be men.*

What a fine and incisive mind. What a resemblance to my own life, my own ideas, my world.

When the bell rang to signal the end of school, I picked up my bag and ran, certain that Severn was coming for me. I ran outside and towards the nearby pasture. I climbed over the barbwire fence and went out into the middle of the field and sat down. A large Limousin bull, which had been shipped over from France, grazed in the distance. Severn had followed me of course. He paused outside the fence and called out, "Hey, Fish Boy, you collecting more bullshit?"

This was a comment full of wit, and I wondered if Severn was smarter than he appeared.

I should have been terrified of Severn, which I was, but also of the bull, because the Limousin is an unpredictable animal and much more dangerous than a Brahma. But I knew this particular bull. Dewey had had several Limousin bulls shipped over the previous year, and it had become my job to care for them, to feed them. It made perfect sense to me, the victim of Severn's violence, to run straight for the pasture near the school where this Limousin, with its broad forehead and wide pelvis and dark brooding eyes, grazed. What fine supple hide. Muscular hindquarters. Testicles like bowling balls. The bull watched me carefully.

The bus arrived and the kids climbed on, and so Severn disappeared. Finally, alone, I moved slowly to the edge of the field, climbed over the fence, and walked home, arriving just in time for supper.

I spent the following week, every lunch hour and after school, in the pasture with the French bull, who came to understand that I was a tepid intruder.

One day at supper my brother said, "Just fight him already. Surprise him."

My mother nodded. She was ruthless, certainly able to see the damage that might be done to her little boy, yet unwilling to protect me. I did not understand her.

My father said, "Let him be."

And I hated him for saying that, because it meant he pitied me.

Finally, two weeks later, full of resolution and dismay, I met Severn behind the outhouse. The whole school population, seventy-seven students, had heard of the fight, and they were present, forming a ring. I removed my glasses and put them in my jeans pocket. I stepped towards Severn and raised my fists in a half-hearted manner. He swung and hit me in the temple. I fell back. He swung again and caught my mouth.

"Fight, you dick," he said.

"It's against my principles," I said.

This infuriated him and he pummelled me until I fell to the ground. The crowd cheered and a few girls, tender souls, gasped and called out for this to stop. Bev was at the edge of the circle. He stood quietly, looking disgusted, hands in his pockets.

To Severn's credit, he did not kick me when I was down. He pulled me to my feet and hit me again and again, in the breadbasket, across the face, around my ears and neck. I fell again and by this time the rabble had grown quieter and Severn was panting.

The crowd dispersed. We all went back to our classes. I cleaned myself up and returned to my homeroom and sat down and pulled out my notebook. I had a loose tooth and I worked at it with my tongue the rest of the afternoon, but it did not fall out. Nettie Runningwolf, who was half Blackfoot and rarely said a word, passed by me on the way out of school and placed a folded piece of paper on my desk. I opened it later at home, in my bedroom, and discovered a pressed flower, yellow, with *Lily* written beneath it.

At supper that evening my mother surprised me when she accused Bev of standing by and doing nothing. "Is that what a brother does?" Earlier, she had iced my jaw and cleaned my face with a warm cloth, muttering all the while about boys and violence. I did not mention my loose tooth because of my oversized fear of our family dentist. The last time I visited him he had found seven cavities and filled them all at once, muttering above me, joking with his assistant, a tall redhead who tittered and snorted and pressed her chest against me as she suctioned up my saliva and blood. Like other women in my life, even those who merely brushed up against me, I loved her.

My mother daubed at my eye and said, "You should take boxing lessons."

"He won't touch me again," I said.

"How can you know that?" she cried.

"He just won't. He garnered no pleasure from this."

"Oh, Arthur, who taught you how to talk?" She shook her head.

I thought it was fair and good that we managed to bewilder each other.

ABOUT ALICE. EVEN AS ISOBEL COURTED ME, MY heart would fling itself sideways towards Alice Dewey whenever she returned for the summer. This was happening less and less, as she now spent time in Wyoming with her extended family, or studied ballet in various cities around the world. Her mother wanted the best for her. But when she came home, she usually found me. I was her *holiday boyfriend*. This is how she put it, and who was I to argue.

Since the age of fourteen, when we were able to get our learner's licence in Alberta, she had been allowed to drive as long as she stayed on the side roads and didn't head off to Calgary or Lethbridge, and so she'd bring me along, though I was never sure why. She had been around for several days during Isobel's last visit, and one time as we drove the country roads she asked me whether "that one" was my girlfriend. I said that Isobel was my adopted cousin, adopted double cousin in fact.

"Doesn't mean you can't be attracted to her."

"True, but how far can it go?"

"Pretty far, I figure."

I asked her if she had a boyfriend. She was striking and full-grown by then, so full-grown that when she wore button-down shirts, the shirt stretched and revealed the laciness of her bra. She complained to me once that dancers shouldn't have big breasts, it was a problem, and to this I had no good response.

"Does that bother you?" she asked. "When I talk about my body?"

I said that it didn't. I was open to all conversations.

She said that her mother was very fond of me. She was impressed with my reading ability. "I don't like to read and that upsets Mother," she said.

At that time I didn't care whether Alice was a reader because I was only interested in sitting next to her and listening to her breathe and hearing her talk about her life away from Alberta and watching her mouth and the profile of her face and her chest. It was my pleasure to be able to sit in the passenger's seat and observe.

She said that she had had several boyfriends but they had been busts. A lot of the boys at the ballet school were not fond of girls in that way. I had been doing some research about dance, in order to have a reasonable conversation with her when she returned, should she return, and now that we were together I talked to her about Russian ballet dancers, and I said that Vaslav Nijinsky had masturbated on stage. She said, "You're funny."

I wasn't as attracted to her as I was to Isobel, perhaps because her mind was not as quick and she didn't challenge me in the same way, and perhaps because I never knew what she truly thought of me. She was full of indirection. In the words of psychoanalysis, she filled me with anxiety, because even as she was rejecting me she made it appear that she wasn't. She wouldn't have understood any of this, her thoughts didn't move in that way. But even so, she was a young woman and I had been intimate with Isobel, and I understood that sexual experience was like a door that opened onto a vast room. Once you knocked and the door was opened, you would go back to that door and keep knocking.

The thing is, Isobel had been the aggressor, and so I had never had to do anything, just sort of lie back and accept her advances. Alice was different. She was shy and refined and careful. One night we watched a movie together at her house. We were in the sitting room. The movie was on CBC and it was a Bond film, though I can't remember the title or even what took place—because I was busy with Alice. She was passionate that night. She held my hand and stroked it and said that she liked my hair, how it was growing out. I asked if I could kiss her and she seemed surprised that I asked.

She said, "Just do it."

And so we kissed. She was harder and less pliable than Isobel, and at first she didn't like my tongue in her mouth, but then she gave in, though she never reciprocated. I felt rather dirty, thinking that perhaps I had violated her mouth. I asked her exactly that. She said, "You're funny." This was her way of saying that I should stop talking.

She had sharp ears for her mother, and perhaps this is why she seemed wary and less enthusiastic than me. Her mother did walk in at one point, throwing a glance at us, but Alice had heard the whispered approach and so we were modestly separated on the couch, nonchalantly watching the film. After her mother left, Alice drew me close and bit my ear and then she said the word *fuck*, quietly, and at first I wasn't sure if I had heard her, but she said it again, and she grabbed my hand and pushed it against her crotch and held it there, and then pushed me away. She was quite unpredictable.

Two days later she left without saying goodbye, and if I had been a more sensitive boy, I would have been hurt. As it stood, I felt a slight ache in my chest and a longing for something indefinable, but after several weeks the longing left me and I remembered Alice vaguely, as if our brief passion had been written on a palimpsest. I loved that word.

I was fifteen when my brother Bev joined the American army to fight in Vietnam.

My mother had a fit. We were at Sunday lunch, and when Bev announced his plans, my mother threw down her napkin, pushed herself back from the table, and went into the kitchen. She banged dishes and threw pots around and called out that he was an idiot, certainly not her blood, and she wouldn't stand for it.

We were eating farmer sausage and macaroni salad, and *zwieback* on which we slathered butter and jam and cheese. Coffee was served from a large silver tureen. There were cherry tarts for dessert.

My father looked at Bev and said, "You're sure about this?"

"I am."

"Where will you sign up?"

"Fort Sill. In Oklahoma."

"How do you know they'll have you?" my father asked.

"I don't. But I am half American, and if they refuse, I'll come back."

My father nodded. He pushed a bun into his mouth, chewed, swallowed, and then said, "She'll come to her senses."

My mother returned to the table. She sat down. "I didn't raise my boy so that he could head off to some unknown land to kill other men who have hearts and souls and hands and feet just like he has. Or to have my boy killed. We come from a people that have always said no to war and to killing. We don't do that. We don't aim a gun at an enemy. We don't have enemies. If you want to save yourself, if you have some sort of guilt that you're trying to soothe, then go build a school or dig a well. Don't shoot people. Thou shalt not kill. Love your neighbour. Oh, listen to me. Listen to your mother."

We were quiet.

We weren't a family given to discussions about politics or world events. Dinner talk, when someone took the time to talk, centred on work and weather and local gossip. Folks in Tomorrow, like us, saw politics as a force from the East, where men in suits made poor decisions based on greed and selfishness. The West, Alberta, was a hinterland, backwards and unacknowledged, but absolutely necessary for the survival of the country, especially now, with the oil crisis. What little news came into our house did so via the CBC and *Time* magazine. We had all seen the images coming out of Vietnam and the States, the protests, the killings at Kent State, but those were events so far removed that they felt like dramas created by a malicious playwright and acted out on a stage by unfortunate players who bore no resemblance to Bev or my father or my mother or me. We were untouched. My mother, though, was wiser. She knew that Bev would be touched by the war, and possibly horrifically, and so she railed and fought. She had one last say, and she spoke it to the ceiling.

"There are young boys, Americans, who are running up to Canada to avoid the draft. And then there's my son who thinks he's better."

"Never said better," Bev said. "Though anyone who'd run from a duty has to be a bit of a weasel."

"A smart weasel then," Mother said. She turned to my father. "Tell him. Tell him he can't go."

"He's a man, Doreen. He'll do what he chooses."

"It's not a choice. That isn't choosing. You might as well shoot me if that's choosing."

PERHAPS BECAUSE SHE WAS ABOUT TO SAY GOODBYE to her eldest son, my mother spent time complaining to me about Bev. She didn't raise him to go off to some fetid land to kill and maim, or worse yet, to *be* killed and maimed. "Don't get it into your head, Arthur, that this is normal or right."

I let her talk. I said nothing. She was educating me in the ways of love and favouritism, for even as she complained about Bev, I understood that we were talking about me.

My father and I drove Bev down to Oklahoma. We crossed the border at Coutts in the pickup, me in the middle between my brother and father, Bev's green suitcase laid out in back. The border guard was an older man with a handlebar moustache and a languid attitude who was proud to meet a Canadian who had made up his mind to eradicate evil in the world.

We slept that first night in a campground near the Wyoming border. Our family had an old canvas baptismal tent with no bottom, and at night the mosquitoes came in through the cracks and attacked us and I heard my father swatting and tossing. Bev slept like a baby. When I woke in the morning my father was tending the fire and making coffee. For breakfast we barbecued wieners on sticks and dipped them into a jar of strawberry jam my mother had sent along. My father said it was the best meal he'd ever had. Bev was quiet.

I'd taken along the *Reader's Digest World Atlas*, and as my father drove I spent time studying the map of Southeast Asia, trying to ascertain the layout of the place. On the inside front cover there was a legend with various coloured rectangles that made it easy to find the country you wanted to explore. I was surprised to discover that Vietnam was not very large. It was shaped like the tail of a cat, the tip of the tail dropping down towards the Gulf of Thailand and the South China Sea. Odd to think that something that small could be the cause of so much trouble. I found various facts and offered them up for everyone's digestion, as if I were back in school making a presentation. Square mileage, GDP, literacy rate, population growth. It turned out that the population was almost three times that of Canada's. This was startling to me, though neither my father nor Bev seemed interested. At some point I found myself in France, poring over the names of various villages, and imagining a life on the coast of Bretagne, perhaps in Saint-Malo, where the tides moved and one walked hand in hand with a beautiful French girl on the wet beach while crabs skittered here and there.

When we dropped Bev off at Fort Sill, we didn't hang around, we just hugged my brother goodbye. And then we drove back towards Alberta. That's when my father became looser and softer. He explained the politics of Vietnam to me, and the politics of the United States. He described the ambitions of the most powerful nation in the world, a place where he had been raised. He said that hegemony produced fear. He used that word and I wrote it down in the notebook that I always carried in my back pocket. He said that the Americans were foolish, though they thought they were wise, but this is what happens when someone has power and little wisdom. He said that no matter what the Americans did, be it good or bad, they would be criticized. There was no winning when you were the king and everyone else was a serf.

I wondered if Bev would be okay, and he said that there was no telling. He said that men liked war. They might say they didn't, but the fact was men liked to fight. He said that if God had made one mistake, it was giving men a love for battle. I had never heard him criticize God in that way and it stirred me in a strange fashion. It made my father seem less predictable. And then he said that he was afraid for Bev, and he turned his face away from me.

We slept in a motel that night. My father said that the tent was useless and we would be better off sleeping in the open air rather than trapping a bunch of mosquitoes and then entering that same trap and offering ourselves up as food. Our family did not have a lot of money and so taking a motel, no matter how cheap the room, was an extravagance that pleased me greatly. The window of our room gave out onto the parking lot where our pickup sat. My father and I shared the only bed, and after we had both showered, he read to me from the book he had with him. It was a novel called *An American Tragedy* by a man named Theodore Dreiser, and though my father was already well into it, he started from the beginning, and at some point I laid my head on his shoulder and followed along as he read, and the words washed over me, but even more so, my father's voice washed over me and entered my ears and I was a child again and we were reading to the horses that he would break in the pasture beyond our little house where our family lived and ate and slept. I would continue to read the book later, back home, taking it from my father's table beside his armchair and reading it innocently, as a story, and only discovering in my later years that it was about ambition and failure and class division. The style was odd, almost simple, and yet it moved me and created in me a longing for the skill to tell a story in that manner: plainly, with force and consequence.

Earlier, coming out of the shower, my father had been naked. I had seen him naked before, but never that close. I saw his penis and it resembled mine though it was slightly larger, and when I saw him naked like that, for some reason I felt sad and ashamed. That is what I felt at that moment, but the feelings, the shame and the sadness, went away when he began to read.

My mother, over the next while, worked her shifts at the hospital and then came home and spent her time cleaning the house and doing laundry and killing chickens, having me push them into boiling water and pluck them, the smell of wet feathers enough to make you sick. She drove into town and came back with fresh paint that she used to freshen up Bev's room, and here too I was her helpmeet. She wrote long letters to him and mailed them off to Fort Sill, from where they would be sent on to Saigon.

An occasional letter came from Bev, brief and of not much use regarding his state and his health and his wants and his fears, but she read and reread each one and then folded it and pushed it back into the envelope and stored it with other valuable papers in a metal box that would protect them from fire should the house burn down. In that box was a photo of Em, black and white, on the beach, looking up at our father, taken the day before she drowned. My mother was not sentimental. She only became so when feeling utterly helpless, and then she was over the top.

I turned into her slave and maid and confidant, and she suffocated me with her anxiety and her will. Sometimes I broke free and spent time with my father, riding out into the pastures to look for cows that were too stupid to know how to birth their calves properly. But mostly, after school and on the weekends, I was with her. She talked to me about Bev and she went on and on about the party we would throw when he returned.

If I were making stuff up rather than telling the truth, I would have Bev killed in Vietnam, which would be more dramatic and create a conflict in our family. That is to say, it would be easier to deal with my mother's grief than to observe the uxorious love she poured all over his absence and the joy she felt upon his return. Her anxiety, her panic, her frenzy, her relief. I recognize all of that now.

THROUGHOUT THIS PERIOD OF MY LIFE, I WROTE letters to Isobel and she wrote back. We slipped photographs of ourselves into the envelopes in order to signal our physical changes. She had grown even taller and her face was more defined and her maturity produced in me a sense of betrayal, dismay, and covetousness. She had acquired a taste for clothes that veered from tomboyish (jeans and plaid shirts and a cowboy hat) to overtly feminine (short shorts, miniskirts and high black boots, tight jeans with embroidered flowers, and tank tops beneath which she was obviously not wearing a bra). In one letter she advised me to grow my hair. "You look like a hick," she wrote. And so I dutifully grew my hair, which discombobulated my father, who took to calling me a hippie, a grave insult in our area. My mother wondered what Isobel and I had to say to each other, what was so important in our lives that we had to write "love" letters back and forth. I said that Isobel was highly intelligent, and that we thought about the same things, and I asked, if Isobel were a boy cousin, would Mother still call them love letters?

"Well, she isn't a boy, is she. There's a whole ocean of girls out there, girls who aren't your double cousin."

"It's not like we're getting married," I said.

"I should think not."

But I did think of it, imagining Isobel eating toast across from me in the morning, her blinking sleepy eyes, the sound of waves falling against the shore outside our villa. We lived in southern France and read Stendhal to each other in the original language, and we drank dark coffee and argued about Camus and the idea of engagement. I had read much of Camus and suggested in a letter that she do so as well. She complied, and then made some joke about how *The Plague* could never be set in a place like Alberta. "You have no rats there," she wrote. She was implying, in a depressing way, that nothing brilliant could come out of my place, my land, my home. Out of me. I didn't disagree.

I began my letters with *Dear Isobel*, or simply *Isobel*, or *Dear Is*, and once I wrote, *Deer Is*. Then I said, *The misspelling of Dear was intentional. Obviously it is an anagram for desire. I've been reading Freud, weird stuff that I usually don't get, though I'm writing down my dreams. Anyways.* I talked about *the moral problem of finding one's own convictions and realizing at the same time that there will always be an element of self-aggrandizement and distortion.* Years later, when we were together in Paris, I asked her how she managed to put up with my pretensions, my naive conviction. She answered very simply, "This is what I loved. Your conviction."

We were never sexually specific in our letters, though when we were face to face we had no problems talking frankly. Writing was different, as if seeing the words on the page made them more forceful, more real.

We saw each other every summer up until the time she was seventeen. Our families visited, and always, just before the vacation, she would write and say, *Time to fool around.* Each time she said this I was surprised, because I kept waiting for her to outgrow me, or for her to find a boyfriend, or for her to dismiss me as backward and ugly. The words themselves, *time to fool around*, were absolutely true. We were fools in time, fooling no one, and we were going around in circles.

We managed to accomplish whatever our imaginations desired, though Isobel, fearful of pregnancy, stubbornly refused to let me find my way inside her. And so we were satisfied with undressing in front of each other and touching and talking and holding each other under the white sky while the sun rose and the horses grazed nearby and the birds sang. Like Julien Sorel and Mathilde de la Mole, when they first make love, our *ecstasies were a bit willed. Passionate love was still a model we were imitating, rather than something real.*

Three summers after my accident, her family came for two weeks, one week of which, in the evenings, both families dressed in finer clothes and attended the evangelistic services in Brooks. At the arena hundreds of metal chairs had been placed in tight rows, and a large stage built beneath the scoreboard, and onto that stage strode a preacher in a light blue suit and white shoes. The preacher's name was Rudy B. Rudy B had the gait of a principal dancer in the Bolshoi Ballet and the voice of a bass who has given himself the role of Paavo, a travelling preacher in a Finnish opera. My father and Isobel's father were slightly dismissive of these revival meetings, but our mothers were keen, and so they dragged everyone else along. Isobel and I sat together near the back of the arena. I was a Christian, as was Isobel. It was the thing to do in our families. Neither of us was yet baptized. The rule in our church was for us to wait until we were adults, or had the mind and decision-making capabilities of adults. I was deeply affected by the evangelist's words, and brought to tears by the final song that was played every night. Though I was already born again, I struggled with whether it was okay for me to step out into the aisle and go forward to *rededicate myself to Jesus.* I did this on a Thursday evening.

That night, the evening of my rededication, riding in the car back to our house, Isobel sat beside me and whispered, "Do you feel any different?"

I shrugged. I showed her the book that I had been given by the woman who had prayed with me in one of the dressing rooms in the back of the arena. There had been numerous others in that dressing room, and I was struck by how I was not special at all, and by how ordinary I felt. Still, I had prayed with the woman, whose name was Loraine. She was barely older than I was and she was quite fetching, and extremely sure of herself. We prayed, I asked for forgiveness, Loraine squeezed my hand, and then she offered me the book, which happened to be a novel with strong religious themes. Still, a book was a book. And this one was free. When I showed Isobel the novel, she studied the title and handed it back to me. "I've read it. It's a piece of crap."

Her mother, my aunt Beth, heard her words and turned her head. "Isobel, please."

Isobel held my hand in the dark and breathed into my ear the most important question. "You'll still meet me tomorrow?"

I squeezed her hand. "Yes," I said.

The following morning we found ourselves alone in a gully with birds circling above us. The previous night and my decision seemed far away and otherworldly in the light of the new day and the immediacy of our desire. I did not see the hypocrisy in this, and neither did Isobel. In any case, we did not speak of it. She said that she wanted to see my leg, the one that had been broken and was now healed. I took off my boots and jeans and sat in the grass while she touched the leg.

"Does it still hurt?"

"It aches sometimes," I said.

She stroked the outside of my thigh. The leg was thin and white and to me it appeared grotesque. She bent to kiss the scar.

"Don't," I said.

"It's okay. I like it."

I had no sensation on the surface of the scar and so I could not feel her mouth or her tongue, but I could see that she was alternating between kissing the scar and licking it, as if she were a small animal tending to her young. The curve of her skull, her hair brushing my skin, the slope of her bent back, the remoteness, the separation between what I saw and what I felt, all of this made me breathless and sad. I felt a tingling at the back of my neck, dizziness, and I saw a flash of light. A red-bellied fish, with the head of a young girl, swam just below the surface of a stream. I closed my eyes and lay back and said that I was feeling sick. I heard her voice and opened my eyes. She was kneeling above me. Her mouth was moving but I could not hear the words. She touched my face, my mouth, my eyes. Stroked my forehead. I heard my name come out of her mouth.

"What is it, Arthur?" she said.

I sat up.

"You fainted," she said.

"No I didn't. I heard your voice the whole time."

"Your eyes were closed and they were fluttering, like this." She closed her own eyes and moved her eyeballs around to show me.

As I was still feeling slightly nauseous, she helped me get dressed. Her hands were strangely quick, and where they touched my bare skin I was overly excited by their softness.

"Weird," I said.

"Very," she said. "Can you ride?"

I shook my head. I had to wait a bit. I said, "I saw my sister, Em. She was under water."

"What do you mean?"

"Her face was under water and she was looking up at me and her mouth was moving like a fish. She had fins and a tail like a fish."

Isobel watched me. "Your sister's dead," she said.

"I know that."

"You were a baby when she died."

"Doesn't matter," I said. "Strange though. I wonder if God is punishing me."

"Oh, Arthur." She touched my face. "Don't think that." Then she held my hands and said, "You should tell your mom."

"What would I say? You were kissing my leg and I had a vision about Em?"

She laughed. Her teeth were white and clean and her tongue was pink. I was tired.

AROUND THAT TIME, MY MOTHER BEGAN WORRYING about my *state of mind*. I was prone to slipping off into reveries, especially when I was working in the barn, or crossing the yard towards the house. She once found me standing beside the clothesline where the sheets flapped in a brisk westerly wind, and she had to shake me several times to get my attention.

"What are you doing? What's wrong, Arthur?"

When I finally noticed her I said that I had been thinking.

"About what?"

I shrugged.

"Well, maybe you should stop thinking and do something more useful."

I agreed with her at that moment, but I didn't agree with her overall. In fact, when she had interrupted me, I had been thinking about the word *ambition*, whose root was *ambire*, which meant "to go round." I imagined myself as ambitious, and if this was so, it meant that I was circling some higher goal. To be ambitious in my town, my church, my tradition, was frowned upon. It meant that I saw myself as better than my people. "Who do you think you are?" my mother asked me more than once.

Being a sensible woman, she took me to an ear, nose, and throat doctor to have my hearing checked. And then we visited my former neurologist, who was still squat and still wore glasses, and though he was ten years older, he was the same gentle man. He sat on a stool before me and looked into my eyes with his light. Blink. Look to the right. Look to the left. Look up. Look down. He placed his instrument on the desk and with both hands he touched my head, moving from the crown to the forehead. The room was silent. I saw the hair in his nostrils and wondered if I too would have that much hair in my nose when I was older. He asked if I had had any bad falls recently. I said no. My last fall had been a few years earlier, when I broke my leg.

"Yes," he said. "I am aware of that. Did you hit your head at that time? When you fell from your horse?"

"I don't remember. I don't think so."

"It is possible, though? That you did?"

His eyes were green. Or blue. They kept changing colour. I said that I didn't know.

"Do you suffer blackouts? Times when you are aware of having lost consciousness?"

"I don't think so."

"Nothing like that then," he said.

I said that one time I had felt a tingling behind my neck and then seen my older sister swimming under water.

"Your older sister."

"She died when I was a baby. She drowned."

"How did you know it was her?"

"I saw her face. I recognized her."

"Where were you when this happened?"

"At home."

"Yes. Where exactly?"

"We had taken the horses out for a ride, and I was lying down by the river, looking up at the sky, and that's when it happened."

"So someone was with you."

"My cousin."

"Was there anything that preceded this? Had you fallen, were you excited?"

I hesitated. "No. Nothing."

"And did your cousin notice anything different about you?"

"My eyes were doing funny things. They were moving around. Like this." I performed for him what Isobel had shown me.

"Does your cousin have a name?"

"Isobel."

"How old is Isobel?"

"A year older than me."

"You two are close?"

"She's my cousin." I said that I didn't want my mother to know.

"About your cousin?"

"My sister."

"Why is that, Arthur?"

"Anything to do with Em makes her upset."

"Don't you think she would be curious about your dream? It might please her."

"I don't think so. She doesn't believe in stuff like that."

Dr. Porter removed his glasses. He wrote something on a piece of paper. "If you say so. Do you mind if I ask her in to talk about how we should proceed?"

"What do you mean?"

"I would like to run some tests. Nothing painful. To do with your head, your brain. You're a smart boy, and we want to keep you that way."

My mother that day was wearing a blue cotton dress with small white flowers that flourished everywhere. Enough to make you dizzy. She wore a wide red belt and her hair was shoulder length and she had flipped the ends before we left the house. I had heard her in the bathroom, toiling and primping. She looked very different that day, perhaps because we were visiting the city, and when she entered the office she sat down and smoothed her dress and crossed her legs. She was wearing her blue high-heeled shoes, the ones she wore every Sunday.

Dr. Porter said that he would like to run a few tests. An EEG, and perhaps, if warranted, a brain scan.

"Does he have a tumour?" my mother asked. She still worked as a nurse, and she liked to get to the heart of the matter.

"Not at all. At least not that I can tell. Don't worry, Doreen, these are simply precautionary steps."

I had not known that Dr. Porter knew my mother's name, and it was almost as if I had forgotten that she had a name, and then I remembered that, yes, my mother was called Doreen. I rarely saw my mother talking to a man other than my father, and this was the first time I realized that she might be attractive to someone other than me. The thought made me protective.

The EEG was scheduled for a Monday morning, and once

again my mother took the day off work and drove me in. My father was down in Wyoming buying horses. In any case, my mother had wanted to keep everything quiet, and so my father was not informed of the tests. She liked to keep him in the dark until it was time to divulge, and then she threw all of the information his way and wondered why he was so confused and slow to pick up on the essentials. She liked to say that he was a bit thick emotionally.

My mother described the test as she drove. She said that once my head had been fitted with various electrodes, I would be shown pictures and asked questions and the technician would observe a series of needles that would indicate and record my brain activity. "They'll want to see if your brain is overexcited in certain areas."

I knew all this. I had found a book on the brain in the school library, and I had talked to my Science teacher about a research project on the brain. Mrs. Enns had been very excited and had shown me various books. I was prepared. And being prepared meant much to me. I wanted to be Dr. Porter's equal. We met again two weeks after the test, and he sat down before me and said that I might be having minor temporal lobe seizures, which would indicate a precondition to some form of epilepsy.

"Not serious at this point, you haven't suffered any grand mal seizures, though it is possible that when you were standing in a reverie by the clothesline, as your mother described you doing, or when your cousin Isobel said that your eyes were rolling about under your lids, you were in fact having a minor seizure. There are medications to prevent further seizures, though at this point I wouldn't prescribe any. Your case doesn't warrant it."

"Why me?" I asked.

He said that any number of factors could be involved. "You had a high fever at a young age, over a long period. You have had a bad fall. These might be instigators. No need to be concerned." He looked at me and touched my shoulder. "Are you worried?"

"Maybe. A little. I don't want to see my sister again."

"Well, you might want to be more curious than afraid. It's just an image of her that you've got locked inside your head, and the seizure is allowing it to surface. The thing is, Arthur, the brain is a mystery. We don't know if it acts like a camera, or a tape recorder, or if it takes in information in a different manner, like a processor, and then translates it into an icon, say a picture or a movie or a sound, so that you, Arthur Wohlgemuht, can understand it and therefore *recall* it." He put great emphasis on the word *recall*, and he smiled at the same time, as if the word, or the series of words he had just used, pleased him. "The incident down by the river, when you saw your sister Em, is an experience that people sometimes have. An event from the past arises, a musical score will start up, a family image will appear. When we go to an art gallery we see sculptures and paintings. These are iconic. Just as an image in our brain is iconic. We require the icon in order to understand the jumble of information. Our brain is a great artist. Which makes you and me artists." He smiled again.

He called my mother into the room and explained in concise terms the results of the tests. He said nothing to her about movies or tape recorders or icons.

"Is he in danger?" she asked.

"Not at all. Keep an eye on him. And you, young man, you must let your mother know if anything untoward occurs. Any tingling of the neck. That sort of thing."

"Tingling of the neck?" my mother asked. "Are there other indicators that will warn us?"

"It happens sometimes," Dr. Porter said, "that a physiological response will alert Arthur that a *reverie* is about to happen. The neck might tingle, the breath shorten, nausea set in. These are warnings of sorts. Arthur understands this."

Driving home, my mother said, "Don't tell your father. He'll just get unnecessarily worried. We don't have to tell anyone. It appears that there is nothing much to tell."

She was embarrassed, and therefore I felt slightly ashamed, though Dr. Porter, whom I trusted, hadn't indicated any need for shame. He had said, half jokingly as we left his office, that I was now in the ranks of the great. I didn't understand what he meant until later that week, when delving into the *World Book Encyclopedia* I discovered that Dostoevsky had been an epileptic. And Flaubert. And Van Gogh. If this was so, I had nothing to fear. Still, I felt fear.

In the car, after my mother announced that my father need not know anything about the doctor's visit, I turned on the radio and landed upon a station where a woman was singing opera. My mother began to sing along, which surprised me because the words were in Italian, and I felt once again, as I had when Dr. Porter called my mother by her name, that she had all along been hiding her real life.

"My father used to play this, after supper," she said. Then, "You're not very happy, are you, Arthur."

She didn't allow any sort of answer, she just kept talking. "Sometimes, when we think we're better than the rest, this makes us unhappy. We become dissatisfied. That might be your problem."

I looked out the window, at the pink tips of the mountains in the distance.

She said, "Don't go thinking that just because of *you know what* that you're special now. Nobody's special." She stopped talking and began to sing again.

I was sixteen at that time. She would have been thirty-nine. On that day she was wearing bright yellow pants that showed off her long legs, cigarette pants they were called, and she wore sandals and her feet were bare. Her feet were very fine, very beautiful. She sang along contentedly to Puccini and tapped the steering wheel. I wondered how she had come to understand that I was dissatisfied.

....

THIRTEEN MONTHS AFTER HE LEFT, BEV RETURNED from Vietnam. At first I did not recognize him. He had lost weight. He was quiet for long periods. He never spoke of his feelings or what he had gone through, except when he drank too much, and then he always related the same story, which wasn't a story at all but a collection of feelings and vague images, in which he described the jungle and the teal sky above him and how luck fell down upon some and not others. When he spoke like this his hands shook. What we did not know then was that over the next years he would be in and out of the psych ward in Edmonton, landing up there the first time when the neighbouring rancher, Felton Granger, found Bev crouching naked down by the river, claiming that *they* were coming to get him.

But now, upon his joyful return, Mother roasted three calves and invited friends and neighbours. The Dewey family came. Alice happened to be home at this time, and so she was there as well, long-legged and thin-armed and dressed in a silk black skirt that, from a certain angle and with the light falling in a particular way, revealed her bare legs and the place high up where her legs met. Her blouse was white and sleeveless. She sat beside me as I ate beef and homemade beans and coleslaw. She ate only a small bun with no butter and she drank water.

She said, "You must be happy, Arthur."

"I am," I said. "You're sitting beside me." I grinned.

"I mean your brother. That he's back."

I said that I didn't really like my brother, he sucked all the oxygen from the earth.

She thought that was mean.

I said that she didn't have a brother.

Later, there was a fiddler and a banjo player and a large fellow playing upright bass, and folks danced. My father, who liked to do a jig now and then, had insisted that there be a dance of sorts. I looked for Alice, with the intention of getting close to her and studying her bare arms. When I finally saw her she was dancing with Bev, and they were leaning into each other, and I saw that Bev was talking into her ear, and Alice would smile and nod and then duck her head as if embarrassed by his words. I went over and interrupted them and said that it was my turn.

Bev looked at me and said, "You're not old enough for her."

Alice released herself and came to me. She looked back at Bev and said thank you.

"Stay away from him," I said. "He's dangerous."

Her eyebrows went up and she clung to me, as if genuinely attracted to me, and I didn't let her go. After, we sat on straw bales at the edge of the dance area, and when we stood to dance again there were pieces of straw stuck to her skirt. I removed them. Her legs, through the gauzy cloth. Her underwear.

Though my mother was throwing the party, and though she didn't drink, there was a liquor table for those who imbibed, and Alice kept returning to that table, pouring vodka into a little plastic glass and pretending it was Canada Dry.

She became looser. She said that she liked my mind. I was smart and witty.

"Did you know that?" she asked.

I said that I had been told this fact by a few people.

"See?" she said, and giggled. She placed her forehead against mine.

We were slow dancing. Her mother was watching from the sideline.

"She's watching us," I said.

"Fuck her," she said. She looped her arms over my shoulders.

"I've always liked you, Arthur," she said. "Remember the frogs we killed? Spearing them down by the dugout?"

I did remember. She had been horrified and mesmerized. I told her this.

"Yes, yes, but that's exactly it. You make no bones."

She had dropped the preposition and the object, and so I had no idea what she was talking about. I held her carefully.

"My mother told me the other day that I will marry someone important."

"It won't be me then, will it?" I said.

She giggled again. I put my hand over her mouth. I did not want to hear that I was funny.

There were lights hanging over the dance area and in the outer regions it was dark. Alice took me there. And then we were on her porch, kissing, and our hands were everywhere. And then we were inside her house, where it was cool and dark, standing beneath the grand chandelier. And then the library, where she leaned against the section where the science books were all lined up. She held my head and kissed me deeply. She drew back and sighed. She was wavering on her feet and so I held her upright. She clutched one of my hands and slipped it up under her white top and inside her bra. It was awkward, and my hand was twisted at such an angle that I felt handcuffed, though I was amazed at the fullness of her. The lights came on and she said, "Shit."

Her mother was standing at the doorway. She said, "I'm going to leave now. I expect that you will do the same, Arthur. Alice, you will go to your room." She turned and left, as she had promised.

I had not looked at her because my back was to her, and even so I could not have faced her. I was thinking of my mother perhaps, who would soon feel the wrath of this woman.

My hand was free now. I stood before Alice and said good night.

"Don't go," she said, and she pulled at my arm.

I let her hold me. She was very relaxed. Almost happy. Only later did I see that she had wanted her mother to find us. It hadn't been about me at all.

I left her there and walked out of that grand house and towards the lights of the party, where folks were still dancing. My brother was sitting with my mother, and she had her arm around his shoulder and she was talking to him. Softly. And I wished that I were Bev.

. . . .

IN A MORE DRAMATIC STORY, ONE FILLED WITH POR-
tent and tragedy, I would receive a summons from Mrs.
Dewey two days later in which she would ask me to join her
in the library at 4 p.m., and we would sit across from each
other. She would be wearing jodhpurs and riding boots and
her hat would rest on the table before us. And she would
finally speak, telling me that I was an intelligent boy but intelligence wouldn't get me her daughter, who was destined for
something more than the wrangler's son. She wouldn't be
a dancer. She was too clumsy, not invested in the necessary
discipline. In fact, she was lazy. Just as she was lazy in love
and sex. She had to be moved to a girls' school in Toronto
where boys were less accessible. Did Alice not tell me? And
then Mrs. Dewey would hold forth on my own future, asking
what I intended to do with myself, and when I would shrug,
not indifferently, she would tell me that I *should* know. I should
be certain. Otherwise I would wander about with no vision
and waste my time and everyone else's. *You have only one life*, she
would say. And then, *You're young. But you are certainly smarter
than your brother, who got lucky and survived the war.* It would be
surprising that she would know my brother to that extent,
and I would see that she knew everything about our family,
and that I knew nothing about hers. This was the privilege of
privacy and wealth. Finally, she would get to her point and say
that I would not see Alice again, and should I talk to her in
private, or should I go for a drive with her, or should I touch
her, or should I even so much as write her, my family would no

longer be welcome on this land. We would be asked to leave. Did I understand?

None of that happened and it disappoints me to not have that kind of theatre and force in my story. The fact is everything was much more banal, and for that reason, sadder. Alice did go away. I did not see her leave. Nothing was said by Mrs. Dewey. I saw her at times, walking from the house to her Oldsmobile to drive into town, or I might have caught a glimpse of her moving through her large rooms at night. She did not address me. She did not look at me. We had an understanding. Or perhaps it was my own fear of Mrs. Dewey that created that understanding. And it affected the most crucial aspect of my life. I no longer entered their house, moving from the portal and walking beneath the grand chandelier and through the heavy walnut doors into the library. And so, I no longer had access to all those books.

My brother took a job at the feedlot and moved into a two-bedroom apartment, sparsely furnished, and sometimes on weekends I slept on a mat in a spare room. Bev didn't mind me hanging around, and once, in what was an outburst of sentimentality for him, he called me *a good shit*. My mother was worried about Bev. A number of times when he was still living at home, he had had nightmares, and she'd found him pacing and shaking and babbling and she'd had to slap him to bring him around. I didn't like the thought of Bev going crazy and so when I did stay over I slept poorly, listening for him to call out.

Bev was riding broncos that summer, and every other weekend he drove his pickup down to Montana and Wyoming to participate in the rodeos there. When he was around on a Friday or Saturday evening, we'd sometimes share a late meal of Kraft Dinner and cold cuts and white bread and milk. Then he'd go out to the bars and seek attention while I stayed home and read late into the evening on an old couch that Bev had found at the local second-hand store. At night, I would often wake and hear a girl's voice and then Bev's voice and some giggling and then the sound of lovemaking, which left me feeling extremely lustful and lonely. Sometimes the girl would still be there in the morning when I got up for work. She would be standing in the kitchen in her underwear, sporting one of Bev's shirts, eating Cheerios or Corn Flakes, and when she saw me she would giggle. They all giggled, and didn't have much to say other than "You're cute," or "You're Arthur, Bev's brother," as if it were a revelation.

I had found work that summer on a ranch where my duties included caring for the extensive irrigation system. I did not like the work, but I was making good money, and the reason for padding my account was to buy myself some freedom. I had decided to leave Alberta. Bev's return, though pleasing at first to my mother, had created in her an anxiousness that spilled onto me. Claustrophobia set in. I imagined that I might travel, preferably to France, where I would spend my days as a *flâneur*, drinking vermouth in small bars and wandering the streets, and then returning to my garret where I would write poetry. My fantasies at that time were illogical and large and deeply romantic.

One evening, Bev and I drove to Brooks where he planned to meet a girl at a bar in town. I was seventeen and couldn't get into the bar, but Bev thought it should be no problem. He knew the bartender. It turned out that the bartender wasn't working that night and so, while my brother went inside and fooled around with his girl, I kept watch over his car and observed the folks enter and then straggle out of the bar. I was regretting my decision to join him, and at some point I went to get myself a hamburger. When I returned, my brother was standing in the parking lot, leaning into a girl who wore a white Stetson.

"This is Candace," my brother said. "Isn't she beautiful? Give my brother a kiss, Candy. He's a young one."

Candace ignored him and told me that Bev wasn't up for driving. "Not up for much of anything," she said, and walked off.

"I can drive," Bev said, and he climbed in. He fumbled with the keys.

"Let me," I said.

"Naww, it's all good."

On the road back to Tomorrow it began to drizzle and then it was raining, one of those rainfalls where the world outside disappears and the wipers become ineffectual and everything closes in on you. I asked Bev if he was okay, and he seemed to be. He had a great capacity for concentration. The Dodge planed across the puddles.

I didn't see the man we hit until we were upon him. He was half on the road, waving his arms, and then we hit him, a quick thud, and my brother said, "Fuck," and braked and pulled to the side.

"You see that?" Bev asked.

Then I was out of the car and running through the rain. The man had been thrown into the ditch and I couldn't find him at first, believing briefly that we had dreamed him up, but then I saw him, in the grass. His left arm was at an odd angle and blood was bubbling up from his mouth and he was trying to speak. He might have been saying sorry. My brother appeared out of the darkness and stood there. He kept saying *fuck* over and over.

I held the man's head. I said, "It's okay, man. Everything's fine. You'll be fine."

My brother was useless. He was talking about the blood and holding his head and pacing up and down in the ditch. I told him to help me. I had managed to get my hands under the man's arms and I instructed Bev to take the feet.

"I can't," he said.

So I dragged the man to the car and told Bev to open the back door. He did this. I slid the man in and tucked his feet up so the door could shut. He moaned every time I touched him. There was blood on my shirt and jeans. I took the keys from Bev and climbed in and told him to do the same. He obeyed. I decided that the nearest hospital was in Calgary, an hour away. I drove fast, breathing rapidly, fearful that the man would die before we arrived.

And he did just that. One minute I could hear him breathing, a slow bubble escaping each time he exhaled, and the next, the sound of the bubbling stopped. I asked Bev to check him.

Bev looked. "I don't know," he said.

"Feel his neck for a pulse."

Bev was quiet, looking straight ahead. His hands were shaking.

I slammed the steering wheel with my hands. "Stupid, stupid, stupid," I cried.

And then we were at the hospital and everything was out of our control and the two of us were huddled on chairs in the waiting room. A policeman approached and introduced himself as Constable Lark.

"You the boys that brought in the fellow that was hit?"

I nodded. "Is he all right?" I asked.

The officer shook his head.

Bev lifted his head, looked at me, and then turned away.

"Were you the driver?" he asked. He was talking to me.

"Yes," I said.

IT TURNED OUT THAT THE MAN IN THE ROAD, JED Armstrong, had stalled out his pickup. The alternator had blown and so he had no power, no hazards, and in the darkness and rain he had stepped out onto the highway to flag us down and we hit him. Those were the facts, and this being so, it was deemed an accident.

The following morning, when we told our parents, my mother blamed Bev for allowing me to drive in a storm like that. And she railed against me. What was I thinking? And why drive all the way to a stupid place like Brooks to chase hussies? Stupid boys. "At least you weren't drinking," she said. "Were you?"

I shook my head. I listened to her go on and on, and I saw that she was afraid for what might be the truth. When she was done I left the kitchen and went to my room and lay on my bed.

Driving back home the night of the accident, after we knew that Jed Armstrong was dead, and after we'd given our statements and I'd blown clean on the Breathalyzer, Bev was quiet. He was sober by then and more clearheaded, and as we pulled into the lot by his apartment, he finally spoke.

"I guess this makes you a hero."

"I don't think so."

"And I guess you want some sort of thanks."

"I don't expect it."

"Course not."

"I didn't do this for you," I said.

"I know that," he said.

....

IN THE MONTHS THAT FOLLOWED, THE WORLD AND nature and weather did what they did regardless of human suffering or bewilderment or grief. There was day and night and day and night and the light fell away earlier and the frost came and then an early blizzard blew in and the cattle in the pastures turned their rumps against the wind and the snow.

Sometimes, on a Sunday, I drove past the Armstrong ranch, slowing down as I passed it by to observe the land and the buildings, the low-slung house, the Ford in the driveway. Sometimes I parked on the road. Everything was silent. I watched the ranch for a bit and then restarted the pickup and drove back into town.

Four months after the funeral I drove to the Armstrong ranch, turned down the driveway and pulled up beside Jed's Ford pickup. A grey mongrel approached, wagging its tail and growling. I climbed down and told the dog to shut its yap. It backed off, happy to acquiesce. A Chinook had settled in over the last number of days, making everyone believe that winter didn't exist. The snow had melted, birds were flitting about madly considering possible nesting places, the smell in the air was fecund, the earth was crying out with joy, and a girl and a boy were throwing a ball over the roof of the house and then chasing each other round and round. When the girl saw me she ran inside. The boy studied me.

"Is your mother around?" I asked.

He motioned at the house.

The front door opened and Stella Armstrong appeared.

She was a young-looking woman, too young to have two children and a dead husband.

I said that I was Arthur Wohlgemuht.

She touched her hand to her mouth and then to the side of her face.

I said, "I've driven by here several times and always been afraid to stop. This time the pickup turned into the driveway." I shrugged.

"Truck has a mind of its own?" she asked.

She went inside. She hadn't told me to follow but she looked back at me as a form of invitation and so I climbed the steps and went through the doorway and stood in the foyer. She had continued down the carpeted hallway to the kitchen. I took off my boots and set them beside another pair that were my size and might have been Jed's. The hallway was narrow and the walls held family photographs that I glanced at and then turned away from. The kitchen had a yellow chrome suite and yellow curtains and a yellow countertop. Stella was standing by the sink, filling the kettle.

"I'll make tea," she said.

Her back was to me. Her shirt was tucked in and I could see the shape of her waist and the jeans hugging her hips and her small feet. She asked if I took sugar.

"Yes, please," I said.

She reached for a bowl from the cabinet and set it before me. The bowl was china with pink flowers etched on the sides. The children came into the kitchen and hung onto her. She said my name and then gave me their names. The boy was Calvin, the girl Carolyn. I had seen them both at the funeral. After she shooed the children she poured the tea and set a cup before me. She sat.

She said, "You were at the funeral. I had all sorts of questions, but it wasn't the time or place. Your mother spoke to me. Did she send you?"

"Oh, no."

"You saw Jed that night?"

"I did."

"Did he say anything? Was he conscious?"

I shook my head. "It was pretty bad."

She bowed her head and then raised it. "How old are you?"

"Seventeen."

"Oh, my. How many are you?"

"Excuse me?"

"How many children in the family?"

"Just my brother Bev, besides me. We had a sister."

"What happened to her?"

"She drowned."

"I'm sorry."

"She passed when I was one."

"Your poor mother." Then she said, "I don't blame you. It was raining. It was dark. Senseless. I don't want you to suffer."

She talked then, about her dead husband's brother, who was helping out on the ranch, and about the children, who were old enough to miss their father but young enough to move on. "He always wanted a ranch," she said. "We're rais-ing Hereford–Angus cross cows and breeding them with Charolais. Jed figured there's a market for tan-coloured cows. So that's what we're doing. We'll get by." She looked around. "He just finished renovating the kitchen. Of course he could do everything. Pull an engine from a truck, fix up a kitchen, frame a barn, pen and rope. I'm just sorry the children won't learn from him. What about you?"

"Excuse me?"

"You're still in school?"

I said that I was. And then I said that I was wondering if she could use a hand on the ranch. On weekends and after school. I said that I was good with horses and cattle. My father had taught me animal husbandry. When I was thirteen he'd had me feed Limousin bulls, which wasn't an easy thing. I knew how to break horses. I was strong. I was willing.

She didn't answer immediately. She asked if I wanted more tea and I said no. She said that she didn't have the money to pay a worker. She was sorry.

I said that I didn't want any pay. I was here to help, just until she got back on her feet, or found someone else.

She said, "I have no plans to remarry."

I thought then that this could not be true, she was too young, her body too inviting to never again have a man.

When we said goodbye, I stood on the stairs and she was in the doorway. I reached up and shook her small hand, which was cool and callused. Her grip was strong. Her sleeves were rolled up past her forearms and I could see the fine blond hairs there. I said goodbye and walked out to my pickup, the grey dog at my heels.

Driving away I saw her standing at the screen door, looking out into the yard. She wasn't looking at me. I don't think she even noticed that I was leaving. She was staring out into the yard, and there wasn't much to look at out there.

Two weeks later she phoned me and said that I could work several evenings a week, and all day Saturday. She said, "The children don't know about your involvement. I don't want them to know." I agreed.

Eventually, on the evenings after school when I worked, she invited me to supper and so I ate with her and the children, who came to accept me and liked the stories I told, usually tall tales such as the one my father liked to tell about his own birth. After his mother gave birth to each of her children, the practice was to weigh the baby on the scale in the barn and then write the weight on the plywood wall alongside the scale. It was a tradition. The name of his great-grandmother was there. His mother. Her mother. I told the Armstrong children that my father had been a large baby, and because of this his mother was tired and sore and didn't have the strength to move. And so my father took matters into his own hands. He leaped up and ran across the yard and into the barn to stand on the farm scale. He picked up the pencil and wrote his weight on the wall. And then he ran back to let his mother know the birth weight, twelve pounds.

Carolyn asked, "Is that true? Your father did that when he was born?"

"Absolutely, my father was very precocious."

"What does that mean?"

"He was clever, an early walker."

"Like a calf," Cal said.

"Exactly."

My father always told his birth story after he had spanked me, in order to reduce his own unhappiness, and perhaps to erase the violence with a sort of magic. I did not tell the children about the spankings, because they had just lost a father and I did not want to give the impression that fathers could be anything but perfect.

STELLA LIKED ME, AND BECAUSE THIS WAS SO, I SPARED no energy in proving myself. I was fond of her as well, and one Saturday afternoon in late spring, while we were branding heifers, I saw the manner in which she held the iron in the fire and then laid it down on the hide. She was quite the catch. I told her this. I may have used exactly those words, thinking they were safe. She smiled and asked if I had a girlfriend. I said no, though I had been seeing someone.

Her name was Sammy, and one weekend when Bev was down in Wyoming and I was staying at his apartment, Sammy came calling late, knocking on the door, crying out Bev's name in a happy way. When I answered the door she looked at me and said, "You're not Bev."

"That's a fact," I said.

Sammy liked that particular locution and she kept saying it throughout the evening, pointing her small finger at me in the living room where we sat drinking beer, calling out, "That's a fact," and then giggling. She was a chubby girl, and a bit of a knockout. Barely eighteen. She didn't think in straight lines or respond in a typical way to a conversation. She knew about the accident, and so we stuck to the details as they were known. She was deeply affected by Jed's death, and death in general, and the idea of surprise.

She said, "It freaks me out. There's you, walking along, or driving, and then bang, there's no more you. Just like that. And you don't even know that there's no more you. That's crazy."

"You might know," I said. "If you believe in some sort of afterlife." I said this carelessly, as if others were believers and I were leaning towards nonbelief.

"Nah, doesn't work for me. I mean, I'd like to think that way, I might be happier, but uh-uh."

The thing is she *was* happy. Even as she gave her little spiel on death she was happy, her face like one of those powerful faraway planets that keeps on shining.

She stayed until the early morning. I didn't think about sleep, or the approaching morning, and at one point she twigged to the fact that we were alone. This excited her.

"Just you and me," she said. And then, before I could say anything, she poked my chest with a finger and said, "That's a fact."

After we kissed she pulled back and wrinkled that nose of hers and then sighed, as if happily defeated, and said, "Okay." That was a green light for sure and so we tore into each other, and though I was fooling around with one of Bev's girls I didn't feel sorry for him at all. I was finally having real sex and this allowed for a brief thought of Isobel and I wondered what she would make of me, and if she would be happy if she knew. All brief, all fleeting, like a small cloud that covers the sun and then moves on.

After, we lay beside each other, and Sammy said that she'd never know, unless someone told her, that Bev and I were brothers. "You're different," she said.

I stood and put one of Bev's records on the turntable and turned it up loud. She lay there like a lamb, smoking a cigarette for a while, then meandered over and bent to kiss me, and I let her. All she had on was her socks.

"I like you," she said.

"You should go," I said. "I gotta get out of here too."

"I'll see you again," she whispered.

And this is how I came to lead a double life, one where I attended school and worked for Stella Armstrong early evenings and weekends, and then sometimes found myself with Sammy, joining her, after that first time at Bev's, at her apartment, a small space that she shared with no one.

One night she said that we needed to talk. Every time she saw Bev she worried and felt bad. I said that I felt bad too, though I truly didn't, and this made me wonder what was wrong with me. And so I felt terrible that I didn't feel terrible. We decided to stop having sex, though we still saw each other, and inevitably, after a week of abstinence, we fell to kissing and holding each other and then falling apart once again. "Ah, man," she would say as we pecked each other's cheeks at the door, "I really like you, Arthur."

Our attraction was physical, though for a time I spoke to her of my thoughts, or I read to her, as if by educating her in some way she might become a true lover. One evening when I read her *The Old Man and the Sea* she cried at the end. "The poor fucking fish," she said.

I told her that she reminded me of my double cousin Isobel, who wasn't my true cousin, and I told her about the shenanigans Isobel and I had gotten up to in our youth. I didn't tell her in a proud way but more as a confession and a curiosity, and she took it that way, in fact she suffered no jealousy. She never did. She thought the name Isobel was exotic and that having sex with a cousin was kind of weird.

"We didn't have sex," I said.

"You think sex is penetration, Arthur. You love her, I can hear it in your voice and the way you describe her. Freckles and flinty eyes, ha."

"Well, you're like her," I said. "That's a compliment."

"Is she smart?"

"She is."

"You like brains more than tits, don't you."

This was true. The year previous, when I discovered that Isobel was reading Kierkegaard's parables, my heart had leaped, and I experienced an attraction to her that moved far beyond the physical. I told Sammy now that though I was typically drawn to all women, I liked best a combination of brains and physique.

She was fond of the word *physique* and she tried to use it in sentences over the next while. "My *physique* is suffering," she announced, studying herself in the mirror. Or, "Your *physique* is thinner than Bev's," she said, stroking my chest.

"Don't tell him about Isobel," I said. "He wouldn't get it."

"Yeah," she said. "He's a blind cunt-sniffer that one." And then she grew melancholy. "Used to be, anyhow."

IT HAD TO HAPPEN OF COURSE THAT MY BROTHER would catch wind of my time with Sammy. Perhaps she told him. One weekend we drove down to Billings to pick up two thoroughbreds for Dewey. It was spring and my father was busy with the calving, and so he sent the two of us to fetch the horses. Going down we drove straight through, but on the return trip we were both tired and so we took a room at a motel in a small town off the highway. We fed and watered the horses and then fell onto the double bed and slept on our backs, fully clothed except for our boots.

Early morning I woke to hear the sound of weeping. I lay in the dim crack of light, and I saw the curtains half drawn over the dusty window and the mirror on the far wall reflecting the rectangle of light. My brother was crying. His body hardly moved, but his shoulders shook slightly, and in the dimness I saw that he held a hand over his mouth as if to obviate the noise. I lay still until he quit crying and eventually began to snore.

I got up then and put on my boots and stepped outside onto the asphalt of the parking lot. Two hawks dipped and wheeled above the highway. I walked over to the nearby restaurant and sat down in a booth and ordered coffee and eggs over easy and toast and five rashers of bacon. The waitress, old like a grandmother, whose name tag said *Dolly*, thought I might want fried potatoes with that, and so she threw some onto the plate as well.

When the food came I was on my third cup of coffee and thinking that I should wake my brother, when he stepped out of the motel room and walked towards the restaurant. I watched him come. He had sloped shoulders and a short neck and wrists thick as my forearms, and he walked with his arms out slightly, as if he might be put upon by something feral at any moment. He slipped into the seat across from me and removed his cowboy hat.

"Slept like a dead man," he said.

Dolly appeared and Bev pointed at my plate. "I'll have that. Make sure to fry up the potatoes nice and crisp."

"Can do," Dolly said. She served him coffee as he held the cup aloft.

He poured sugar, kept pouring, brimmed the cup with cream, and then took a teaspoon and stirred the coffee, his eyes looking out the window into the distance. "Had the weirdest dream," he said. "I was a kid with a puppy and we were playing fetch. Me throwing a stick and the little mongrel running out and bringing the stick back. I kept throwing it farther and farther and the last time I threw it the mutt didn't come back. He disappeared. I cried and cried and when I woke up I was actually crying. You heard me?"

"Didn't hear a thing. I was out."

He drank his coffee. I wiped up the last bit of egg yolk with my toast. Sat back. When his plate came I watched him eat. When he was done he pushed his plate away and said, as if this were a continuation of a conversation, that the mosquitoes in Vietnam made no noise.

"In the darkness you never knew where they were, you just knew that they were there. And then they bit. It was a mad world."

This was the first time that he had spoken so clearly of his time in Vietnam, and I was anxious that he might reveal something I didn't want to hear.

But he was done with that. He said, "What's with Stella Armstrong? You crawling your way to heaven? That your intention?"

"Who said I have intentions?"

"You do have 'em, and you should know what they are. You tell her what actually happened?"

"Now that's a stupid question. Anyways, it's not my story to tell."

"You save my sorry ass and now it's up to me to tell everyone what a goddamn fine fellow you are?"

I looked at him carefully and then asked, "Where'd you get to be so fucked up?"

"At fucked-up school." His nose had been broken long ago in a fight and it was set sideways. He had broken a wrist the previous summer, riding broncos. And there were cracked ribs, and a hip that was askew. And then there was all that stuff inside that was broken, but couldn't be proved, and that was the worst of it, the scariest part, because it made him unpredictable, someone to be feared. I was sitting there thinking about all his broken parts, maybe even feeling sorry for him a little, when he said, "You like to hide things."

"Whaddya mean?"

"Mean exactly that. Sammy for instance." He took up his coffee again.

I said nothing, though my breathing was quick and short.

"You been touching her?" he asked.

"Screw you. You have a harem traipsing through your bedroom."

"No crime in that. All those girls know there are others coming down the chute. I don't hide nothin'. You, on the other hand, you think you're better. Better than Sammy, better than your family. Better than most everyone in Southern Alberta. Sammy might be dumber than a sack of hammers but she's a sweetheart. When we get back home you find Sammy and tell her sorry. She deserves to know that you ain't worth a penny to the hunnert."

"Go to hell. Sammy's brighter than you think, and if you can't see that then you're the sack holding the hammers. Anyways, she *likes* me." I stood and walked out. Leaned against the pickup and watched Bev chatting up Dolly as he paid the bill.

When he came out, he walked over to me and said, "Take off your glasses."

"Don't be an ass," I said.

He hit me in the jaw. I took a swing back at him but he pushed my arm aside and hit me in the gut. And then once more across the side of the head. Short sharp blows that deliberately missed my glasses but hurt nonetheless. He was quick and powerful and the first hit would have sufficed, but as he said later in the pickup, "Had to set you to rights, you self-righteous prick."

And nothing more was said of that.

IN MY EIGHTEENTH SUMMER STELLA ARMSTRONG hired me and paid me a salary because, as she told me, I was a dependable boy. She was raising Red and Black Angus cattle, and she grew forage. My job was to move cows and calves from pasture to pasture on horseback. Many of the ranchers in the area had begun to use quads to move the cattle, but Stella was traditional and she insisted on her hired hands using horses.

Severn Turk was the other hire that summer, and so the two of us were thrown together by chance, though in a small place like Tomorrow, chance was hardly a factor. We became friends. He was good with words, even though he could barely read. His wit was quick and we founded our friendship on wordplay. He also loved to argue, though his technique, especially when he was wrong and realized it, was based on volume and name-calling. It was a hot dry summer, and in the late afternoons when we found ourselves near Flat Creek, we dismounted, undressed, and swam. After, we lay on the earth, our heads resting on our saddles. Severn had a hard strong body and his hands were rough and he smelled of cigarillos, which he liked to smoke. He wasn't Mennonite or Christian in any sense, and that pleased me. I saw him as being very different, from somewhere else entirely, though we had both grown up in the same place. His older brother Stu was already married and had a kid, and Severn had plans to get married and own a ranch in the area. I told him that I intended to move to a country where no one knew me, where a different language was spoken.

That made no sense to him. "Why would you leave?" he asked. "Where would you go?"

We argued one time about education and reading and university, things he had no respect for. My mother wanted me to study in university, but I had already decided that I would travel instead. This didn't mean that I couldn't argue for an ideal and a future that I was postponing.

"What good is it?" he asked. "Do them professors profess knowledge about reboring piston cylinders, or castrating a bull?"

"Might learn you how to rebore your soul," I said.

"Soul is fine." He grinned. "I could rebore something. So fucking horny." He stood and pranced about, showing off his hard-on.

This was not unusual or abnormal. In that time and in that place our bodies were something to behold. We partook in pissing contests, and one time Severn masturbated right in front of me, shooting off into the river with a bright exclamation.

Now, when he said he was horny, the sun was dazzling and I had to shield my eyes so as to see him better, and what I saw was the sharp edges of his hip bones and his flat stomach and his frontal nudity and the tufts of hair at his nipples. He wore his cowboy hat. He was barefoot. He said he was going up to Calgary on the weekend, to the Stampede, where he hoped to meet a sweet little buckle bunny.

"Wanna come?" He looked down at me.

At that time I was a conflagration of emotions and desires. I was of course still in touch with Isobel, who had revealed her body to me numerous times, as I had revealed mine to her. And there had been Sammy, now gone from my life. My fascination with sex was almost debilitating, and yet every day I anticipated various possibilities, like the ill man who keeps feeding himself the exact thing that makes him ill. I said that I was busy.

Another time, in the late afternoon by Flat Creek, Severn brought up the beating he had given me. He was pulling on his boots, which were Lucchese American Alligator Belly Bias-Cut. Only the best for Severn. He said, "Time I beat the shit out of you again."

"Other way round, wasn't it?" I grinned.

"You were useless. Flapping your hands like dishrags. Like beating a scarecrow."

He told me to stand up. When I obeyed, he took my hands and lifted them, placing them near my temples, elbows in. He circled me and touched the backs of my knees and told me to crouch slightly. "Not big-time, but ya gotta be ready to spring. Up on the balls of your feet. Yeah, like that." He stood before me and held up a palm. "Take a jab," he said. I did, but it was ineffectual. "Again," he said. "Make it sting."

I hit his palm hard, forcing him back.

"Better," he said.

And so, over several weeks, he taught me the bare bones of fighting, moving from make-believe to outright battle, where we danced around each other wearing only jeans. One time, only once, I caught him good in the eye and cut him. He sat down then and said that it had been a clean shot. He'd left himself open.

I kneeled and studied the blood trickling from his eyebrow. "Shit, I'm sorry," I said.

"Don't be." He got up and washed his head and face in the river. Rose and shook out his hair, all golden and fine.

I WROTE IN MY NOTEBOOK THE NAMES OF THE GIRLS and women I had loved and still loved. *Hildegaard, Mother, Em, Tamiko, Miss Chou, Nettie Runningwolf, Alice Dewey, Sammy, Stella Armstrong, Isobel, Isobel, Isobel, Isobel.* My mind wandered, but my pen kept writing Isobel's name, over and over again. She was honest. She did not make me anxious. She did not pretend to love me. She did not ask for anything. She let me see her naked. She let me be naked.

At that time, through letter writing, Isobel and I had agreed that we needed contact with intellectuals and writers and poets. People who could offer us a higher sense of thinking. And so we decided to write those authors whom we admired the most. She wrote to Susan Sontag. She received a letter back from someone at a publishing house in New York. A lovely letter that thanked her for hers and for her interest in Ms. Sontag's *oeuvre*. Unfortunately, Ms. Sontag was in Europe and wasn't available. A work of Ms. Sontag's was enclosed in the mail, a book of essays that Isobel cherished and that made her further worship Sontag.

I had considered writing W. H. Auden because I loved his poetry, but he had just died. In any case, I was mostly interested in the best of the French writers, most of whom were dead as well. Baudelaire died at forty-six after suffering a stroke and aphasia. Camus died in a car crash. Flaubert died at Croisset of a cerebral hemorrhage in 1880 at the age of fifty-eight. I did write a few letters to Samuel Beckett, who was still alive. He was Irish but wrote in French, and therefore I felt some affinity towards him. I wrote long letters in English, asking him about his ideas and the tremendous silences of his characters. I never heard from him or his publisher, which was a tremendous silence in itself. I assumed that my letters never found him. Finally, I wrote a letter to Jean-Paul Sartre, and in my letter I asked Monsieur Sartre if he had any advice for a young man who came from the provinces but also had a hunger for literature and the higher meaning of life.

> *I have great affection for Stendhal and Flaubert, especially Flaubert, and I know from my reading about you that you have a high appreciation for Flaubert. I admire this in you. My inclinations lean towards the French writers, even though my French is non-existent. I make do with translations. I recently read your play* No Exit *and I want to ask you if you believe in hell. Perhaps this is too obvious.*

I wrote this letter in French, translating it from English with the help of the French teacher at my high school. I did not tell Madame Manches to whom the letter was written, I simply explained that I was practising my French. She was pleased to help me, and so the words I used were raised to a new level.

One day, several months later, having assumed that my letter to Sartre had also gotten lost during its trip over the ocean, I came home from school and found a letter addressed to *Monsieur Arthur Wohlgemuht*, with a return address from Éditions Gallimard, Paris. I went to my room, locked my door, and ripped open the envelope. It was not from Monsieur Sartre but from someone at the publishing house who was named Laurent. The letter was brief and to the point. "Monsieur Sartre, unfortunately, does not do correspondence. Thank you for the letter, and please be assured that we wish you all the best."

I was disappointed and also relieved. And being relieved I was able to set my mind at ease and ascend to a place where I composed the letter that might have been written had Monsieur Sartre *done* correspondence.

Dear Monsieur W.,

Thank you for your honest letter. And thank you for your interest in literature. This is the first letter I have received from a young man in Western Canada (I receive many letters from readers in France), a young man who shows a keen interest in humanity, and a shared love of Flaubert, and a commitment to action. For commitment is not just an idea, it is an act. Regarding the writing of novels, here is some advice. A novel is like a dinner party. You need a solid place upon which to set your table. This is your foundation.

And then you organize the table according to the number of settings, and the people you invite. Invite characters of surprising and moral character, or at least those who grapple with what is right, or those who make decisions that shock. Typically, the struggle is of a moral nature. The character suffers anxiety, or has a fear of death, or sex, or violence, or perhaps there is a synthesis of all of these, but in the end the story hinges on a working out of despair and hope. There can be no shrinking from the truth, or from the absurdity of that truth. Those who cower simply want escapism. Don't cozy up to the reader. Don't patronize. And finally, if you can say what a story is "about," the story isn't worth reading. And, yes, narrative is tyrannical. It demands bread crumbs be dropped along the path. Learn how to drop the crumbs without revealing that you are dropping them. Know this, that a character (just like man) makes himself, in spite of eventualities in a meaningless world.

I wrote Isobel and gave her the whole of what I had imagined Monsieur Sartre's response might be. She was impressed by the description of novel writing and asked me where I had stolen this from. I wrote back and told her that I had made it up, which I had, and this impressed her even more, which made me happy, because it has always been my goal to win Isobel's affection through the working of my mind. Monsieur Sartre's final sentence in that fabricated letter, the notion that a person must make oneself in spite of the *eventualities in a meaningless world*, became true for me—because this is what I intended for myself. My first seventeen years or so had been fat with ideas and occurrence and wonder and imagination. A cacophony of pleasure, the absorption of knowledge, the stretching of the sinew of my mind, the mind diseased yet sharp. What a marvel. But then came a few thin years. And I call them thin because I lived a repetitive and inauthentic existence. My mind contracted, and I fell into the tedium of work and the temptation of lucre and the appeal of the body. I learned that for every action there is a reaction, and that sometimes the reaction is no action at all. I discovered my double self, and there were times, when I faced one of my selves, that I did not like what I saw. And yet, throughout this, I was still able to consider myself a bright star in the sky that hung like a black curtain over those plains.

2.

....

Leaving

At the age of nineteen, after spending a year getting to know a very emotionally constant girl named Dorothy, and falling back for a time on tradition and religion, I decided one day to *throw off my traces*. I kissed Dorothy goodbye at the airport in Calgary and flew to Toronto and then on to Paris, where I was to live with a French family and earn my keep by teaching English to their eight-year-old son.

Dorothy had long straight dark hair that she let cascade to her waist, or sometimes pulled into braids. Her father owned the saddlery in town and she worked for him. She immediately fell for my wit, and I was attracted to her calm nature and her awareness of the ordinary world and her keenness for objects. She had brilliant recall for names of flowers and trees and different types of grasses and of course for all the parts of a saddle. I was also quite lonely, and twice a week in the evenings, after I had finished work, we met at a local restaurant where we indulged in warm food and soft conversation that usually circled around our days and my sore muscles and the house that she would build someday. She wanted a two-storey with twin dormers and, of all things, a rose window. We never spoke of our deeper thoughts or the nature of death or what would become of our physical bodies in heaven, perhaps because this did not appeal to her. I was her sole interest. At the end of the meal, when I had finally finished my helping of mashed potatoes and meat loaf and washed everything down with a cold glass of milk, she pushed her long dark hair back behind her ears and reached across the table to clutch my hands.

She was eighteen and was looking for a man who might help her escape her father's grasp, and though she was all manner of warmth and desire and she let me nibble at her body, only once, in a flurry of passion, did she unbuckle and kiss me. She was confused by my thoughts and often said, "I don't know who you are, Arthur."

Bev was in a hospital in Edmonton at the time—he'd suffered what my mother called a "breakdown"—and on Sunday afternoons Dorothy and I visited him. And it was there that I saw Dorothy come alive in a manner that she never was with me. On one of our visits, my mother had sent along cupcakes and we ate these and drank pop and my brother talked. He had discovered God. He admitted that he was clearly a sinner, but he had been forgiven. Dorothy leaned forward and touched his hand and said that this was amazing. On our way back to Tomorrow later, she slid over and leaned her small head against my shoulder as I drove, and she talked about Bev's penitence.

"Like Raskolnikov," I said. "Only he doesn't have Nietzsche's sense of Superman. In the end he's still just Bev Wohlgemuht."

She didn't know Raskolnikov and she didn't ask. She became thoughtful. She kissed my cheek. This bothered me, that I could insult her in an underhanded sort of way, and then she would forgive me by showing affection.

She said, "I'd marry you, Arthur. In a jiffy."

"Why?" I asked.

She began to cry. I wrapped my free arm around her and said sorry, and I added that I would marry her but first I just had to get rid of some wanderlust.

"What do you mean?"

"I have to go away. Just for a while."

"Why?"

"I will die otherwise."

THE PLAN WAS THAT I WOULD BE GONE FOR A YEAR, rid myself of my wanderlust, and then return to marry Dorothy and we would settle down in Tomorrow, Alberta, where we would live lives of somnolent satisfaction and eventually die of old age. After I kissed Dorothy goodbye and was finally in the air, I was so relieved to be gone from her that I wrote her a letter telling her how much I missed her. I folded this brief letter and placed it in an envelope and tucked it into my briefcase, which was made from steer hide, a dark brown satchel that I had designed and sewn back in Tomorrow.

And then I took out another piece of paper and wrote a letter to Isobel.

Dear Isobel,

"The period of falling in love is surely the most interesting time, during which (after the total impression has been made by the first stroke of enchantment) from every encounter, from every glance of the eye, one fetches something home, like the bird which in its busy season fetches one piece after another to its nest and yet constantly feels overwhelmed by the great wealth at its disposal."

This from the unsurpassable Kierkegaard. I love it. And want to capture it. Along with the truer emotions that enter later: melancholy, desperation, longing. The sense of "if only."

I imagine writing a novel in the style of Flaubert or Stendhal, a Bildungsroman that will be from the perspective of a young man who grows up in the provinces and runs away to Paris, where he falls in love with an older woman.

I have a new briefcase, a beautiful possession that holds my other possessions within it, and I will sling it over my

shoulder and stroll the boulevards of Paris. I plan to purchase
a silk foulard.

Love,
Arthur

I HAD ARRANGED, VIA LETTERS AND HALTING TELE-
phone conversations that took place in broken French and
English, to live with a family named Godbout (*Carmine
et Pierre et leur petit fils Christian*) in the suburb of Rueil-
Malmaison. *Nous habitons en banlieue,* Carmine wrote in one of
her letters, and I dutifully translated this with the help of my
French–English dictionary, discovering that I would be living in the suburbs, a long Metro ride from the centre of Paris
where the centre of the world existed. I discovered that the
Godbout house was not far from the Château de Malmaison,
the summerhouse of Napoleon's first wife, and upon learning
this I was amazed and moved. I knew that Julien Sorel had
been very fond of Napoleon, had even seen him in real life,
and given that I was modelling myself in a slight way after
Monsieur Sorel, one of Stendhal's greatest creations, I believed
that providence had led me to Rueil–Malmaison.

The connection to the Godbout family had come about
by chance. A distant cousin of mine, Greg, who worked at
a school in Germany's Black Forest, came home on holiday,
and one Sunday, while he was eating lunch at our house, my

mother said that I had unrealistic dreams to live in France. She chuckled, as if this were farfetched and impossible, and just one more impractical dream that her youngest son harboured. Greg didn't see it as farfetched. He said that he knew a couple in France who were looking for an English speaker, a young man preferably, who could teach their eight-year-old son. And so I made contact with Pierre and Carmine, and the chips began to fall into place. In one of her letters Carmine wrote, "I am happy to know that you grew up in a religious home. That is important. We want our son to be influenced by someone wholesome."

Carmine was an anxious woman with a thin face and smooth arms who always dressed as if she were waiting for something grand just around the next corner. I never saw her in anything but dresses of various subdued colours, or blouses and skirts, of which my favourite was night-green and pleated, verging on too short. Her hair was dark, and when streaks of grey appeared, she resorted to applying a medium-brown dye that accented her dark eyes. She had some Tunisian blood in her. She wore flat shoes, alternating between black and brown, and the shoes were always dully polished. She was a very conservative dresser. Her husband, Pierre, was often absent. He worked for an aid agency and travelled in sub-Sahara Africa.

Eventually it became a habit, when Pierre was travelling, that once or twice a week Carmine invited me to eat with her and Christian, the son, who was polite and timid and quite intelligent, though he was prone to mixing up his personal pronouns when speaking English. We always ate late, *à peu prés neuf heures*, and Carmine insisted we speak English for her sake, and for the sake of Christian, though her rule was often broken, and so I became immersed in the pitter-patter of their language, which centred around the domestic.

After, Christian took a bath while Carmine and I remained at the table and drank espresso. Christian called often from the bath, asking for help with the shampoo, or a toy, or the soap, or he wondered if Arthur was *toujours là*, and then Carmine remonstrated in her soft gentle fashion, calling out, "Of course Arthur is still here," and every time my name fell out of her mouth, I marvelled. Eventually, we finished with a *pousse-café*, and then said good night.

I lived behind the main house in a small coach house that was furnished and self-sufficient. There was a kitchen, a bath, a small dining area with a terrace, and a bedroom with a double bed covered with a white spread. I had carried with me, in my large cloth suitcase, my favourite books, and these I placed on the shelves in the dining area. When I was lonely, and I was often lonely, I looked to these books for comfort, though at some point I understood that human company could never be replaced by the stories I had come to love as a young boy. This worried me, and made me wonder if I was losing touch with the world of art.

I took the RER to Paris every morning at 7 a.m., walking from the house to the station, often in a rain that was constant that autumn. The women on the train put on their makeup, spreading out complete kits on their narrow laps, and the men read newspapers. Nobody on the train made eye contact, and so I rode, often standing, looking down at the people in a strange country that I had fallen in love with from a distance. I noticed that many of the women had dandruff, and that the men often wore trench coats with dirty collars. I was taller than most of the men and though this gave me a sense of physical superiority, I believed that I would never be able to match a French man's intellectual breadth. They had studied Latin in school. I hadn't. They read *Le Figaro* and *Le Monde* while I paged through the *International Herald Tribune*. Eventually I took to slipping the *Tribune* inside the covers of *Le Monde* so as to give the appearance of someone who, though foreign, was *prepared*.

For three hours every morning, five days a week, I studied at Alliance Française. There were nine of us in the class. I was the only male. Our teacher, Madame Flamand, was a sallow-faced woman in her late thirties who wore bright red and yellow blazers, and she stood like a sun within the circle that her students, the planets, formed. She leaned forward and beat the words into us, her spit landing on our faces and shirts. The women in the class were all older than me, hailing from Venice and Barcelona and Budapest. They were chattels of their husbands, whose companies had lent them to French businesses, and all of them, save for Helena, who came from Rome, were indifferent to their studies.

Several times, because she asked me and because I had

nothing better to do for lunch, I ate a ham-and-cheese croissant and drank an espresso with Helena at a café near the
school. She wore black leather pants and a fur stole, and as we
sat and smoked Marlboros she told me in a mixture of French,
Italian, and English, with Italian predominating, about her
husband, the businessman, who had "forced" her to live in the
land of Gaul. She said that I was *giovane* and *bellissimo*. The *o*
in *bellissimo* was round and full, like the O of her brightly coloured mouth as she released the vowel. She was bored with her
life, and though I might have been a distraction, I was a minor
distraction, someone to be tossed aside when something better came along. This would be a swarthy athletic-looking man
whom I at first mistook for her husband, Felice. He drove up
to the coffee shop in his Mercedes, rolled down the window
and waved, and she unwrapped her legs and stood and gathered her purse and fur, and bent to kiss me once, twice, three
times, and then swayed off, her buttocks moving through her
leather pants like the flanks of a horse.

I rode the RER back to Rueil-Malmaison after lunch
and from 3 to 6 p.m. I taught Christian. We studied in the
drawing room of the large house while Carmine moved above
and around us. I was, like Christian, constantly aware of her
presence, and I was aware of the scent of her, at times a very
subtle hint of tobacco, indicating that she had stepped outside
to smoke a Gauloise.

I was not a teacher and therefore my methodology was
based on curiosity rather than rigour, and so Christian and

I spent time playing games and conversing, and for an hour each day I would read to him from the novels of my youth, Hemingway and London. Sometimes, when I felt that he might imagine me as lazy and incompetent, we worked on memorizing verbs. He was bright and willing, and he never complained, though there were times when I looked up from the novel I was reading and found him sleeping, his delicate French head resting on my rural Canadian shoulder. I did not disturb him then, but let him sleep, and he inevitably woke with a yawn and a desire for something to drink, and so we made our way to the Godbout kitchen and poured ourselves sparkling water from green bottles that were stored in rows in the refrigerator.

I envied him his life, the habitude, his composure at such a young age, the practice of greeting his mother with a kiss every afternoon when he returned from school. He called out *maman*, sought her out, and he approached her and they kissed, once, twice, and then exchanged niceties about their mornings. Whenever I observed this, for there were days when I would be sitting with Carmine in the kitchen as I attended Christian, I felt a commotion in my chest, and a longing for a mother who wore dully polished flat shoes and simple dresses and sometimes a too-short skirt, and who, because she trusted me, would *reveal* herself.

Christian was very sheltered. He had not travelled, save to Bretagne to visit his maternal grandmother, and he knew nothing of the Great Plains, or of the Rockies, and he had never milked a cow or sat on a horse or held a gun. He loved stories of cowboys and so I told him about breaking horses, and I drew for him a horse and labelled its parts, just as I had done so many years ago for Miss Chou, and I told him the story of Moby, my American quarter horse stallion, who had fallen and broken his leg and was shot by my brother.

Christian was so impressed by this story that he asked me to retell it on one of those evenings when his father was out of town and his mother had invited me to join them for dinner, *environ twenty-one hours*. Carmine, who saw in me the opportunity to practise her execrable English, tended to jumble the two languages so that she ended up speaking a *mélange* that, if kept brief, was comprehensible. I told the story once again, aware of Christian's excitement not so much for the narrative this time but for his mother's response. As I spoke he kept looking at his *maman* and waiting for her to nod or exclaim or laugh, and not surprisingly she did all of these things, not because the story was brilliant or terribly interesting, but because Christian expected it of her.

When I was done, she said, "This is why you walk with a limp." She said it in French and I understood everything except for the word *clopiner*, and so she demonstrated, standing and walking around the table with a slight push off her right leg. Christian thought this was wonderful and he too stood and imitated his *maman*, who was imitating me, who had been, in a subconscious manner, imitating Philip Carey from *Of Human Bondage*. I had read the book as a boy and had experienced the heartbreak of an innocent, and up until I was older I called Mr. Maugham *Mog-ham*, and then there came the day when my English teacher introduced a writer called Maugham, and I raised my hand and said that it was *Mog-ham*, not Maugham, and our teacher, Mr. Suderman, with his crew cut and his thin jaw and his distaste for curriculum, told the class that indeed, from now on it would be Somerset Mog-ham, because Mr. Wohlgemuht had pronounced it so.

And now, here was Carmine, hobbling around the table, on which there were the remains of a baguette and three different cheeses, and a compote, and several untouched *patisseries* that we were about to take with our coffee, and the sensations I experienced at that moment were of conviviality and shame and joy, all three, of which the greatest was joy, because in imitating my walk, Carmine had become a part of me, she had entered my physical self, and the image of her skirt pressing against her thighs, and her hip jutting out, and her stocking feet, for she had removed her shoes for dinner, left me with a warmth in my heart that bordered on ecstasy.

She paused and touched my shoulder lightly, near the left clavicle, and she said, almost mournfully, "*Je suis désolé, Arthur. Je plaisante.*"

I motioned grandly with my arms, taking in Carmine and Christian and the room we were in, and I said it was like theatre. "I do," I said, "I limp." Here I used the French word, with what I hoped was the correct conjugation.

"The horse," she said. "This is sad."

"It is. It was mine from when I was very young."

"Children receive horses, where you live?"

"On the ranch. Though most children, like Christian, have never touched a horse."

"Pierre likes a lot the westerns," she said.

"Films?"

"Yes, and books. He thinks if he is a cowboy, he will carry a six-shooter." She smiled at me as if we were in cahoots, both of us slightly amused by her husband's extravagant wishes, or perhaps she was simply pleased to have me nearby.

I was handsome. I had gained some weight during my time working back home, and my arms were stronger; in fact my forearms were muscular and when I wore T-shirts I was aware of people noticing my forearms, though no one remarked outright, except for Carmine, who had one time, in the evening, perhaps after she had had too much wine, said that she admired the veins on the insides of my forearms, how they stood out in relief, or something like that. I did not understand every word and she may, in fact, have been talking about how her own arms were tired of holding her child and her husband and that she was envious of my freedom, my strength, and this is when she motioned at my arms. Or perhaps she was talking about my naïveté, which she mistook for strength, the brave move to Paris, the individual as hero.

Carmine and I became fond of each other, or she may merely have been lonely and seen me as a companion with whom she could converse at a deeper level than she could with Christian, or even with Pierre, who was a bit of a philistine. We watched television together on Friday evenings, and one Friday, while Christian was in his bath, she invited me to watch a film with her. It was *Claire's Knee*, by a director called Eric Rohmer, whom I had of course never heard of. Carmine and I sat side by side on the couch. She crossed her legs and palmed her skirt and explained that she had seen this film before and she loved it.

"It's about nothing really, except the desire of one man to touch the knee of the girl he adores. In fact, the man adores women in general, *et alors* the knee is a stand-in for all women."

I did not understand everything she said, particularly the word for *stand-in*, and so I asked her to explain, which she did once more, using the words *replacement* and *symbol*. This I understood.

The film was like nothing I had ever seen in my short life as a moviegoer. There was no violence, no fighting, no great movement of plot or story, just a man who falls in love with a sixteen-year-old girl named Laura, and then falls in love with Claire, the step-sister of Laura. I was struck by the beauty of the girls and the beauty of the background in the film, the lake and the hills behind the actors as they spoke. The man who was in love with these two sisters, and who was in fact engaged to be married to a third woman, said, "Every woman has her most vulnerable part. For some it is the nape of the neck, the waist, the hands. For Claire, in that position, in that light, it was her knee."

Carmine tried to explain this concept to me in a more elementary French, and as she did so I watched her mouth because it was easier to comprehend when I saw the movement of her lips. I was aware of Carmine's hand lying on her lap, and I understood that if I had been Julien Sorel I would have taken that hand in mine and let nature take its course. Or was it Julien's lover Mathilde who reached for his hand? In any case, at that moment Christian called out from upstairs, and as Carmine left the room I was aware of the hole in the heel of her right stocking, and that the stoop of her back (she was wearing a sweater that was quite rumpled) made her appear older. When she returned she sat once again beside me, and as she pulled at the hem of her skirt she became younger again.

While she was gone, the film had kept playing, and though I had caught a few words here and there, I did not understand much, but that did not seem to matter, as the characters in the film spoke and moved in a way that allowed me to grasp that all of them were full of want and indecision and desire.

Carmine said that Jerôme, the man who loved all the women, was a bit vulgar and not to be trusted. She gave a mock shudder and said that she did not like him, but she said it in a jaunty manner and so it seemed that she might in fact like him. It was confusing. Later, back in my room and in my overwrought manner, I thought about Carmine's most vulnerable part, certainly her neck, and about the film itself, about how nothing truly happens and yet everything under the surface is in turmoil.

FOR THE MOST PART, EXCEPT DURING THE WEEKDAY afternoon hours when I was teaching English to Christian and taking him to museums or reading with him or playing Monopoly or Scrabble, I was alone. At noon, walking back from the Metro to the house, I would stop in for a coffee and a croissant at a local café, and then pick up a fresh baguette at a boulangerie, and this would be my supper, which I would eat alone, at the small table in the kitchen. The overhead light was fluorescent and it hummed and the light it gave was blue and bleak, and so I bought a small table lamp, and within the light that the lamp offered, I broke my bread and opened a little jar of confiture, and I cut some Gouda, and I ate slowly, prolonging the hour, sometimes writing, sometimes reading.

I was attempting to read Flaubert's letters to Louise Colet. They were of course in French and I methodically translated them, transposing them back and forth, so that by the seventh time, I had memorized various letters and could write them out verbatim in the original. This was my manner of acquiring another language. Because I was a visual learner I did not easily pick up speaking. In fact, I did not understand what someone was saying until I had seen it written. In the beginning I translated literally. When my professor at Alliance Française leaned in and spat the question *Qui?* five times into my face, all I could imagine was the key that opened a door. And so, alone in my room, I took great pleasure and comfort in plodding through Flaubert, sometimes managing to translate two or three sentences in one evening.

I was writing letters home to Dorothy, who would then pass them on to my mother. And I was working at writing stories. Ever since my great success in middle school, when I had won that short story contest in which I imitated another writer, I had dabbled at writing, but now, here in Paris, I was determined to find my way as a writer, to move beyond dabbling, and to produce work that was original and full of force. It was difficult, but there were brief moments when I descended into art and believed that I had produced something worthwhile, even if that might be a paragraph or two. By the end of an evening, after hours of writing, my back was sore and my fingers stiff. As a reward I would make a coffee and then sit on the terrace in the cold, and drink the coffee and smoke a Marlboro. I would watch the lights in the Godbout residence, and slowly they would go out, first downstairs, and then finally in the upstairs bedroom, and I would imagine Carmine undressing and slipping into a chemise and lying down on her back and thinking of me. When Monsieur was home, I did not think of her.

I HAD COME TO FRANCE FOR ALL THE NECESSARY REASONS. I would learn the language and read and write and I would wander the streets of Paris and discover the place I had coveted since I was a young boy lying in traction, staring at an atlas and memorizing the names of French cities and imagining myself plowing through those same cities. I would be modern, and like Baudelaire strolling through this same city, I would pursue *the transitory, the fugitive, the contingent which make up one half of art, the other being the eternal and the immutable.* What I had failed to understand is that I had been in love with the idea of a place that was unmoved by Arthur Wohlgemuht, a place that had held no spot for me, and that try as I might, the indifference could not be shaken. I had had plans to go up to Rouen to visit Flaubert's museum. I had had great intentions to wander the large halls of the Louvre and to visit La Musée d'Orsay, and about this I had done little. I had caught several glimpses of Monet and Picasso during brief visits to several museums, and I had studied the Parisians who walked the sidewalks, facing them with bright expectancy, but I had found there only grimness and arrogance and dismissal.

I set out on a quest to catch a glimpse of Monsieur Sartre. I went to Café de Flore and sat at a table drinking coffee and reading *Madame Bovary*, hoping that Sartre, should he be present and writing at his own small table, might notice Flaubert in my hands. I went to Café de la Mairie, where Sartre and Camus met for the last time in 1951. And on to La Palette on Rue de Seine, where de Beauvoir and Sartre also spent time. Of course I never did see the man, or his lover, but the search itself was vigorous and true, as all important quests are.

I had also thought that I might meet others my age, travellers who were lonely as I was, and who were looking for camaraderie or conversation over a glass of wine in one of the many *brasseries* that lined the wide boulevards of the famous streets of Paris. I don't know where I got this idea. Perhaps I imagined that in my French class there might be one or two students like me, wanderers who had come to this city with the aim of immersing themselves in art and culture and the language, and who had read the same French novelists that I had read, and who would be anxious to discuss these writers and their ideas. I found no one like this. Once or twice a week, after I had finished teaching Christian, I showered and dressed—often I wore Levi's and cowboy boots and a snap-button shirt that reminded me of where I came from—and I walked over to the RER station and took the train into Paris. I wandered the streets then, moving from one *arrondissement* to another, looking into the windows of restaurants and studying the menus as if I were a sophisticated diner who knew his *goûts*. One time, in a little café in Montmartre, I took a seat at a table for two and ordered a cheese plate and a beer.

"What sort of beer?" the waiter asked.

I did not know. I had never been a big drinker, in fact I wasn't terribly fond of alcohol, but I forged ahead and said, in my formal French, "It is up to you to decide."

He brought me a bottle that said *1664* on it and he poured it into a glass for me.

I thanked him.

"It is nothing," he said, though it appeared to be everything.

He knew from my accent and my stumbling French that I was a foreigner, certainly American, and I sensed his disdain, the same condescension I had experienced since my arrival. The French, I had discovered, were suspicious of the Americans, foremost because of the war in Vietnam, which was nearing its conclusion, but also because the *franc* was suffering even as the dollar strengthened. To this waiter's mind I was just another one of *them*. I might have protested but my claims would have been ineffectual. In any case, I was clearly more American than French, and in my naiveté I experienced a certain pride and defensiveness.

The cheese on the plate was quite strong and one smelled of cow dung, but I ate everything, spreading it onto little discs of bread that had been cut from a baguette. I had a book before me and it was to this book that I bowed as I ate, though I found it hard to concentrate, because I was distracted by the other diners, who were loud and full of argument and goodwill. The café was crowded, and I was forced to sit shoulder to shoulder with those who flanked me. The man on my right, who was eating with another man, was tall and bald and he wore glasses that resembled welder's goggles, and he kept pushing the goggles up onto his forehead, where they rested as he bent to his pasta. I wondered, as I ate and pretended to read, if anyone was aware of me, and I hoped this was not the case. I was nervous, and my stomach ached because I had eaten the cheese too quickly.

The waiter returned and asked if I wanted another beer. I shook my head and said that I wanted the *addition*, please. When I spoke, the man in the welding glasses looked over at me and then returned to his conversation.

The next time I went to the city, I wandered the streets in the same manner, pausing before the restaurant windows to study the menus, and eventually found myself in a very simple café full of schoolgirls who were so scrubbed and clean looking that they reminded me of Dorothy, my girlfriend. I missed her in an enormous way, though it was only the idea of her that I missed. I did not want her to be there in Paris with me.

A letter had arrived from her that week, and in the letter, which was short and to the point, she said that she had been spending time with my brother Bev. They had become very close. She said that it did not make her happy to tell me in this way, by letter, but she and Bev had fallen in love. They planned to marry soon. *I am sorry*, she said. And she signed only with her name, *Dorothy*.

Always, in her previous letters, she would write, *All my love*, or *Kisses and hugs*, or *Thinking always of you forever and ever*. Sweet sappy sentimental thoughts that I willingly accepted. And now she wrote only her name. Quite simply. I was not devastated by the news, in fact I might have been relieved, but I felt that I *should* be hurt because it was the thing to feel and so I allowed myself to despise Dorothy. About Bev, I felt nothing. Or wanted to feel nothing. The fact was I saw him as ungrateful. He was selfish. He had no honour.

And then my mother wrote as well, addressing Bev's surprising good fortune and my own abandonment of Dorothy. She said, "You didn't really love her, Arthur. If you did, you would be here and not there." My mother was too alone, too sequestered, too much governed by the narrowness of a morality that could never admit the need for both love and the *daimonic*.

OVER THE COURSE OF THE PREVIOUS YEAR, OCCASIONALLY in Paris but also back home in Alberta, I had been suffering what I will refer to as petit mal seizures. They did not happen often, and there were times when I was only aware of the occurrence *after the fact*, so slight was the effect. My knowledge of the petit mal came about due to the feeling of recollection during the seizures. When I was still back home and working as a carpenter's helper, I tried to augment my existence by reading in the evening before falling into a dead sleep. One evening, while reading a novel, I came upon a paragraph that so impressed me that I reread it, repeating certain phrases aloud to myself, and in so doing I experienced an unpleasant taste of sulphur in my mouth. When I was next aware of myself, I was driving my pickup through the countryside and beside me on the seat was the book I had been reading. I was aware that my actions—rising from the chair, picking up the book, stepping out of the apartment door, and climbing into my pickup and beginning to drive—had occurred outside of my consciousness, even though I had succeeded in physically moving through the world unimpeded. It was as if I had been of two minds. I was also aware that during my vacant period I had experienced a "recollection" in which I recalled a childhood incident. I had been lying on a vast bed between my mother and father and at the foot of the bed stood my sister and my brother. The recollection was vivid and surprisingly satisfactory. It was as if I had, in my absent state, achieved a double self.

In December 1963, Wilder Penfield, a neurosurgeon, published a one-hundred-page article based on a thirty-year study of patients who had experienced temporal lobe epileptic seizures. The study involved direct physical stimulation, after craniotomy, of the cortical grey matter. The patients were conscious during stimulation and they often reported a *remembrance* of their past waking life.

Regarding these remembrances, Penfield writes, "It may have been a time of listening to music, a time of looking in at the door of a dance hall, a time of imagining the action of robbers from a comic strip, a time of waking from a vivid dream, a time of laughing conversation with friends, a time of listening to a little son to make sure he was safe, a time of watching illuminated signs, a time of lying in the delivery room at childbirth, a time of being frightened by a menacing man, a time of watching people enter the room with snow on their clothes.

"It may have been a time of hearing someone call your husband's name, a time of listening to your mother scold your brother, a time of watching a guy crawl through a hole in the fence at a baseball game, a time of standing on the corner of 'Jacob and Washington, South Bend, Indiana,' a time of telling the doctor the sensation you had when you got 'the disease from water,' a time of grabbing a stick out of a dog's mouth, a time of listening to (and watching) your mother speed the parting guests ... a time of seeing the nurses of the hospital as you lay in bed and hearing what they say...."

And so on. All case studies. All recorded while the patient lay on a table with the top of his skull removed.

Not all experiences are recalled. "For example, the times of making up one's mind to do this or that do not appear in the record. Times of carrying out skilled acts, times of speaking or saying this and that, or of writing messages and adding figures—these things are not recorded. Times of eating and tasting food, times of sexual excitement or experience—these things have been absent as well as periods of painful suffering or weeping. Modesty does not explain these silences."

There was much to conclude from this, about my self, the absences, my double.

THAT NIGHT, AFTER I HAD READ MY MOTHER'S LETTER in which she accused me of being here and not there, I had one of my seizures. Perhaps it was because of the news in the letter, or maybe because I had been lackadaisical with my medication. Carbatrol was the anticonvulsant my neurologist had prescribed for me when he determined that I had reached the point where medication was necessary, and it left me with ringing in my ears and a sense of malaise. Because I disliked the side effects, I had become careless. Sometime after reading the letter, I felt a slight tingling on the back of my neck followed by a sense of nausea, and when I woke I was lying in the bathroom. I had a bump on my forehead from where I had hit the toilet. There was blood in my mouth. I managed to get up and rinse my mouth and find the bed. I slept, and woke, and remembered clearly the image of my mother reaching down to pluck me from her womb. It was a beautiful image, and I held onto it.

OVER THE NEXT MONTHS, I SUFFERED AN ONSET OF graphomania during which time I was constantly scribbling, jotting down notes on blank pieces of paper, writing free association, filling notebooks, completing stories and poems and immediately beginning new ones, beginning my novel, and writing letters to Isobel. I told her that writing was an artificial process, difficult, and that it required a certain kind of brain. I said that my own brain interested me deeply. I was experiencing auras in which I caught glimpses of my past, as I had years earlier, near the Little Bow, when she kissed my scar and I had a vision of Em. Do you recall? I said that I was committed to art because art heightens life. *She gives deeper joy, she consumes more swiftly. She engraves adventures of the spirit and* the mind in the faces of her votaries; let them lead outwardly a life of the most cloistered calm, she will in the end produce in them a fastidiousness, an over-refinement, a nervous fever and exhaustion, such as a career of extravagant passions and pleasure can hardly show. This from *Death in Venice*, which Helena had given me one day in class when she saw me with a book.

"Wonderful," Helena said. "I love a man who understands nature, the nature of the ego, the soul, sympathy, love, art, the nature of art." She said this in her brazen mixture of four languages and so perhaps I am conjuring what she said, or putting words in her mouth. Perhaps she said that she liked my eyebrows, and that she wanted to have sex with me, because at that time I was longing for a woman, any woman, to take me in her arms and make love to me, and me to her, and then we would lounge on the bed, the afternoon light falling onto our tangled feet. That is what I wished for. Helena's long fingers, with their finely shaped knuckles, waved about and fell lightly upon my bare arms with the fine veins that Carmine so admired.

The following day she pressed into my hands a tattered paperback English translation of *Death in Venice*. "He wrote in German," she said.

I did not know Thomas Mann. I concluded that I must have failed to notice him in Mrs. Dewey's library.

That evening I read the story, with a furious passion, in one sitting. It is about an older man, a writer, an artist, who is wanton and swims in the realm of feeling. He travels to Venice and discovers a young boy of fourteen, Tadzio, who is staying at the same hotel. He falls in love with the boy. It is an ideal and unrequited love, where ugliness is paired with beauty, and desperation with grace. The story ends abruptly, with the older man dying of cholera, perhaps because he ate some overripe strawberries that he had bought on the street while out surreptitiously following Tadzio. When I finished the story, I reread it more slowly, and when I had finished for a second time it was going on three o'clock. Still, I was not tired. I sat down and I wrote a story about an artist who travels to Berlin, where he meets a young girl, much too young, and falls in love with her. He hides this love from others and from himself, he follows her, and he ruminates on *the subtlest thing of all; that the lover was nearer the divine than the beloved.* I copied this straight from Mann. While following the young girl he is hit by a car and dies.

The next day, upon rereading it, I discovered that where I had been aiming for sadness and loss I had only achieved bathos. The story was empty and had no deeper thoughts. I had not faced the truth. The sadness was unearned. And so I tore it up.

With the news that I was no longer responsible in love, that Dorothy had chosen someone else, I felt freer and I began to wander the streets of Paris with an eye to making myself accessible. I had some extra money from the small salary I received from Carmine, and with this fund I purchased a pair of handmade shoes, Italian, and I ordered a suit from a tailor on Rue des Saints-Pères and a number of cotton shirts and several ties of silk and wool. I sat in coffee shops and feigned idleness, writing and reading, drinking espresso, aware of the comings and goings of the various customers around me. I was a handsome boy (for I was in essence still a boy), and I swept my hair back so that my well-shaped ears and my jaw and my dark eyes were evident. I no longer wore my cowboy boots or my snap-button shirts. They were vestiges of my rural past, of my lack of refinement, an admission of everything in me that was anti-cosmopolitan. *Modernité* beckoned. I knew in my heart that the world I had left would always remain, that I could wander back and the rodeo riders and ranchers and girls in pickups would wave at me and I would wave in return and it would be as it always was, even unto the end of the earth. But my soul was elsewhere.

Women found me attractive in my new clothes. One afternoon, sitting in the sunshine at a small table at a café on Boulevard du Montparnasse, an older woman carrying a white poodle approached me and paused and leaned forward and announced that I was beautiful. She placed some francs on the table, said thank you, and strode off. She wore a dark green wool skirt with a matching jacket, and her grey hair was combed back, and she carried herself and her dog with complete poise. She did not turn to look back at me. I wondered if anyone had seen this small exchange. I glanced at the other customers and saw that they were all engaged with their newspapers or deep in conversation. I picked up the money she had left. It was not a small sum.

On another day, I met Max, a young American who had lived in Paris for a year. He sat down at my table without asking and began to talk. "I've seen you 'round," he said. "Here and there." He said his name and held out a hand for me to shake, and I did so, a little wary, torn between my desire to have friendship and my distrust of his straggly quality and enthusiasm. I wondered what he wanted. It turned out that he wanted to hold court. He made his way in Paris by playing a banjo in the subway, eking out a few *sous*, and drawing sketches of tourists alongside the Pont Neuf.

"American tourists like me because I speak their language, and so I earn their trust. The competition is fierce. I came here believing that I would be Picasso or Monet, and that the world would kiss my feet, but in fact artists are like sewage here, we flow in the gutter and people turn away from us. The French, they hate Americans. When a country suffers it looks for a scapegoat, and I am that scapegoat. What are you?"

He did not ask my name, or wonder where I was from, or ask what I did, but he wanted to know *what* I was, as if he were querying my reason for being on this earth. A good question, necessary and often overlooked, and for this reason I ignored the possibility that this Max might be a mountebank and I answered him. I toned down my response. I did not want to show him all my cards, and so I explained my job as a teacher of a young boy, and my French language studies.

"A good gig," he said, and nodded wisely. And then he spoke of himself. He had grown up the son of diplomats, and he was wandering through the world before he settled down to a life of acquisition and glut. "You and me, we are young and carefree. The chains of commerce haven't yet attached themselves. Will you buy me a coffee?" He motioned at the waiter and ordered an espresso and water. His French was fine and smooth. His face was mostly eyes, which were dark discs, full of longing and understanding. These eyes took in the spaces and the characters around him, and in a cheap novel rife with clichés his eyes would be fathomless. His dark hair was cut and trimmed. His clothes were ragged. It was as if his head had been attached to a mismatched body. Reason versus passion.

We talked for two hours, or he talked, and then we walked for many blocks and ate at a poorly lit restaurant that held two tables and a small bar. He insisted on paying for the food, steak and fries, and I insisted on buying the wine. We drank three bottles and so it happened that the cost of the wine surpassed that of the food, but by the time the bill came, I was utterly generous.

He had gone to boarding schools. "Since I was five I only saw my parents on holidays. A great independence was fostered. At six I contracted malaria and every now and then, off and on, the fevers return. Just last month I lay in my room and had visions of monkeys with oversized genitals while watching myself float out the window. I called myself back. That close to death." He rubbed his hands gleefully. Max had found an ear to spill his words into and so he talked and talked. He had attended a boarding school with a view of Kilimanjaro. "Always there. Forever. I never climbed it. In any case here is a story for you. To help you understand how life works. In this boarding school where I was sent, there were rats, and the poor rats were starving, and at night these rats roamed the dormitories and gnawed on the callused feet of the students. On my feet. We tried everything to kill these rats. Traps, poison, sentries. Nothing worked. These were intelligent rats, boarding school rats that avoided traps, turned their noses up at the poison, and eluded the sentries. And so I, at the age of fourteen, came up with a plan. Lay out grain for the rats, but mix the grain with plaster of Paris. The rats, discovering this feast, gorged themselves. But the plaster of Paris made the rats thirsty and so they drank and drank. You know what happened of course. The water mixed with the plaster of Paris became a paste in the stomachs of these rats, and of course it hardened, and the rats were killed in this manner. This is thinking. This is facing a problem not with a hammer, but with an idea. One must appeal to the avarice of the rat. It is a simpler thing to have the rat kill himself. The rats of Paris are numerous, by the way. I have approached the authorities with my plan, offering my services for a small fee, but they are bureaucrats, not given to invention."

He poured more wine. His fingernails required trimming. He must have caught me noticing, because he explained that he did not have banjo picks and that is why he needed long nails. He played bluegrass. Certain Parisians appreciated low culture from the southern states. "Though I have never been to Kentucky."

He had had a girlfriend for a time who also attended boarding school, and they graduated together and travelled throughout Africa, though not in Uganda, which was full of madness and bloodshed. "We travelled to Zanzibar, a jewel of an island, where we swam with the jellyfish and feasted on kingfish. My girlfriend at the time, Sarah, she met the Tanzanian minister of culture who was visiting the island, and he offered her a good amount of money to share his room. Not to have sex with him, but simply to give the appearance that they were having sex. Rumple the sheets, leave her underwear on the floor, let the maid see that this was a bedroom of iniquity, and so she stayed with him for two weeks, completely chaste, while I slept in a hammock in a cheap hotel nearby, and this is how we lived. She would spend the day with me, and the night with the minister. Some might see this as a compromise on my part, but I trusted her."

"Is she here with you?" I asked.

"Oh, no. She married a Swiss businessman and lives in Zurich. Classic bourgeois. Do you like women?" he asked.

An odd question, but I dutifully answered that of course I did. I was also quite drunk, and perhaps to impress him, or perhaps to gain some purchase in the arena of storytelling, I told him about my adopted double cousin Isobel and our youthful love, and even as I told him, I felt shame for having offered up a piece of Isobel that was not mine to disclose.

He leaned forward and ate me up with his mournful eyes and said that he knew a young woman who would love me. "You are perfect for her. Your strong arms, your idealism, your good heart. Let me show you." He steered me out of the restaurant and onto the Metro and then off the Metro and down a small dark street where men urinated against the walls of buildings and women gathered on the sidewalks. He seemed to know these women, for they called out his name, Max, and he addressed them all, as if he were a ragged god who might mete out favours. He stopped before a younger woman, close to my own age, and spoke to her in French, and she looked away and then turned to me and eyed my shoes and my tie and my new shirt. My sartorial panache appeared to win her over because she said, "Agreed."

"This is a good friend of mine," Max said. "She'll show you some fun."

"I'm okay," I said. "I should go home."

"No, no. She's sweet. Don't worry." And he pressed a condom into my hand and whispered in my ear. "Give her a little something after. As a treat." He patted my back and slipped off into the darkness. And so I stood facing the girl, who was smoking and lifting her eyes to the sky as if to say, *What manner of fool is this?*

She was slight, her hair was thin and dark and short, and her face was angular. She wore bright red elf boots and her bare legs were crossed at the ankles as if affecting nonchalance. She put out her cigarette and asked me my age. I immediately liked her voice. Perhaps because she was talking to *me*.

"Twenty-one," I said.

"English," she said.

"Yes."

She made a little shooing motion with her hand and led me to a building and up a series of stairs and down a hallway with numerous doors and into a room in which there was a bed, a dresser, and in the corner a sink and a bidet. As I followed her I was aware of her walk, and of my own walk. I pulled myself more erect in order to diminish my limp.

She closed the door and turned to me and said, "*Et alors.*"

"I would like to make love," I said, using the phrase I had been practising as I followed her. Even in my inebriated state I was aware that she was a prostitute and that Max was her pimp. I did not care.

Her teeth were small and her nose was tiny.

"Just make love," she said. She called me romantic. She touched my jaw and said, "What a surprise."

I took out the money I had received that one afternoon from the woman in the café and I forced it on her.

She counted it, slipped it into her purse. I wondered if I had overpaid, though I was not concerned.

She said that I could undress while she bathed. I sat on the edge of the bed, removed my tie, and began to unbutton my shirt. She was wearing a thin yellow dress and she pulled this over her head and draped it over a chair. She wore no bra. She slid her underwear to her knees and sat on the bidet. I paused and watched her. Her matter-of-factness, her elf boots and the underwear, and the sluicing of the water as she bowed her head and scrubbed herself, all of this filled me with an unexpected tenderness. She stood and dried herself and then bent to remove her boots and underwear, and as she did so I was reminded of the cage that held Isobel's heart down by the Little Bow so long ago. The young woman was completely naked now and drops of water glistened in the hair between her legs.

"*Vos vêtements,*" she said, standing before me.

I stood and removed my clothes, neatly folding them and placing them on a nearby chair.

We were standing, facing each other, and she looked me up and down and said that I was young and beautiful. "*C'est bon.*"

I did not have an erection. This didn't seem to worry her. We went to the bed and she lay there as I kissed her neck and her jaw and her shoulders. I kissed her nipples. She touched my arms and she touched my penis and she said that my hair was so soft. She took my penis in her mouth and I got hard and came very quickly, pulling her head away just before so that she would not have to suffer the humiliation of spitting out my semen.

"Is that all?" she asked.

I was stroking her back, running my fingers along her rib cage. She was frail, and she was hardy. She rose and picked up her dress and slipped it over her head. Her bare chest disappeared. She picked up the towel she had used earlier and handed it to me and with it I wiped my stomach. I got dressed as she watched herself in the mirror above the sink, applying makeup, touching up her hair with her small hands.

"How are you called?" I asked.

She lifted her eyebrows. I saw this in the reflection of the mirror. "Renée," she said. "*Et vous?*" She insisted on being formal.

"Arthur." I said it the English way, with the *th* sound. She didn't understand. I said it again. "Are-toor."

"Ah, Artur. *Au revoir*, Artur."

She let me out and closed the door. She remained in the room. I found my own way down the stairs.

I was alone in the car on the Metro riding back to Rueil–Malmaison, save for a homeless man who stood in the back corner, sighing. I stood and walked through to the next carriage and took a seat. It was raining. Outside, there were the lights of the passing cars and houses and streetlights. I was thinking of the manner in which Renée's bare knees pressed together as she first alighted like a bird on the bidet. As if my presence hadn't mattered at all, as if, in fact, I hadn't existed.

The next time I went to find her, seven days later, she said my name, *Are-toor*, and called me over and we smoked in the darkness and she asked me where I came from. I told her, and she asked a few more questions, and so it was revealed to her that I came from a ranch and that I rode horses.

"A cowboy," she said in English. She said that she would like to visit my country.

I asked her about Max, whom I had not seen since he patted me on the back and disappeared into the darkness. She didn't want to talk about him.

Up in the room she undressed me first and then told me to lie down and watch her wash. She suffered no shame, and for me, the country boy born into a religion that depended upon shame, this was a marvel to witness. She appeared to find nothing ridiculous or indecent about her own behaviour, perhaps it was habit or routine, while I, the observer and hesitant participant, experienced humiliation, even distress—though by the time she was towelling herself dry I had an erection. Her forthright manner, her clarity, her *here I am* nature, filled me with desire because she was my opposite. She asked if I wanted to put myself inside her *cul*, though it would cost more. I said that I would be happy to make love in the habitual manner. I sounded very formal but she understood and accepted my wish, though she seemed slightly disappointed. It was clear that she saw me as having a certain wealth.

This time, when I left her, she touched my chin and said, "It is important to know what you want." She said it in French and she said it quickly and the clack of *ce que* disorientated me and so I thought she was telling me what *she* wanted. But she wasn't. I realized all of this later, alone in my own bed, as I repeated her words to myself. On the Metro, riding home, I had discovered that my cash had been lifted from my wallet, not a large amount, but I felt humiliation once again, and sadness. I did not blame Renée. She was desperate and poor. Though I did consider finding Max and confronting him. But I did nothing. I thought that what had come my way had been justly deserved.

Something had been loosed in me. I was in the middle of Flaubert's letters, his *Voyage en Orient*, and as much as I was disgusted by his whoring, I was intrigued as well. In Beirut he has a woman with *a spray of jasmine in her frizzy black hair*, and *a bit of matter beside the inner pupil of her right eye*. In Jerusalem he visits the Holy Sepulchre and leaves with a cold sour feeling: *hypocrisy, cupidity, falsification, impudence.* He returns home, reads the Sermon on the Mount, his *heart touched as though nothing had ever touched it before.*

My mother read the Sermon to us in the evenings, during devotions. It *does* touch you. I had become a Christian at the age of six, my mother's thigh pressing against mine as I bowed my head to pray. I was baptized at eighteen, just after meeting Dorothy. We were baptized the same Sunday morning. But she was the force. My heart was not all there. She walked down into the baptistery ahead of me, wearing a purple choir gown, and when she was lifted from the water by the bald pastor, she sputtered and gasped and the water streamed from her long braids. The gown clung to her chest and her navel, and I admired her body and then turned away. There is a stark and dangerous beauty when the sacred meets the profane. That evening, in the darkness of my pickup, she took my hands and placed them on her breasts. "These are yours," she said.

As a boy, on Sunday afternoons after church and lunch, I would ride Moby, and later, in the dim coolness of the stable, I would remove Moby's bit and bridle, loosen the cinch and heft the saddle from his back and remove the blanket, and then groom him and lead him out to the pasture and set him free. He ran then, full speed up to the far fence and then back again, straight at me where I stood. I always feared that he would run me over, but at the last moment he pulled up and swung his large head, blowing through his nostrils, his eyes wild and heated. And then off he went again, running.

IN MY LETTERS TO ISOBEL I HAD BECOME MORE FAMILIAR. I began each letter with *My dear little girl*, which was how Sartre addressed de Beauvoir when he was first wooing her. I admitted my theft, but I said that I was also willing to borrow from a master.

> *And it is such a beautiful phrase, isn't it? Living here, in this place where I do not know anyone, has made me both more self-conscious and freer. I can be anyone I want to be and though this should allow me more freedom, it sometimes falls on my head heavily. I believe I am choosing, and then immediately I question my choice. Everything is random. My*

birth, who my parents are, you as my cousin who aren't really my cousin, my place here in Paris, whether I choose to buy a baguette at this boulangerie or that one, the words I pour onto this paper and the order of those words, the voyage of this letter across the ocean and the various hands that will touch it, your response to my words, et cetera, et cetera. I slept with a prostitute named Renée. Why a prostitute? Why Renée? Why not a different woman, older, darker, wealthier, uglier? And then I went back a second time, quite happily. I wanted the experience. I wanted to feel something, and so I did. I felt hunger and lust and desolation and guilt and relief and happiness. There was a moment, when she removed her underwear and sat on the bidet, that I felt purity, as if Renée's lack of shame had overcome my own feelings of indignity. When I was with her I thought of you.

Isobel wrote back.

My dear Arthur,

Let us be clear, I am not your little whore. And I think that your notion of the random is nonsense. For if this is true then you are saying that you have absolutely no choice. I think it is funny that you, with all your fears, slept with a whore named Renée. And don't think that you can excuse your behaviour by saying that you had no choice. I am happy for you. See? I could choose to be jealous, which I was when I

first read your letter, but then I decided that jealousy would
only make me anxious, and so I chose to be happy for you.
Good for you, you wanton boy. I envy your freedom. I want
to be there with you. I hang onto your smell and your smile
and your bravery.

Love,
Isobel

ONE SUNDAY MORNING I WENT TO CHURCH WITH
Carmine and Pierre and Christian. Carmine had been
insisting that Christian was insisting that I join them, and so
on this morning I did so, though my feelings were not with
the family. They were focused on myself, and the joy I felt for
myself, and my thoughts of Isobel.

Carmine wore a black sleeveless dress and flat black shoes
with velvet bows. Her face was pale. I assumed that she did
not wear makeup to church. Her plainness, her sombre manner, and the music of the chanting priest created a hole in me
and a longing for a bond with Carmine that I knew would
never take place, even though she was aware of me and kept
turning her small head to gauge my presence and my proximity to Christian, who sat beside me in the pew and held my
hand, sweet boy.

I had been raised, as I said, Mennonite, where the
churches were pared down. Images were forbidden, the singing

was four-part harmony with piano as accompaniment. I had never experienced the grandeur and pomp and smells of a Catholic service. I imitated Carmine. When she genuflected at the entrance and touched her fingers to the holy water, I copied her. When she kneeled, I did the same. When she rose, along with Christian and Pierre, to take communion, I followed. The priest was swathed in white robes with gold piping. He offered the body and blood of Christ, and I accepted it. The wine was wine. In my church back home the wine was grape juice in the smallest of glasses that nested in a silver salver, and from which the individual plucked the glass, and to which, after drinking, he returned it. As Anabaptists we were our own priests. We butchered the body of Christ, blessed it ourselves, and ate it. We drained the blood, poured it into tiny glasses, and drank it. Here, in this cold stone church in Rueil–Malmaison, near to Joséphine de Beauharnais' summerhouse, the emissary of God served us, and even as we were served I understood that I had crossed over from faith into doubt. I was no longer a believer. How could I be? It was all a game. A farce. I could not reconcile my life as a sexual being with this fantastic diversion of Christ's body and blood. I wanted the real body and the real blood. Renée's body and blood, the solidity of lust and sex and the frenzy of love.

Poor Christ, who never knew a woman.

In the afternoon, after a lunch of cold soup, chilled white wine, potatoes roasted with olive oil and rosemary, and tiny sausages wrapped in pastry, Pierre and Carmine retired to their room for a rest, or perhaps to make love, while Christian and I played a game of *boules* in the backyard.

That evening I wrote my mother and told her that I no longer believed in God. I said that it was impossible to stay in a locked house when outside that house there was a vista full of life. My metaphor was weak, and so I compensated by capitalizing *LIFE*, as if that might distract my mother. *Don't worry about me*, I wrote. *I haven't gone off the deep end.* I asked about Bev and Dorothy. I said that I held no grudge against them, and she was right to say that I was here and they were there.

When I reread what I had written, I felt calm. I knew that she would be upset, but she would also deny everything I had just said. She would say I was in a state. I didn't know what I was saying. I would come around to see the truth. She would pray for me. All this and more. Of course, my confession of atheism was guiding my mother down the wrong path. What I really wanted to tell her was that I was of greater moral character than Bev, and why couldn't she see that? But instead, I told her that I was now an atheist.

I had chosen Renée because I had had no luck with French girls. They were flirtatious and sometimes coy and then suddenly cold and indifferent. My looks, my manner, appeared to have no effect. And there was also the question of my spoken French, which while passable was neither debonair nor smooth. I did not possess the language of wooing.

One day, at dinner with the Godbout family, Pierre, who was back from his travels, asked me with a wink if I had had any chance with the French women. He asked this question when Carmine was in the kitchen firing up the crème brûlée.

I said that all was fine.

"You see," he said, "it is important to know that a French woman likes to be pulled. A simple look is not sufficient. You must be insistent. They expect it. Desire it. You must be vigorous. It makes for a little game, you see. Do not accept that no is the answer she wants to give. You must try, and try again." He drank from his wine. His throat was quite active when he swallowed.

Throughout his little speech Christian was watching and listening.

Carmine returned and said that she was not completely pleased with the crème brûlée. It should be colder in the interior. She made a slight motion with her small mouth, the mouth that I loved to watch as she spoke. I was wondering at that moment if she had wanted me to be more aggressive with her, if indeed Pierre was correct and Carmine wanted me to pull at her. I sincerely doubted it, and would have been embarrassed to attempt anything uncouth.

At that time, every lunch hour I went to a café near Alliance Française, where I ate a boiled egg and croissant and drank espresso. Aniane worked as a waitress in the café, and at some point, when she took my order or perhaps when she cleared my plate, we began to talk. She was older than me by several years, not a knockout at all, hair in little ringlets the colour of the prairie grassland in fall, a pale brown. Her face was round and she had a crooked tooth, and all these mishmash of parts, especially her ordinary face topped by her dun-coloured curls, made her powerfully attractive. Or it might have been that her plainness made her less intimidating. She was very friendly, something I had not experienced with Parisians, and she went out of her way to make sure everything was all right with me. She knew from my spoken French that I was not from France, and eventually she asked me my origins and I told her, and she told me that she came from a small village near Avignon. "Provincial," she said.

I loved her name, *Aniane*. I loved the feel of it in my mouth, all those vowels, the repetition itself. She had no interest in things literary. She was not conceited or hollow. Her mind worked sideways. She was not good at argument or debate, but she often surprised me with her ideas, which arrived unexpectedly and sharply. Her mouth was very expressive, and when we spoke my eyes kept focusing on her mouth and her top lip, which stuck out in a fetching manner, and she must have noticed me looking there. Though I did like her eyes as well, which were dark, and her eyebrows were thick and tan, like the soft hair of a newborn calf.

And so I was interested in her. She talked to me, and this was no small matter. I was still lonely for company. I had asked her once if she would like to meet for coffee or a drink after work, but she said that she was very busy.

After my conversation with Pierre, I decided that I would like to pull at her, and so one lunch hour, when she delivered my croissant and egg and coffee, I asked again if we could meet sometime.

"I don't think so," she said. "I have different tastes."

"Today," I said. "I will wait for you after work. When do you get off?"

"At seven," she said. "If I am here, I am here."

She wore a black apron over her skirt. The stocking of her right leg had a run in it. I sat and read, looking up from my book to watch her work. She was aware of me watching her, and she didn't seem to mind, because she kept looking my way.

That afternoon I went home and taught Christian. I was conscious of the clock on the wall and the hour at which I would have to leave. Finally, I patted Christian on the head and said, "I must go." I showered and changed to nicer clothes. I returned to the café and stood on the sidewalk and observed Aniane move among the customers. When she appeared on the street she did not seem surprised to see me.

We walked side by side up the street to a restaurant, where we drank beer and ate a small pizza. I told her that I liked her manner. She was simple and approachable in the best of ways.

"What is the best of ways?" she asked.

"Well, for example, you talk to me, a stranger from another country who does not speak your language very well."

"Oh, you do," she said. Her round face looked up at me and I wanted to put my hands on her.

Outside later, again on the street, Aniane placed her hand in the crook of my elbow and in this manner we slowly walked. On that street, I believe it was Rue Madame, in the shadows created by a dim street lamp, she told me that she had been married for a time but now she lived by herself. She had a child of three called Bernadette, who moved between her apartment and the father's place. She said that she did not leave one man to become involved with another so quickly.

"In any case, you are young," she said.

I was extremely disappointed. She was telling me that I was insufficient, that I was not worth the effort. I did not speak and so she stroked my face and clutched my arm and whispered that all was fine, I was handsome and young and everything lay before me. "You are a killer," she said.

She said this in English. It made no sense.

I said that I didn't want to be a killer, I was looking for love.

"Perhaps," she said, and it was that one word, *perhaps*, that lifted my spirits. My imagination had always been extreme. With each female I met, I created a story of love and passion and bliss. I fit them into my world, put them in my arms, loved them, gave my soul over to them, and had us living out a life of affection and care and desire. I was prodigiously generous. I wanted all women to love me, and I would love them back.

WE KEPT SEEING EACH OTHER. WE WENT TO MOVIES that I did not understand, and Aniane and I sat in deep leather seats near the back of the theatre and drank beer as she informed me of the important details. The softness of her breath on my neck. On Sunday afternoons, when she cared for Bernadette, we met in the Jardin du Luxembourg and ambled about, observing the tennis players, and then I sat on a bench as Aniane pushed Bernadette on a swing in the playground. Bernadette, when she was first introduced to me, tilted her head, and then I stepped forward and lowered my head to her level and she kissed me on the cheeks. She smelled like her mother. She wore a bright yellow coat over an off-white dress. And white stockings, and black shoes. Later, after she had finished with the playground, I wiped the dust from her shoes with my shirtsleeve. Her legs were firm and round. Once, when Bernadette fell in the playground and began to cry, Aniane picked her up and brushed her off and held her and spoke into her ear, and then held her at arm's length, and finally held her close again.

I BELIEVED THAT IT WOULD BE A SIMPLE THING, IN A foreign country, where you are not known, to remake yourself. This proved to be difficult. Yes, no one recognized my visage, and not one person, other than Helena, my Italian colleague with the leather pants, and the Godbout family, and now Aniane, knew that I had been raised on a ranch in Alberta and that I was essentially a plebeian striving for aristocratic grace. But, as I came to understand, I was still Arthur Wohlgemuht, and I still had vestiges of my Mennonite upbringing in me, which led to bouts of guilt and conflict and boundless desire. I was also the Arthur Wohlgemuht with the brainpan that was slightly sick, the one who suffered auras, and the one who occasionally fell into deleterious seizures.

If my relationship with Aniane circled around movies and visits to the park with Bernadette, and if I had not yet fallen into her arms and found myself buried between her legs in a paroxysm of gratitude and lust, it was my own fault, the fault of my lack of know-how, my lack of aggression and insistence, and certainly my lack of ability to speak her language. Literally. I have always depended on words to get me what I want. I can be eloquent and smooth in my own language, English, but now here I was, spending time with a French girl who did not speak English. I was attempting to communicate desire and love without the aid of my wit and my beautiful sentences, and of course I was failing. I began to fear that Renée, my sweet whore, for this is how I thought of her, would be my one and only sexual gratification in France. She was sweet, to be sure, but she required money, which meant that sex would always and only be a form of barter, and I didn't want my singular sexual experience to be mercantile. I was still a romantic.

One Saturday afternoon Aniane picked me up and we rode in her ex-husband's Citroën to a hospital in the Yonne region, an hour's drive southeast of Paris. The previous day, in the café, I had asked her when I could see her again, and she had deferred and postponed and had once again said how we did not have the same tastes, a statement that still confused me, and though I said that I was willing to change my tastes, she shook her head and said that it was impossible. When she said the word *impossible* in French, I was aware of how much more beautiful the French language was than English, and how a simple word like *impossible* seemed to hold so much more promise when said in French, with its incrementally rising third syllable and the softness of its refusal. It is not surprising then that French is the language of diplomacy, and in this case it was Aniane who was being diplomatic, for she finally gave in and said that she was travelling up to visit a friend in the hospital the following day and I was welcome to join her.

"It will be regular, not terribly exciting," she said, and when I expressed interest, she gave me the street and address where I should be waiting. She would be driving the red Citroën.

I arrived at the meeting place early. It was a warm day for that time of year, and it was raining. I did not have an umbrella and so took refuge beneath the awning of a shop that sold kitchenware and sinks and bathroom tiles and marble countertops. An older woman was visible through the window. She sat at a desk, and then she stood and moved about the shop. She wore a shockingly blue dress with shoes that matched. She looked as if she were attending a wedding or a special social event. Perhaps meeting the president of the Republic. That is how certain French women dressed, and I pictured them toiling at their toilettes, primping and preening in order to meet the head of state, or, in this case, preparing to sell bathroom tiles.

I imagined that the woman in blue might step outside and ask me what I wanted, or she might attempt to shoo me away as if I were a vagabond, and then I would explain that I was waiting for a ride, and that while I was waiting I had been watching and admiring her. I would say that I had been wanting her to step outside to ask me the exact question that she had just posed, and now that she had made her way outside, I would like to ask her name, because I was in the process of writing a novel, and she would appear in the novel, and perhaps she might want her name to be written into the story. But she didn't step outside, in fact she simply moved about the grand space that was her shop, or someone else's shop, for she was only the worker, and so her name remains unknown, and it is possible that she will never again have the chance to appear in a novel. But then, perhaps this was not her ambition.

By the time Aniane appeared, half an hour later, I was soaked from the rain. She had packed a little lunch, which we planned to eat in a park, should the rain stop, but before that she wanted to pay a visit to the friend she knew in an institution. She called it an institution, though I might have called it something else. When we entered the place, a large brick building of five storeys, I saw immediately that the residents there were lonely and alone and that most of them sat on benches in the corridors, staring straight ahead. There were nurses and orderlies strolling about. What manner of place this was, I could not tell, but I assumed that most of the patients were mentally deficient. The girl we visited was named Rosalyn and she was about twenty, though her face looked thirty, except when she smiled and then she became thirteen. She had some sort of palsy. Her hands didn't work properly. They were curled inward like claws. Aniane was constantly wiping her mouth with a little cloth, as there was a perpetual flow of saliva. Rosalyn seemed to recognize Aniane because she began to grunt and move her slippered feet in an excited fashion when Aniane bent to kiss her.

Aniane introduced me. "This is Arthur, my friend," she said.

I felt that I must also greet Rosalyn, and so I bent to kiss her cheeks, because *it was the thing to do*. Immediately, Rosalyn set to howling. Aniane pulled me away and comforted Rosalyn, whispering in her ear that it was okay, this was a friend, no need to be frightened. Aniane stood and said that Rosalyn wasn't used to strangers. Perhaps I should sit at a distance, and she motioned at a bench, on which there was an old woman wearing a plaid shirt and green pants that were too large for her.

I sat beside this woman while Aniane crouched before Rosalyn and talked softly to her. The air, hot and stuffy, smelled of antiseptic and urine. I grew groggy and faint. Perhaps I slept, perhaps I dreamed, for I found myself once again on the ward of the hospital where I had stayed when I broke my leg years earlier. I had lain in traction waiting for my mother to come to me, her clothes and hair smelling of the ranch, of the outside world that kept grinding on its cogs while I, on my back, read and slept and read some more, and suffered fantastic fantasies. And then I found myself on the infant's ward where Hildegaard, my first love, nursed me. She offered first one full breast, and then the other, and she punched me softly on the thigh and told me that I would be great.

When I roused myself, Aniane was feeding Rosalyn from a large orange bowl, a mash of sorts that pleased Rosalyn greatly, for her slippered feet crossed and uncrossed with each spoonful. After, Aniane set the bowl on the floor and carefully wiped Rosalyn's mouth with a cloth. Aniane stood. She looked over at me and nodded. I did not know what this nod signified, but nevertheless I stood and waited for another signal. Perhaps I was to draw near. Perhaps disappear. Aniane bent to kiss Rosalyn's forehead and then she said goodbye, approached me and took my hand, and together we walked out of the building. The rain had finished, the sun was shining.

Aniane did not say anything until we were in the car and driving once again. Finally, she spoke. She said, "Rosalyn is my ex-husband's sister. She was born with severe cerebral palsy and was immediately placed in an institution by her parents. They did not want her. No one from the family visits her. It is like she doesn't exist. When my husband first told me about her I was appalled and angry, and I asked him if he had ever visited and he said it was forbidden. 'How old are you?' I asked him. 'Don't you have a conscience, a mind of your own, compassion?' And so each week I visit Rosalyn. Even though

I am no longer part of the family, I visit her. She has no one else." She was sending me a signal. She was telling me that if I wanted her, I would have to take all of her. The Citroën and the ex-husband, Bernadette with her pudgy legs, Rosalyn, the palsy-ridden woman that no one wanted, and finally, her, Aniane, the waitress with the ripped hose who served me desultory looking croissants and cold eggs. This was the tableau she was offering, and if I expected that everything would be romance and roses and making love in the afternoon while Piaf played faintly in the background, I might as well forget it. *Choose*, she appeared to say, *just remember, we have different tastes.*

I ignored the signal. I took her hand and said that she was kind and generous. She wanted to hear that, needed to. Her head nodded, her top lip stuck out as she drove. She thanked me.

I continued. "It's a wonderful thing you do, taking care of a stranger."

"She's not a stranger," Aniane cried.

I saw my mistake but I pushed forward. "Well, in a way she is. She belongs to a family that has rejected both you and Rosalyn. You said they have money. Of which you have none. Of which she has been cut out." My French was humbled and slow. I had trouble with prepositions, even though I respected them, especially the preposition *dont*. About the wealth, the riches, she had told me this. The family had old money, made from rubber plantations in Vietnam. Way back. The money now sat in investments, in real estate. She had received nothing. Not a pittance. *Rien*. She had never officially married and so had no rights.

"I love that girl," she said. "Did you see her, all alone? She responds. She smiles. She has no one."

I wanted to say that I too had no one. Look at me. But I nodded and said that she, Aniane, had worked magic with Rosalyn. "When we first got there she looked old. When we left she had lost years. She was fifteen."

"She was, wasn't she?" Aniane took my left hand in her right and she squeezed. "Let's find a park," she said.

"Yes," I said.

We drove and drove but found nothing but small patches of grass surrounded by large tenements, or parks where children played and where there was not enough privacy, and little crops of land that looked inviting but were not for the public, until finally she pulled onto a small side road and found a patch of pasture with cows grazing nearby. She parked the Citroën in a copse of trees, away from the prying eyes of passersby. She laid out a white blanket on the wet ground, and on this we sat and ate boiled eggs, of course, and croissants and fresh strawberries and bits of chocolate with raisins buried deep inside. She had a bottle of wine and a corkscrew and we drank and spilled onto the white blanket, but no matter, she would clean it with hydrogen peroxide and soap. She was a fixer. She knew what to do. She was like my mother in that way.

She lay back on the blanket and I lay beside her and soon we were nibbling at each other's lips and eyes and ears. She was warm and open. She unbuttoned her blouse and removed her bra and said, "Now," as she held my head against her chest. I was amazed. What manner of gift was this? What had I done? In fact, I lifted my head at one point and asked, "Why now?" but thankfully she didn't engage me. Her eyes were looking up at the blue sky, and she shook her head and forced me back against her breast.

In that shadowed place, surrounded by the hum of traffic in the distance, and the Lourdais chewing their cud, and the scrape of a backhoe against the tarmac somewhere far away, she dipped and whispered, and so my sweet Aniane and I, we made love on a stained blanket, in the countryside, while the Citroën and a few dairy cows stood guard. I had a condom. This pleased her. She said, "Don't want anything tricky to happen." I was of the same mind. Her body was surprisingly hungry. I had not experienced outright passion before in a woman. She almost didn't need me, she was so good at love.

OVER THE NEXT WHILE I DISCOVERED THAT ANIANE was most ardent after we paid visits to Rosalyn. We would drive out to the institution and spend several hours with Rosalyn, who had become used to my presence. I was now allowed to sit on a wooden chair nearby, though I still did not touch her or talk to her. Aniane would feed her and tell her about her day, the weather outside, the little sayings that her daughter Bernadette had come up with, while I observed from a small distance. Then, Aniane and I would leave the building, and Aniane, softened by despondency or longing or the cruelty of fate, would cling to me until inevitably we ended up making love somewhere, anywhere: the Citroën; a cramped hotel room in the Arab quarter where foreign voices hollered in the adjoining space; another pasture on another warm day, though in that instance a farmer discovered us and chased us from his property, Aniane screaming that the farmer should just fuck off already; the Citroën again; and, finally, in my bed, in my lodgings, on a Saturday afternoon when the sun fell through my bedroom window onto her bare knee, a glorious moment tinged with amour and needs and pleasure and agreement.

I had been hesitant to draw her back to my place. It was private, the space where I wrote and read and dreamed and ate and shat. Also, there was Carmine to consider. I didn't want to disappoint her, to let her down, nor did I want her to think that because I now had a lover, I had given up on her. She was still my ideal, the woman upon whom I projected my yearnings and fantasies. She should not lose sight of this. Regardless, on that Saturday in late August, Aniane and I were desperate for someplace to have sex, and when I suggested my apartment, she hesitated and asked if I was sure.

"It's a secret," she said.

"What's a secret?" I asked.

"Your apartment. You are keeping it a secret from me."

"No. Not at all. You can come. Do. Let's go."

My enthusiasm was too strong. She knew, via previous conversations, that my lodgings were off-limits.

"You are sure?" she asked.

"Absolutely."

She loved that my space was suffused with light. About my large collection of books she said nothing, though later, when her presence in my place became one of habit, I would pull one of my favourite books from the shelf and read to her while she sat on a chair in the sun. And fell asleep.

She was tired, certainly. She worked long hours at the café. She cared for her daughter most of the week. Whereas she had many responsibilities, I had only one, teaching Christian. The rest of my time was taken up with tending to my own needs. Even so, when I noticed that she had fallen asleep, I was hurt. I closed the book and studied her as she slept, her chest rising and falling, her head lolling to one side. I saw that we had little in common other than a desire to share our bodies, and even that was suspect, because I sensed that I took more pleasure from her than she did from me. What excited her was companionship, evenings drinking red wine on a sidewalk café and possessively holding my hand and talking about her work, or about Bernadette who was drawing wonderful pictures at such a young age, and then worrying about Rosalyn who seemed depressed and had stopped eating.

I had imagined finding a woman with whom I might have deep conversations about books and art and ideas, a woman who had grown up in an apartment on Rue du Montparnasse or some such place, with an architect for a father and a psychiatrist for a mother, where the walls held various studies by famous painters and numerous books on art, and the wine-soaked evenings ended with murmurs of intellectual satisfaction. Aniane had known none of this, and was not interested in the least. Her life was unyielding and dull and of slight consequence. Her thoughts had no solidity, she did not attach her ideas to any larger scheme. She had no interest in motivation. She did not know what motivated her.

One evening, sitting and holding her hand in a café where we sat side by side, facing the street, I experienced a certain melancholy. And this being so, I said, "What will you be?"

She wrinkled her small nose and looked at me. "What are you saying?"

"What do you want to be? Surely you must want to be something."

"But I am something. I am Aniane. I am the mother of Bernadette. I am your lover."

"Is that enough?"

She laughed. She thought I was being silly. She kissed me on the cheek.

I said that I wanted experience and adventure. "That is the only way to become a writer. Then the world will see me. They will see Arthur Wohlgemuht."

She touched my jaw and said that I was a peasant just like her. I was a handsome farmer who thought that just because he could read and write and think a little, he was better than the other peasants. "You are full of vanity," she said. She shrugged, amused by my desires.

Vanité. I was six when my mother read to me the words of John Bunyan. Little Christian comes to a place called Vanity Fair, where all is frivolity, pointless amusement, and empty acts. Everything is hollow. Was that me? Why, when I held something good, did I always want more and more and more?

I took Aniane's hand, the one that held mine, lifted it to my mouth, and kissed it.

That night we rode the RER back to my place. It was late. At one of the stops, two young men entered our car and sat down nearby. Aniane and I had been talking and laughing. I was anticipating sex. I had recently become fascinated by her motherhood, the stark realization that when we made love, I was entering a place from which Bernadette had come. The marvel of opposites, the creator, the coming in and the going out. On the train, side by side, she was holding my hand, and then she wasn't, and then she was. It was a cool evening and she wore my trench coat over a leather vest. I was wearing a thin shirt and jeans and running shoes. The two young men were louche and aggressive, and it became clear that they were watching us and making comments and laughing. We ignored them. We got off at our stop and the two men got off as well. Aniane kept looking back. I told her not to worry. But she was worried. And so we walked quickly, but the two men caught us up and one of them, wide-eyed with a small mouth, said that he would like to see my flower. I think that's what he said. I didn't understand for certain. I understood *flower*, but he may have said *her flower*.

Aniane turned to face them. "Fuck off," she said.

I pulled at her arm and said, "Let's go."

"I'd like to see your flower," the wide-eyed fellow said again. He was talking to me. He was obviously the spokesperson. His friend hung back, though he stood on tiptoes and danced about slightly, and I thought that he might be more dangerous than the small-mouthed wide-eyed one.

I looked at the small-mouthed one's nose and then I studied the dancer's nose. It was all very simple, though they didn't know it yet, and I felt calm because it was so simple.

I said, "This is not your affair." I said it in French of course and I may have said that my flower was not his affair, I can't remember exactly, but I wanted to distract him with my poor French, and I managed to do this. He tilted his head slightly, and that's when I hit him. A straight jab to the nose, the tenderest area on the face. Severn had taught me this. *Don't wait for a signal, or for him to throw the first punch. Pretend as if you don't care. Maybe look away so that he thinks you aren't paying attention. And then take one little step forward, and as you step forward, aim at the nose. Don't swing. That's a giveaway. Throw the punch directly from the shoulder, straight on. A jab. Shift your weight towards the target as you jab. More power that way. Hit the nose square. It won't hurt your hand, but if you hit well, it'll hurt him for sure. Surprise is important. It gives you the advantage.* And this is how I hit the small-mouthed fellow. Blood spurted immediately and he howled and bent forward. I hit him once more, across the right ear, which is also tender. My fist formed a slight parabola through the air. It wasn't a straight jab, but it no longer mattered. The small-mouthed fellow wasn't paying attention. He groaned and covered his head. He was now on his knees. The dancer leaned back, leaned forward, studied his friend, and then took one step in reverse.

I held Aniane's arm and led her away. She wanted to look back but I forbade it. "You'll encourage them," I said.

We turned down my street and walked on through the circles of light that fell from the street lamps onto the pavement. I was shaking. I felt no pleasure. I felt no fear.

Aniane was making noises of appreciation and wonder. She was excited. She did a little dance to the right and jabbed with one hand, and then danced to the left. "My boxer," she said. "Marvellous. Where did you learn that?" She laughed. "You surely got your adventure." And she took my hand and said that she loved me.

WHEN ANIANE SAID THAT SHE LOVED ME, AFTER MY scuffle with the men on the street, I wanted to tell her that it was not love she felt but a base desire triggered by watching a young good-looking man win a boxing match. As we walked she kept exclaiming. She touched my chest and said that I was powerful. She stopped me in the middle of the quiet street and kissed me on the mouth.

"You have courage," she said. She giggled in a nervous manner. On the other side of the street a solitary man washed the sidewalks.

When we arrived at my apartment, I let us in, and as soon as the door was closed Aniane undressed me. She meandered over my body, kissing each part as it appeared. She was very warm, not at all reserved. She had seen the scar on my leg before, had even asked about it, but she had always seemed squeamish. This time, overwhelmed by passion and pride, she touched it. "Oh," she said. I felt a tingling on the back of my neck and closed my eyes. My mother was leaning over me, her face in a grimace, and her hands were reaching for my head. When I opened my eyes again I saw Aniane standing by the window, smoking. My head ached. My mouth tasted of tin and blood. I slept some more and when I woke again Aniane was frying eggs. I sat up. She said my name and came to sit beside me.

"You were sick," she said. "You became unconscious. I thought I might call an ambulance, but then you stopped thrashing and you slept. For a long time."

Over coffee, I told her about Isobel and the time she had kissed my scar and the vision I had had of my sister Em. I spoke of the man who was my neurologist and the tests he had done on my brain. I presented it as a romantic problem, one of dreaminess and inspiration and intelligence. I did not use the word *epilepsy*, neither did I tell her that I had been off and on with my medication. For the first time, I spoke about my past. I told her about my brother who had fought in Vietnam, and I told her about his breakdown. I did not have a large vocabulary and so it came to be understood that my brother had a *nervous brain*.

"*Fou*," Aniane said, and she made a twirling motion with her finger by her temple to indicate madness.

"A little," I said. I wanted to speak of the accident, and of working for Stella Armstrong, and why I had chosen to work for her, but I didn't have the words for all of that, and so I simply let Aniane touch my poor head and hold me.

Two days later, returning from my French classes, Carmine met me as I passed by her house on the path to my lodgings. She leaned forward and in her soft and refined manner she wondered if we might have a tête-à-tête. I paused. What did she want?

"The visitor. Your visitor. It was understood when you first came here to live that you wouldn't bring home girls."

"It's one girl," I said. "She's a friend."

"Yes, well. Pierre and I have discussed this and we would like you to stop. It's out of place. And Christian. You understand."

I nodded.

"You are an intelligent boy, Arthur. You have dreams and aspirations."

I agreed with her, though I said that Aniane certainly had aspirations as well.

"You come from a different place, Arthur." She said my name each time she made a statement, as if this would lend her more force. "This girl, from when she was a child, was guided in a certain way. She will be a worker. She will not go to university, this is not in her cards. You, Arthur, on the other hand, are blossoming. You have a vision. I have seen that in our conversations."

I had been told this before, that a French child's life was determined from birth. This one would be a dentist, that one a chef, this one a surgeon, that one a lawyer, this one a tradesman. I said, "My parents are ranchers, they raise cattle, they farm. That doesn't mean I have to be the same. And just because Aniane comes from peasant stock doesn't mean she can't remake herself."

Carmine was amused by my passion and naïveté. "She might want to go back home with you. This can happen."

"It's not like that," I said, and immediately felt sorry for Aniane. I was betraying her.

"For you, perhaps. For her, who knows?"

Carmine might have been jealous. But she was also rigid, and clean, and Catholic.

I agreed. I would no longer bring the girl back to the apartment.

When I told Aniane she grew angry and spiteful. "Who does she think I am? Some whore you bed? A slut without a name?" She said that she detested bourgeois folks with their boring squeaky clean lives in the suburbs who never fuck and who ignore the poor. Where did they think their luxuries came from? She said it was men like my Pierre Godbout who came to her restaurant and ate their little meal and offered a small tip and for this they thought they had the right to tap her ass and talk dirty to her.

I did not understand all of this. She said it quickly and with tremendous passion, her voice going up and down, her hands moving there and here, and I understood about the poor and how men expected something from her, but it may have been me that she was talking about, how I touched her ass and talked dirty to her. Such is the terror of translation.

What she said next I understood. "What did you tell her?"

I ducked my head. And then I regarded her fiery face and said that I had agreed not to bring visitors again.

"That's incredible," she said. "You are like them."

"I don't think so."

"You don't know what you are." She had shifted her disgust for Carmine and Pierre onto me, the man she thought she might have loved.

"Of course they're wrong," I said. "But I need a place to live. What will I do?"

"Live with me."

"I don't think so." I was repeating myself. I was failing. She saw me as a charlatan.

"You're afraid of love."

"No. No."

She smiled, but it was not a happy smile. We were sitting side by side in a café that looked out over the Seine. Tourists passed by, and there was the rattle of many languages. Artists sold little watercolours on the *pont*. Images of characters sitting over an espresso in a café, romance, ecstasy, lovers holding hands. I had arrived.

She continued her theme and whispered fiercely, "You don't love me."

"But I do."

"You don't love Bernadette. Or Rosalyn. You love only yourself."

"Why Rosalyn? What does she have to do with us? Is this a test?"

She closed her wide mouth and turned away. I stroked her ear. She pushed my hand aside. A gypsy appeared at our side and offered roses. I purchased a single red rose and laid it on the table before Aniane. Her anger had delighted me. This was truth.

She regarded the rose. Picked it up and smelled it. Softer now. She had tears in her eyes that she wiped with the back of her wrist. "You'll go home. Back to your ranch, your freedom, your mountains and horses. You'll forget me."

"I'll never forget."

"You see? You are already gone."

"Come with me." Ah, foolishness. Impulse and chivalry and silly proclamations.

"Do you mean that? You know I can't bear it, the trickery."

"No tricks," I said. I kissed her temple. Her hair was dirty.

"Do they have nursery schools for girls like Bernadette where you live? For her age?"

"Absolutely. Any age. We are rich. Milk and honey."

"I sometimes think of this."

"You do." I did not ask about the father, what he would say about Bernadette disappearing. We were working out a fantasy, one that Carmine had warned me about. This left me longing for what I would be leaving behind.

My mother wrote once a month. I had been waiting for a response to my confession of atheism, but she never addressed it, silence being a fine critic. In one of her letters, she advised me of the world I had left. She spoke of the spring rains, and she said that the river was rising and some flooding was expected. She said that Bev and Dorothy, Lord willing, were planning a wedding for the summer and that perhaps I might be back home at that time.

I remember the day you were born, Arthur. And how later I left you in the hospital. It broke my heart. I prayed to God to take care of you and if he did so I promised him that you would be good and strong and create something in the world. Make something good. You would be a giver, not a taker. There is too much selfishness. Mrs. Ernie Unger, our neighbour? She up and leaves Ernie for this young man who sells vehicles at the Ford dealership. Who wears yellow suits. Seersucker. And fancy shoes from Italy. Never trust a man in handmade Italian shoes. She leaves four children under six. What for? Because she needs to find herself. Well, good luck to her. Oh, the number of times I could have left your father to find myself. But I didn't. People don't. Are you eating?

AND THEN ISOBEL WROTE TO SAY THAT SHE WOULD BE coming to Paris within the week. She was travelling and in previous letters she had said that she was in London, and then Amsterdam, and then Mannheim. And now she was coming to Paris. I prepared for her arrival. I washed my windows, cleaned the cupboards, swept, and hung my laundry out in the sun. I warned Carmine that my cousin Isobel would be visiting, and she asked immediately if I needed a cot for her, an extra bed. Out of modesty, I agreed. And so, one day, I found that a small cot had been placed in my reading room, next to my bookshelf. Clean sheets, a white blanket, two pillows. Isobel would be allowed to stay with me because she was my cousin, and what, indeed, can cousins get up to?

I met her at the airport the day she arrived. She was robust and vigorous and we talked non-stop during the Metro ride. I felt immediately the kinship of my people. My tongue was loosed. My heart was open. I told her about Christian and Carmine and Pierre. I said that I was in love with Carmine. "You'll see. She's elegant and graceful. We eat cheese and baguette together in the evenings when her husband is travelling."

She wanted to know where I hung out, who my friends were.

I had not mentioned Aniane in any of my letters and so I spoke of her now. "Ah, Arthur," she said. "A French lover."

"She has a girl who's three. Name's Bernadette."

"You motherfucker."

"She wants to meet you. She might be jealous." I had told Aniane that I would be busy for a time with my double cousin. She pouted and clung to me and then let me go.

"She *should* be jealous," Isobel said, and she kissed me, on the cheek. She tousled my hair and said my name, "Arthur," and then, "How do you taste?" and she kissed me on the mouth. "Same old," she said. Her flinty eyes gleamed.

For some reason I felt anxious.

We had hugged at the airport, and as we did so it was as if we had always been together. Our bodies fit. She wore old jeans and cowboy boots. A tank top and no bra. Her forearms were like mine, ropy. She walked with a swagger. She didn't care about the pretensions of Parisians. She spoke English and expected them to figure out what she was saying.

She had spent the last year in Missoula, going to college there and living near her birth mother, whom she had found after months of searching. "She lives in a dingy house in a dingy neighbourhood. Doesn't really work, but she gets by. She has a man who shows up once in a blue moon for favours. She puts up with this. Funny thing, she wasn't exactly happy to see me. First thing she asked was did I have any money."

There was a sister, a year younger, who treated Isobel poorly. "She couldn't figure out why I would show up after so many years. She said I was lucky to have another family."

She told this tale too forcefully, with a detached cold sadness, and it left me with a feeling of gloom.

We were to switch trains at Châtelet–Les Halles, but we decided to take in the city and so we walked the streets for a time. It was spring, the air was fine, the smell of food, the taste of beer in a *brasserie*, Marlboros, her hands fidgeting across the suit jacket I had worn, brushing my shoulders, playing with my ears.

"You're nervous, Arthur," she said. We were sitting shoulder to shoulder. Her backpack lay at our feet.

"It's very strange being here with you. We've never been together in public."

"Then it's about time, my dear little boy."

She held my hand. She said that she planned to stay two weeks, if that was okay, and then take a bus down to Rome and then Athens and fly over to Cairo. "Come with me," she said.

I thought of Aniane and what she would make of me just up and running away. She'd hinted at it, though, that I was that kind of fellow. I didn't want to be that kind of fellow.

"I've got responsibilities here. Christian, Carmine, Aniane."

"So, you're going to marry this girl? You have a contract?"

"No contract. But she likes me."

"That's something, isn't it? And it goes both ways?"

"I don't know." I felt sick saying this. Three hours with Isobel and I was already making plans, betraying Aniane. "I've got quite the set-up here. An apartment, a job, time to read." I said that I was translating Flaubert's letters from French to English. "When he was working on *Madame Bovary* there were days when he wrote only three words. One week he wrote half a page."

"Flaubert wants you to feel sorry for him. Poor fat man sits at his desk and writes five words and then crosses them out. Don't be derivative."

Isobel didn't understand my love for the older French writers. Still, I was thrilled to finally be talking to someone about literature. I'd missed it. I said, "Aniane doesn't read. I mean, she can read, but she chooses not to read."

"Lots of people choose not to read. That's okay. If everybody read, Arthur, you wouldn't feel special." She fetched her backpack and dug for a book. She handed it to me. "I stole it from this guy on the plane. He was sitting beside me reading and I pretended to sleep, even laid my head on his shoulder, which he didn't mind. He was an older man. Fifty maybe. I have no idea really, but he was older, and he seemed to like this strange girl using his shoulder. Anyway, I pretended to sleep but I made my eyes into slits." Here she narrowed her eyes to show me. "And I read along with him. Got trapped by the story, which is amazing by the way. Just before we landed in London he went to the bathroom, and I took the book and put it in my purse. He never noticed. We parted ways. I thanked him for his shoulder. He said that it was his pleasure. So, I gave him pleasure and he gave me a book. I finished it at Heathrow. It's yours now."

It was *Goodbye, Columbus*. I had never heard of it.

"Try it," she said. "It will remind you of you. Only he's Jewish."

It was wonderful to hear English. To speak it. Not to have to parse every word, rearrange my thoughts, strain and decipher, miss out. My views over the last months had been jumbled and simple. Because I was working in French, I had not had the chance to practise deeper reasoning, wordplay, thinking, thinking about my thinking. My head was full again, my heart warm.

THAT NIGHT ISOBEL IGNORED THE LITTLE COT IN THE reading room and climbed into bed with me.

"You're naked," I said.

"I've taken off my clothes—how can I put them on again?"

She shivered and I held her and breathed warm air onto the top of her head and then on each of her shoulders. She fell asleep quickly. I read her stolen book all in one go by the light of my small lamp. When I finished I lay there for a long time thinking about Neil and Brenda, the characters in the novella by this Roth fellow, who had impressed me deeply. A story of class and longing. When I finally turned out the lamp, Isobel raised her head, said my name, kissed me on the mouth, and then turned away and fell asleep again. My hand lay on her left hip. She had showered earlier and then, very much at home, walked around my apartment in her underwear and a shirt of mine. For a long time I couldn't sleep. The smell of soap in her hair. The shadows of her shoulder blades, the back of her neck.

When I woke, she was lying on her left side, facing me, her eyes wide open. She spoke first.

"Hi."

"Hey."

She said my name and touched my mouth. "You gotta hard-on. I peeked."

"Always do in the morning."

"My mother, not Aunt Beth but my real mother, is large. Big head with little eyes. It was weird. I didn't know her."

"Why should you?"

"I looked at her and I wanted to leave. Run. And then I felt guilty."

"I read *Goodbye, Columbus.*"

"And?"

"It made me jealous."

"How's that?"

"I don't know how he does it. It's such a simple story, isn't it."

"The shame isn't simple."

"I know. I got that. It's what I feel sometimes with Carmine, that her existence is high above me and there might be ladders here and there that would allow me to reach her, but I can't climb those ladders."

"Just because she's sophisticated doesn't mean she's better."

"But she is. I feel so small." This was the crux of my existence, and explaining it now to Isobel, putting words to feelings I had had over the last months, helped me understand my desolation. But there was pride too. "It's not all despair. I flap about, sometimes full of longing and panic, other times certain that I am strong and interesting. I don't want to just act."

We were lying on our sides, facing each other. "Are we going to have sex?" I asked.

"No," she said.

And for some reason this made me happy. All this striving and getting had exhausted me. I was grateful to Isobel, who was so certain and sure of herself. The need to be loved and spoiled and indulged was like a great wound within me, and now here was this girl who had wrapped a bandage around my wound. I told her this.

"Oh, I have had practise wrapping wounds," she said, and she kissed my chest.

She was tender. "You're pale and thin and diminished. This is not you. If you want to be true to yourself, Arthur, if you want to tell a true story, it is not the story of a young artist who comes to Paris and finds a lover and visits the haunts of famous dead writers. That is trite. Your story is back home. Those are your facts."

I said that they were uninteresting facts. "I'm a different person at home."

"Better, maybe."

"I don't think so."

"You're a very moral boy." She laughed and drew the blanket over her chest.

I agreed. Especially when it came to books. I said that I had promised myself that I would not sit in judgment of a book or a writer until I had come to understand what the writer was attempting. I sat up in bed then, as if the force of my thoughts had elevated my physical self. "And I've discovered this. That many writers don't approach their subjects with the necessary seriousness. They don't respect their characters. They refuse to take on the large questions of life and death, of love and hate, and the biggest question of all, Why am I on this earth? What is my purpose?"

WE SPENT THAT DAY, SUNDAY, IN MY APARTMENT, reading, eating, sleeping, and talking. I made my way out into the streets to look for food and returned with a block of cheese and some bread and a few pastries. We dripped coffee into a pale porcelain pot and we cut the bread and on it we spread butter and raspberry jam spooned from a jar that Isobel struggled to open.

"Here," she said, "tighter than a bull's ass in fly time." She handed it to me. Contentedly vulgar, she still used the expressions of her upbringing. I sprung the lid from the jar and handed it back to her. She spooned large amounts onto her bread and pushed the food into her mouth. She sat cross-legged on my bed and said, "How beautiful you are, my darling, how beautiful."

I loved her.

In the evening, we dressed in proper clothes and I knocked at the Godbout door in order to introduce Isobel to Carmine and Christian. Pierre was travelling. Little Christian opened, softly shy, and I said, "This is my cousin Isobel. This is Christian."

He dutifully kissed her and she was obviously pleased. What a sweet boy. Carmine appeared, wearing a plaid outfit and brown shoes. She welcomed Isobel. "Enchanted," she said.

I reflected on that word and wondered if this were indeed possible.

We sat in the drawing room and talked banalities while Christian served us coffee with little squares of sugar and small spoons laid out on the saucers. He was fascinated by Isobel, I could see, and I recalled my childhood and my fascination for all things female. He studied her bare legs, her bright orange sleeveless dress, her feathered earrings, her gold sandals. He practised his halting English. "Your eyes are blue," he said to Isobel.

In the morning I went to my French class while Isobel slept. I returned home to find the bed unmade, Isobel's clothes strewn about, and the apartment empty. I taught Christian that afternoon, but my heart was not in it. I kept listening for Isobel to return. The reading room window was open and Isobel would have had to pass directly beneath it, but I did not hear her, and so I became restless and cut the lesson short. I made pasta and sauce for supper. A salad of tomato and onion and cucumber. I ate at 10 p.m., alone, in the quiet of my room, looking out through my window to the lights at the Godbout house.

Isobel returned late, around midnight. She climbed into bed beside me. She smelled of alcohol and smoke. She was very excited. She had met a group of men and women her age, and they'd shared drinks and then gone dancing.

"What an amazing city," she said. "I got completely lost coming home. I was going in the opposite direction and had to ask everyone for help. Great people. One man took me over to the other side of the tracks and rode with me back into the city. He played harmonica. Made up a French song for me and played it right there, on the train. God, I could live here. One of the girls I met, her name is Bérénice. She is sophisticated and beautiful. You will love her."

"I didn't know where you were."

"I'm sorry."

"I made pasta for us."

"Aww, Arthur. How was I to know? You didn't have to."

"I wanted to."

She was quiet. "Tomorrow. I'll meet you after class and we'll go out for lunch. You can show me your favourite places."

"I don't have favourite places. You probably have more favourite places after one day than I do after ten months."

"You're upset."

"I'm not. How old was the harmonica player?"

She laughed. "You're jealous. Oh, sweet Arthur." She kissed my shoulder, then leaned across me and kissed the other. Her bare chest was pressed against my bare chest. "Sweet Arthur," she said again.

About Isobel. She had four sisters, there were no brothers, and she was the eldest, the one upon whom the family's dreams had been set. She was adopted before it was finally divined that Aunt Beth might in fact be able to have children, and so she became both the special child and the outside child.

Aunt Beth was rigorous and demanding. She expected her girls to be all things. They would rope and ride and wrangle and brand and break horses and nurse calves and rise before the sun and pitch hay and even with all that they would roll out pastry and can pickles and wash floors and wring laundry and sew the dresses that they wore every Sunday, matching dresses that were godawful revolting. Sometimes purple with printed flowers, sometimes virginal white, always with long hems to hide the knees from the view of the lascivious. Jeans were allowed when they roped and wrangled. Line the five girls up and they were a muscular gang, all of them big-boned, save for Isobel, whose genes, though they came from a large woman, had somehow produced a lean and ravenous girl who, from the back, looked like a boy. As she grew older, she insisted on wearing her hair short. The other sisters had long blond hair plaited in braids, all matching. Like a clutch of Paraguayan Mennonite *femmes fatales*.

Aunt Beth, fanatical about her daughters' weight, kept Tupperware containers in the fridge, and each container had a girl's name on it, *Sue Ann, Faith, Alison, Amy, Isobel*, and in each container there were pounds of butter, and these bricks of butter represented the number of pounds that each girl must lose in order to reach her ideal weight. Poor Sue Ann, whose container brimmed with nine pounds of butter. Amy's fluctuated between three and five. And so on. Isobel's container was empty. She was a rake. The other girls mocked her. She had no tits. She had the legs of a foal. Her hips were too narrow, she could never bear children. She was uglier than a cow's rear. Not true, of course. They wanted her to think it true.

And so, thinking she might be homely, she went out of her way to prove it both true and false. She became hard and intemperate, and she acquired an attitude that was forthright and strong. She took up boxing and fought the boys in her weight class because there were no girls to fight. She wasn't particularly powerful, but she was quick and her footwork was excellent. She was the finest skipper her trainer had ever seen. She also took up rodeo and rode the broncos, and one summer, in Cheyenne, Wyoming, she won first place in her age group. After that, she quit.

That was the last summer as a boy that I saw her naked, only because it was the last time she made the trip up to

Alberta with her family. We had lain one fine morning with our heads resting on our saddles, talking to the blue sky, still clothed, and then with a yell she stood and stripped and ran down into the water. To see her body flashing and twirling in the sunlight—for she did twirl several times before arriving at the river's edge so as to give me a complete survey—was a fearful thing. I pulled off my clothes more slowly and walked down towards the river in my underwear.

"Come on, Arthur," she yelled. "Strip. Let me see you. Nothing new."

I pulled my underwear off and walked down to the water's edge with my hands in front of my crotch. She'd seen me before, up close, but for some reason the distance, her perspective from down in the river, shed a different light on my self. She, on the other hand, seemed to feel no embarrassment. One time, out riding, she had stopped and climbed down off her horse and, while I watched, dropped her jeans and underwear and squatted beside the horse and peed into a gopher hole. She had grinned up at me. "You like that," she said.

"You're weird," I said.

"Uh-huh."

It came to me at one point that if I was jealous at all, it wasn't of her sexuality, but of the big buckets of bravery she carried around with her, her great desire for experience, and her ability to just go out and grab at the world. I, on the other hand, was simply an observer. Poor me. How can greatness come from standing on the sideline? And so, I admired Isobel's vision for herself, though she would have denied any deliberate vision. She simply lived.

The following evening she was to meet her new friends at a café in the Sixth. I tagged along. And this is where I met Bérénice, the girl Isobel said I would love. She spoke English. She had gone to college in America and had travelled through the States, her favourite place being the plains. "All that space," she said, and she stretched out her arms. She was full of grand gestures, her arms constantly moving, her hands describing her ideas as she spoke, and she spoke very well. She was the woman I had been looking for in Paris, refined, educated, beautiful, cultured, and now here she was, sitting beside me in a café on Boulevard Saint-Germaine.

Oysters were ordered and I approached them with trepidation, attempting to hide the fact that the texture alone was despicable. Bérénice squeezed lemon over each of her oysters and slid them into her mouth just so, talking, laughing, drinking, her pretty mouth both a portal and a fount. Her forearms were soft with down and she wore numerous rings, and if she had been married I wouldn't have known. But of course she wasn't married. French girls did not marry at such a young age. So taken was I with her that I went home that evening with no ability to remember her physically. I had some vague recollection of her face and the manner in which her hair fell across it, and I of course recalled the rings, and the fine hair on her arms, but beyond that I could not even remember what she was wearing. A dress, I believe, and sandals.

She accommodated me, this is what I recall from that first evening together. She remembered my name, and she turned to me occasionally and looked into my eyes, but no more than she looked into the eyes of Isobel, who sat across from her. Her voice was quite low. This pleased me. She knew everything. We spoke in English. She talked of Ionesco and Brecht and Genet and Beethoven and Brando all at the same time, as if there were a certain space reserved in heaven for a select few. She turned to me and asked if I had seen *Last Tango* and of course I hadn't. I didn't know what she was referring to. The contemporary world held no interest for me. I may even have said this.

Isobel, who overheard, interrupted and said, "Oh, he's an old soul."

We laughed. I saw that my ignorance was a defect. I had always played with people when it came to knowledge. I begged off and claimed that I preferred the full glass of the nineteenth century and that if you poured today's ideas into a glass, it would be half full. Or something like that. It was an image I'd heard from Max, the pimp, and I realized, sitting beside Bérénice, that some notions are half-baked, and this might be one of them. I laughed at myself and said that of course my biggest problem was that I only respected dead writers and yet I myself was not yet dead. I hadn't even written anything of worth. It was all a contradiction, I knew that.

I wanted desperately to engage Bérénice, to impress her. She was studying art history at the Sorbonne. About art, I knew nothing, though I did describe my grade three teacher and her insistence that we study Alexandre Cabanel.

Yes, she said, Cabanel, and she said that it was wonderful to have had such a teacher at such a young age. "In the country," she said.

I didn't understand. "I'm sorry?"

"You grew up on a farm. Isn't that how you say it? 'In the country.'"

"Yes, we do. And I did. But I've left home."

This was so obvious, and such a true fact, that she didn't understand.

"Left home. What do you mean?"

"Well, I am here."

"You won't go back?"

"No, I won't." This was shocking to me. I had never realized the truth of my exodus, and only now, sitting next to Bérénice, did I feel the elation of my decision.

My admission was shocking to Bérénice as well. She said that she could not fathom the idea of leaving home. "Paris will always be my home. I might leave for a time, for a trip perhaps, or to study, but inevitably I return."

And then someone said her name and she was torn away from the intimacy we had created. It was Tom. He was seated to her right and all evening he had been clamouring for her attention, and of course they knew each other, had met when she lived in the States, and so they were close, perhaps even lovers, I did not know, and neither did I care, for I saw that Tom had nothing on me. He was pretty and he spoke well, but his ideas were flat, and this made his soul flat, and so he was boring.

We left the bar and went dancing. I had never gone dancing before, except to the dance that took place on Dewey's ranch, celebrating Bev's return from the war, and that night the bluegrass band had played and everyone danced outside in the darkness, or near the bonfire, but for me it was the darkness and Alice Dewey's proximity that allowed me to move my feet. Now, here I was, in the din of a club in Paris, and as it was with all things in my life, I determined to learn by imitation. I danced beside Isobel and watched her carefully. I moved my feet as she moved hers and my elbows went out slightly, though at some point I became self-conscious and lost my confidence and simply began to shuffle.

She touched my arm and pulled my head down towards her mouth and shouted, "Stop thinking."

I saw Bérénice nearby, moving towards Tom and then moving away, and then touching his elbow and drawing him near. I turned away from her. I discovered that I was looser when I was unaware of others around me, or when I imitated strangers.

There is a madness that grips the one who has been suppressed and then, all in one moment, has been set free. This was me on the dance floor. I became mad. Wild. I trailed after a tall black man whose moves beguiled me. I rolled my shoulders, bent forward, slid my feet, discovered the beat of the music in my stomach. This was life.

For two hours I danced, throwing myself here and there, and when I finally came to rest on a stool near Isobel, she wiped at my brow and said, "Crazy hick."

I kissed her on the mouth.

Bérénice appeared and held Isobel's arm. She was leaving. I would never see her again. Tom was waiting impatiently at the door. I said that I planned to visit the Louvre, I was interested in the Italian masters, and would she join me. I said that she could teach me a thing or two. I said that line exactly, *a thing or two*, and as soon as I said it I cringed. But she seemed not to notice.

She shrugged coolly and said that it was possible but not tomorrow. In three days. Saturday. Perhaps we would meet at 2 p.m., near the entrance.

And I said, "Yes, yes, yes."

She turned to Isobel and kissed her and waved at me and she left.

On the train, riding back to the suburbs, Isobel fell asleep with her head on my shoulder.

MAN WITH A GLOVE, BY TITIAN, SHOWS A YOUNG MAN of about eighteen casually leaning on a block of marble. His face is wan, his hands are detailed and fine. His eyes are dark and full of sensitivity and self-confidence. He is possibly an aristocrat from Venice. The world is his to have.

Andrea Solari's *Madonna with the Green Cushion* is an image of Mary lowering her breast into baby Jesus' mouth. She holds the breast for him as he reaches up to suckle. A rich blend of colour. The love between child and mother. They gaze into each other's eyes. All is tender and well.

In preparation for my appointment with Bérénice I had visited the Louvre two days running and had headed straight for the section that held the Italian masters. I spoke to the museum guards who were very knowledgeable, and this offered me the opportunity to understand the source of certain paintings and the methods used and the history of specific artists. On Saturday, when we met outside in the sunshine, Bérénice's radiance bowled me over. Her certainty, the manner in which she walked, the clothes she wore, which were quite plain but well thought out. Her top was sleeveless and she had casually flung a sweater over her shoulders. Her hair was both organized and in disarray.

She went up on tiptoes and kissed me on both cheeks. She smelled of lilacs. I knew the scent from my youth when the lilac shrub outside our kitchen window blossomed briefly in early June. Every afternoon, during that time of flowering, my mother would cut blossoms from the shrub with her kitchen scissors and place them in a sealer jar full of water on the dining room table, so that when we ate later in the evening, the smell of lilac would overwhelm the smell of chicken or farmer sausage or the slices of roast that lay on our plates. And here again was the lilac.

She said that the day was formidable, the sun, the breeze, the optimism, and she didn't have the desire to go into a building and stand around and get sore legs and talk shop. Was that okay? Why not walk outside, find a park, take a coffee in a café? She would show me Paris.

I agreed. My slight and anxious knowledge would have to wait for another time and another place to be displayed. I was disappointed. I had wanted her to *talk shop*, to educate me, to make me a better person. I may in fact have said this to her, but more subtly.

"Oh, there will be lots of time for that," she said, and my heart was happy, for she was implying that we would see each other again and again. Or was it simply an expression that she used?

We walked and we talked. She was eloquent and clear-minded. She was like one of those people who, because she at first does not want to reveal much about herself, asks a barrage of questions. About my past, where I was from, and why I was in Paris. About Isobel, whom I appeared to love.

"I've only known her a short time, but I can see that she is special."

I said that I did love her, but she was my cousin, though she was adopted. She eyed me sneakily and said that in the ways of love there were times when taboos went flying away. Here her hands flew into the air like the taboos she had just set free. I said that we were summer cousins and that we had seen each other every August for many years. We rode horses together, shot at tin cans with a slingshot, that sort of thing. She did not know the word *slingshot*, and when I explained she said that this was *wild*, and she said it in English of course and it sounded forced and wrong, as if she were trying out a colloquialism that she had learned during her year in America. And then it slipped out that she might have a man in Montpellier who was older and who was an *avocat* and who wanted to marry her. She gave me the goods on marriage. It was a form of prison where husband and wife consumed each other. There was no freedom. I agreed, one must be free.

At a sidewalk café we ate various cheeses that were superior to those on the cheese plate I had eaten one night in Montmartre when my loneliness plagued me. We drank wine, a rosé, and I admired the manner in which she held her glass as she lifted it to her lips. So delicate. We took the Metro late in the afternoon to her *arrondissement* and she brought me to her house where she lived with her father. Her mother was dead. She had died alone two years earlier at the summer home near Lake Geneva. This is what she said, and I wondered if she had misspoken, the expression was so strange. To die *alone*. Then she moved on to something else and though I wanted to, I did not ask about the mother or the manner of her death. She said that her father was quite protective, and it was he in the end who wanted her to consider the *avocat* from Montpellier. *Avocat* was the only

French word in her sentence, and I offered her the English word, *lawyer*, and she said that she knew this was the word. She seemed put off by my correction.

Her house was the house I had dreamed of. It was in fact an apartment on the main floor situated on a small side street in Montparnasse, and upon entering one was confronted by an enormous bookshelf that ran floor to ceiling. In the sitting room there was a small original study by Picasso. There was a dog of a singular breed, pure white, panting for water. *As the hart panteth after the waterbrooks.* She took care of the dog, crouching to play with its ears, and a slip of her flesh was revealed between her shirt and her jeans as she stooped forward. I looked away.

We read. She sat in a chair and I on a couch, and she read a book on Dutch art while I picked my way through a page of Stendhal in French. It was glorious. My mind drifted and I imagined that I was like Meno's uneducated slave boy, who proved the Pythagorean theorem merely by answering Socrates' questions. Bérénice would be my Socrates. It was as if truth and knowledge already existed in my mind, and because Bérénice and I would see each other more and more and because we would converse at an intimate level and because we would have a relationship, I would become awake to ideas that I never knew I had.

I was aware of her hand turning the pages. I snuck looks and saw how her pink tongue touched her upper lip as she concentrated. She also had a habit of pushing out her jaw, indicating determination, or perhaps it was just a habit she had picked up from her childhood.

She closed her book and said that she was meeting some friends. "Thank you for the afternoon. It was lovely."

When we said goodbye I shook her hand. She smiled and kissed my cheeks.

I was happy to leave, for I could now fantasize and dream and walk, leaning forward like a boxer on the balls of my feet. She would be mine. She would inhabit me, she would appear to know my thoughts even though she didn't truly, but I would behave as if she were inside me, as if she were a witness to my actions and my desires and even my ignorance. Her eyes (I recall that they were like the dark chocolate that one sees through the window of a *chocolatier*) saw into my soul, and if I wanted her to appreciate what she saw, I would have to improve myself. I did not want her to find there a disappointed life, a life of regret, ignorance, naiveté, silliness, shame, poverty of the soul, weakness, lustiness, vulgarity. And so I walked about the city, and all the while she occupied my thoughts. *What would Bérénice think? What would Bérénice say? What would she do? Would she posit a thought? An exclamation? Would she revolt?* My eyes were her eyes. When I saw something extraordinary, such as the six-year-old boy juggling in the tunnel of the Metro with a baby sleeping on a rag at his feet, I wanted her to witness this. And we might discuss how this was possible here in Paris and not where I came from. And we would agree that just as a dumb animal can neither sink too low nor rise too high, so a place like Tomorrow is mediocre and is not the place for extreme brilliance nor abject paucity of the mind.

I HAD NOT SEEN ANIANE FOR SEVERAL WEEKS AND I suffered guilt, and I dropped by the café one day with Isobel. Aniane saw us come in but ignored us for a time. She finally walked over and stood by the table and looked down at me, and then over at Isobel. She was suffering an onset of acne, which happened to her sometimes, especially when she was anxious. I had never seen it so pronounced. Her face was very red.

"This is Isobel, my cousin," I said.

Isobel reached out a hand to shake and Aniane touched it lightly and then asked if Isobel's visit was happy.

"Are you enjoying yourself?" I translated.

"Oh, yes, absolutely," Isobel said.

"She doesn't speak French," Aniane said.

I shook my head.

"I'm sorry," Aniane said. "About my face."

I said that it was fine.

She shrugged. "I'm visiting Rosalyn tonight." This was a statement of fact. I wasn't sure what she wanted. She said, "You're taking care of your cousin."

I said that I was.

She nodded. "Well, perhaps in two weeks my face will be better and you will like me again."

"If you want me to come with you tonight, I will."

"No. No. Please. She's very beautiful, your cousin. Her face is clean. You will help her find adventure."

"My god," I said. "She's my cousin."

Throughout this conversation Isobel was regarding us with a bemused expression.

"She's upset," Isobel announced.

I shook my head.

"I think so," Isobel said. "Tell her not to worry about me."

"What do you mean?"

"Don't worry about me. You should take care of her. It's a bit of a pickle for you. I'm sorry. She's very sweet."

"How do you know if she's sweet? You can't understand her. All you have is the visual image. She sometimes suffers these outbreaks of acne. Like now. She's got a great heart. She visits a girl with cerebral palsy every week. Her ex-husband's sister."

I turned to Aniane and said that Isobel was leaving Paris in several days and then I would have more time.

She nodded.

"And Bernadette?" I asked. "How is she?"

"She is the same." She said that my eyes were contented. "You are happy."

This was a fact and she was acknowledging that fact. She had never expected much, which is why she was able to recognize my happiness and accept it. I saw it as a flaw, her dumb approval of my grasping.

When we said goodbye, she shook Isobel's hand and then she drew me close and put one arm around my neck and whispered in my ear, "See you again, Arthur."

My breathing in the last while had become shallow and difficult and any form of exertion left me weak, so that walking down the street I had to sit on a bench or lean against a wall and gather both my breath and my thoughts. Melancholy was all around me, and inside me, though I didn't recognize it inside me. The world in general was a confusing place, and it became even more confusing during Isobel's last full day in Paris, when I went with her to the American Express office. She wanted to phone her mother to announce her travel plans. She sat in a small booth and waited for the call to go through. After a long while the connection was made. I sat on a chair and watched her talk and push her hair back from her face with her free hand. It was with pleasure and regret that I watched the movement of her hand and her mouth. At one point, she turned to me with a certain look, a glance of concern, and then she turned away. When we arrived she had suggested that I might want to call my family as well, but I said that talking to my mother frightened me.

When Isobel finally hung up and came to where I was waiting, she told me that my brother Bev was back in the hospital. He'd gone on a shooting spree in downtown Tomorrow. "No one was hurt," she said. "But he frightened a lot of people."

It turned out that Bev had driven into town early morning, stationed himself in a sniper position alongside his pickup, and proceeded to shoot the tires of passing vehicles. And then he shot out the street lights. And the windows of various businesses. The only thing that had saved him from being shot by the police was Dorothy, who had talked to him, and approached and taken the rifle from his hands.

"You should call home," Isobel said.

"Why?"

"So they know that you know."

"Your mother will tell them."

"That's just shitty," she said.

"Shitty is all I have."

"Poor Bev," she said, and she walked outside.

I caught up to her on the sidewalk and kept pace, though she was half running, trying to escape me.

"I don't get you, Arthur," she said.

"I don't get myself," I said. Then I said that she didn't know everything about me, or my brother.

"Course I don't, because you won't tell me. What are you afraid of?"

I had no answer.

Finally, she slowed down.

I told her what she had looked like as she spoke on the phone, and what pleasure I had found in observing her hand touch the side of her face, and her hair, and how beautiful she was, and I said that whenever I was with someone else,

Aniane, or Bérénice, I compared them to her, Isobel, and they came up short. Did she know that? And before she could answer I began to speak again, and I said I was like the honeybee that gorges itself on the sweet flowers in spring, this one, no that one, and there, over there, let us try that one. Fat and sated, unable to find his way back to the hive. Be aware of the existence of a flower. It might not be there when you set out to find it again.

She shook her head. "You're obfuscating, Arthur. I ask you to tell me about your brother, and you speak of honeybees."

"I'm talking to you," I said. "I can't just give you the straight goods in a straight line. Life's not like that."

"It is. It can be. And if you weren't so in love with words you would see that you can't ever speak the truth."

"What's the truth?"

"You see? You should know that."

"Well, I just told you that I love you."

She stopped and faced me. We were on a busy street. Cars honked and sped past. Walkers pushed up against us. Everything we heard around us was in another language, not our language, and this made me feel lost.

"Did you?"

"I think so."

"You think so." She grinned.

We found a sidewalk café and drank white wine from glasses with thin stems. We spoke no more of love, perhaps because it was too frightening and might loose some wild animal that we might never catch again. It was as if a heavy door in a castle made of stone had opened a crack and allowed us a view of the bucolic world beyond our prison, and though we smelled and saw the green world out there, we did not sally forth. Instead we stepped back.

And she spoke again of my brother. "It's so sad," she said.

"My mother will be going crazy about now," I said.

"I wonder if Bev ever feels it coming, if he knows what's happening."

"He's always been volatile. Even before Vietnam."

"Why do you hate him?"

"I don't."

"My mom told me once that your mom was always the rebel in the family. Everyone thought she'd run off somewhere to some strange place and marry an artist, or be an artist."

"My mom?"

"Yeah."

"Never heard that before."

"Maybe you don't know her."

"I wrote and told her I was an atheist. She never said a word about it."

"Why would you tell her that?"

"She should know the truth."

"Bullshit." Isobel grabbed my jaw and looked me in the eyes. "Not everything's just about you, Arthur."

. . . .

WE HAD MADE PLANS TO GO TO A DINNER PARTY THAT night at Bérénice's house, but Isobel suggested that as it was her last night in Paris we should go out just the two of us. "That group tires me out," she said. She touched my jaw and said, "I worry for you, Arthur. Bérénice is worldly and she has flair and she's rich and you're attracted to her mystery, but she's got other plans."

Still, I convinced her to go, and was immediately sorry. The evening, so brimming with possibility, turned into a conflagration of revelations, ideas, and argument that left me reeling and depressed. There were seven of us at the table, Isobel and I, Bérénice and her father, and her father's girlfriend, who was a young woman close to Bérénice's age, Bérénice's fiancé, Alain, the *avocat* from Montpellier, who was suave and angular and well-heeled, and Tom, the American, looking as forlorn as I felt.

Upon our arrival Bérénice introduced Alain. "This is my fiancé," she said, and of course all my dreams tumbled down around my head.

Isobel was aware of my melancholy and she stayed by my side and during the meal held my hand under the table, much like she had years earlier at our family lunch after we had lain naked down by the river. Only this time I was not comforted. I drank too much and became garrulous and difficult, especially with Bérénice's father, who was in fact quite polite and asked me questions about my home in Canada and about ranching and livestock and my family. And then someone, perhaps Alain, or perhaps the father, spoke disparagingly of America, and a discussion ensued that encompassed American imperialism and the student riots of '68 and Marx and the rights of the individual and Vietnam. The discussion began in English, but as often happens when passions take over, the speaker reverted to his mother tongue. Also, Bérénice's father's girlfriend did not speak English, and so a lot of what was said, most of what stung me and cut at me, was said in French. Isobel was lost, and I was half-lost.

I said, for no good reason other than to provoke and to deliberately lower myself in their estimation, that my brother had fought with the Americans in Vietnam. Alain said that it was bizarre that my brother would volunteer to fight. He said this in English. A quick translation ensued for the father's girlfriend, who had long thin arms holding many bracelets that banged and clattered.

Tom, the American friend of Bérénice, agreed. He had been sitting quietly, watching and waiting, and when I mentioned my brother, he sat up suddenly as if bitten. He said, "Wow." And then he said it again. "Wow."

"Well," I said. "It was his choice."

Bérénice turned to Tom and asked him if was true that he too had been drafted.

Tom said that he had, but his name had been far down on the list, and then Nixon began to withdraw the troops and so he was saved. And then he came to Paris.

"Lucky you," I said.

Tom stared at me. And then he called me a fucking cliché. A writer who wasn't a writer who ended up in Paris wanting to write. "You're a joke," he said. This was said quickly, in English and in a low tone that only Isobel and I understood.

"That's true," I said. And I shared a smile with everyone at the table.

"Well, I believe that Arthur's brother was brave," Bérénice said. She looked upset, and I thought then that she had probably just realized that she had chosen the wrong man to marry, or perhaps she understood what Tom had said and therefore felt sorry for me.

"It's a moral equation," her father said. "Does one follow the dictates of the government or the stirring of the conscience?" He said this in French and I understood it because I had recently translated a letter from Flaubert to Colet in which Flaubert had written, *Your letters stir me to my entrails.* I translated for Isobel, and I may have used the word *entrails* as well, for effect, for power, to make everything more visceral, but I also used the word *conscience*, because it was important and because the father had used it. Also, I wanted Tom to see that though I might be a joke, I had at least learned a little of the language of the country.

Isobel's face reddened and she set her spoon down beside her bowl of bouillabaisse and said that conscience didn't flow just one way, like a river going downstream. She said that my brother might have a supremely stirred conscience.

"It is possible," said the father. He was attracted to Isobel.

Bérénice wondered what required greater bravery, to say yes, or to say no.

"No, evidently," said Alain.

"No to what?" Bérénice asked. "To the state? To oneself? Let us be clear."

Alain said Americans were bullies, that was clear.

Tom took umbrage. "We have to do all the dirty work in the world," he said.

"That's ridiculous," said the father. And this was when he descended into a long speech in his own language about these specious arguments, and language such as *dirty work*, and how the Americans liked to make a mess, like a person who shits on the linoleum and then scoops it up and looks around as if to say, *I am doing everyone else's dirty work.* "It's disgusting," he said.

Bérénice translated for Isobel and me and Tom. I was quiet and disquieted, and I was feeling nauseous. Isobel was upset. And when she is upset her hands gesticulate and she speaks quickly. She did that now. She said that a man like my brother would have no interest in sitting in a beautiful parlour surrounded by books and paintings, talking about ideas and criticizing others and passing judgment.

"There is belief and there is action, and Bev, Arthur's brother, even though he wasn't drafted, chose to act." She said that my brother had suffered, and that he had courage, the courage of his beliefs. She said that he had commitment. When she was finished speaking she reached into her canvas satchel and pulled out her cigarettes and lit one.

"Commitment to a foolish endeavour, perhaps," said Alain.

Bérénice's father clapped his hands slowly and said to Isobel, "*Bravo.*" He leaned into the ear of his girlfriend and whispered a translation. She nodded and made a small moue with her mouth. The father looked at me and said that he was sorry about my brother.

I said nothing.

Bérénice said, "Is it true? He suffered?"

Isobel said, "Of course it's true. He still does."

"I'm sorry, Arthur," Bérénice said. "I did not know."

I was aware of her pity, and of how she might now see me as more "interesting," and for this I had my brother to thank. But as it was, my brother was far from me and he knew little about me and we didn't speak, and so I didn't know much about him, other than the simple fact that Dorothy was now taking care of him, and that Dorothy had once been mine, and in the latest nasty bit of news, my brother had imagined that car tires and shop windows were the Viet Cong. My head ached. My mouth was dry. I drank some water.

And then, as if the discussion had been a game, and the ideas academic, we moved on to other topics, mostly trite and inconsequential. I saw that money and education will give you many things, many pleasures and conveniences, and it may even give you a longer life, but that does not mean that you will not live a disappointed life. In the metaphysical sense. But most folks don't care about the metaphysical.

We ate a lamb dish with rosemary, and then we had the

richest confection of thin layers of puff pastry and a filling of jam and cream, a true *mille-feuille*, and the conversation turned, and we drank fine wine, and we were regaled with stories from the father's youth, and we finished off with coffee and a liqueur, all very civilized, and by the time we departed it was late.

On the Metro, riding back to our apartment, Isobel held my hand and whispered that she was sorry. I did not ask her what there was to be sorry about, but I too felt sorry. For myself, for her, for Bérénice's father's girlfriend, who was in the end a beautiful dolt who could not see what was in store for her, and especially for Bérénice, who would be marrying a bourgeois cow. The blindness of greed. The seeking of status. The collecting of objects. A miserable state of affairs.

And then the train stopped. This had never happened before in my travels. We sat in the silence. The only other person in our car rose and walked through to the next carriage. We were alone. The lights of nearby apartment buildings lit up the sky. We were halfway between Paris and Rueil–Malmaison. The lights went out in the carriage, came back on, and then went out again and stayed out.

"Are we in danger?" Isobel asked.

"They'd tell us if we were," I said.

As we sat in the darkness I told Isobel the story of when I was six and how my family took a train through the Rockies to the West Coast. It was Christmas and there were deep banks of snow and millions of trees bearing more snow. The train stopped for the longest time on the track high up near Roger's

Pass because the snow was too deep to proceed. All the passengers gathered at the windows and spoke in whispers. I said that there was something communal and comforting about trains.

She was holding my hand. She leaned her head on my shoulder. I kissed the top of her head. I said that I wanted to tell her something but I was afraid. She began to speak. I said, "Don't talk, please." And then I told her the story of Jed Armstrong's death. She of course had heard the story in one form, but I gave her the facts. I said that my brother had frightened me that night, and he had been drunk, and that I had taken the blame for the accident. I said, "A number of months after the funeral I went to work for Sally Armstrong, the widow. I helped her out. I got to know her kids. And all along Sally believed I was the one who was driving. I was looking for something, atonement maybe, and she gave it to me. Only it was Bev she should have given it to. I was a chicken shit. Yeah, so, that's what I wanted to tell you."

When I stopped talking Isobel was still holding my hand. In the shadows I was aware of her facing me, and of the outline of her jaw, but I couldn't see her eyes.

She hugged me and then withdrew and held my face between her hands. Then she said, "Does your mother know what really happened? Your father?"

"They know what I told them. That I was driving. I always hoped my mother might figure it out, but she didn't."

"Maybe she didn't want to know. Poor you. Making things so complicated."

I said nothing.

Then she said, "Poor Bev."

"You think so?"

"Yeah, I think so."

"Him going crazy?"

"Yeah."

"You think I should go home. To see them?"

"Maybe. It's just sad. Everything."

I WENT TO THE AIRPORT WITH ISOBEL THE FOLLOW-
ing morning and she held my hand the whole way. The night
before she had lain beside me in bed and read to me. *For one
human being to love another: that is perhaps the most difficult of all
our tasks, the ultimate, the last test and proof, the work for which
all other work is but preparation. Love is at first not anything that
means merging, giving over, and uniting with another—it is a high
inducement to the individual to ripen, to become something in himself,
to become world, to become world in himself for another's sake, it is a
great exacting claim upon him, something that chooses him and calls
him to vast things.* This from Rilke. And then she said, "I don't
know very much about love."

I did not speak. I was happy to have her near. To smell her,
to hear her voice. We were both naked. She put the book aside
and leaned in and kissed me. She lingered there. I held the
back of her head. It was our best kiss ever, full of wonder and
exclamation and softness. And then we made love and she was

very different from the girl down by the river where the horses watered, and I was a different boy, as if we had stripped away all that willed effort and now were flowing into one another. She gathered herself up and flung herself at me and I threw myself back at her with tenderness and abandonment and it was one the happiest moments of my life.

After, when she had fallen asleep, her head resting on my shoulder, I looked again at what she had read to me and I wondered how it was possible for a writer to be both so sentimental and so profound. I knew then that I loved Isobel, "my" human being, as much as I loved words and stories and books.

At the airport Isobel hugged me a long time and I held her and then we said goodbye.

Later, on the train, looking out the window at the passing tenements, my happiness surprised me. I still did not know all of my feelings, or where they came from.

That morning I went to class and then I returned home to teach Christian. Lately, I had been telling him stories from the Old Testament, Joseph and his cruel brothers, Samson and Delilah, David and Goliath, stories I had grown up with, but that he had never heard before. A secular education has its limits. Perhaps he loved the moral quality of the stories, or perhaps this is what I loved. One cannot be sure. In any case, he usually begged for a story, and so I offered what I had, always in English. His vocabulary had improved and he was beginning to acquire subtlety and nuance, difficult when learning a new language.

In the evening, Carmine addressed me officially. She said because Christian would be attending school both in the morning and the afternoon come September, I, Arthur, would no longer be needed as a tutor, and therefore my time as a teacher would end in August, and yes, thanks to me Christian's English had been ameliorated, and moreover if I was willing to pay rent for my apartment I could stay on of course, and as a reward for my hard work the family would love for me to join them on holiday in Bretagne, at the family summer house in Saint-Malo, because Christian wanted me to come, I was welcome, Arthur.

All of this was said in French and it fell onto my ears much in the manner I have written it. The personal pronoun was *vous*, because she was addressing me directly and formally. The words came quickly, like water flowing down rapids where rocks are hidden beneath the surface. And yet, the sentiments were so sincere and my dismissal from my job so easily done, and perhaps because I was so delighted to understand every word Carmine said, and pleased as well to be standing face to face with her, once again aware of her mouth and my name in her mouth and her brown shoes and brown skirt, that I nodded as she spoke and when she had finished I said, "Yes, I will come."

"Marvellous." She touched my forearm, with its muscles and veins, and though a year of lassitude and reading and study had slightly diminished the definition in my arms, she didn't seem to notice.

Only later did I realize that everything was changing in my life. Isobel was gone, and within a month I would no longer have a job, or the means to pay for my apartment. I had no plans for my future. My life.

I WAS TO SEE ANIANE THE FOLLOWING EVENING. SHE was wary of me. I had told her about Bérénice and Bérénice's family and that I had fallen for the whole package, in a romantic way, like a fantasy, and then the fantasy had tumbled away. I had said that Bérénice was getting married to an arrogant man. I would not be invited to dinners there anymore because they thought I supported the war in Vietnam, and I was once again a foreigner from a province in Canada who had little purchase in French society. Aniane had laughed at me. Of course, I told the story of Bérénice as if the whole matter were a joke, but I was hiding the truth, and I so wanted to be truthful in some real way.

I arrived early, with a strong plan that I would not be duplicitous. I would tell her the facts. I was not in love with her. I had to find myself before I could possess another. But what was this notion of possession anyway, the idea that we can own someone as we might own a car or a house or a horse or a watch? She exited the café and saw me, and even as she kissed me once, twice, I began to speak and I explained myself. I spoke of possession and love and my own failure to find both. I said that I had failed to be faithful. I could not. I had affairs to settle. I was in love with Isobel. I made a face. I was painfully obvious. I blathered. I begged. I retreated.

Aniane stepped forward and held my arm. "What are you saying?"

Was I not clear? I searched through my limited vocabulary to find the words to tell her that I no longer loved her. This was not true, because standing there in the dark, beneath a dim light, I realized that I still did love her, and how could this happen? And of course I had always found it difficult to say something in the negative in French. And then add to that the word *longer*, as in *I no longer love you*, and it became even more difficult. *Non plus*. That was the phrase. *I you love no longer.* I said this. She said that she understood. She had known this for some time.

When she said this I was amazed and I loved her again. She knew me better than I knew myself. I began to speak English then, a genuine torrent, and I said that I had to go home to see my family once again, to acknowledge them, and then to leave once more. I said that there were times when I wished that I did not have a family, because then I would be free, but of course I wouldn't be truly free because there was still me, wasn't there?

When I finished speaking I realized that I was quite emotional and that my hands were at my sides, helpless things, and she was reaching for me and holding me and saying, "Poor Arthur, my poor Arthur." She might have slapped me and called me a cheat and a liar, but instead we stood in the rain, and she kissed my cheeks and wiped the rain from my eyes and she whispered and consoled me. Not because she had understood my words, but because she had witnessed my confusion.

"I was correct?" she said. Her face was rueful, but her eyes were clear. "We have different tastes."

"No, not necessarily."

"Yes. Evidently." She touched my arm. "You will be all right?" she asked. "You will find your way home?"

"Yes."

"Goodbye, then."

"Is that all?"

"Nothing more," she said, and she turned and walked away.

Her back to me, the sound of her shoes on the sidewalk, the smell of the Parisian air, her words, *nothing more*, all of this truly affected me.

In a long letter that Isobel sent me from Rome, where she was reading ancient philosophers, for she liked to read the writers of the country she was visiting, she told me that she missed me in a big way, though this was not a bad thing. *There is something delicious about longing for you, Arthur. To know that you miss me as well and that we will see each other again.* She said that regarding what I had told her about the accident and my brother, it was important to understand myself first and foremost. *You have no control over other people's actions. This is where we get into trouble. No matter what you say, or what you feel, or what you say you feel, or what you believe, or what you say you believe,* you are only what you do. *As simple as that. And I can see, my dear Arthur, that you are doing well.*

I RETURNED TO CANADA AND FELL BACK INTO MY LIFE there. I slept in my childhood room and covered my bed each morning with the green chenille bedspread that had existed since my birth. Nothing had changed. We drank coffee from the same chipped ceramic cups, the supper plates were still plain and white, and though the switch on the old kettle had broken, my father had fixed it with a twist tie. The physicality, the sameness, depressed me.

I rose early that first morning and found my father drinking coffee alone. My mother was still sleeping. We sat together then and talked. I told him a little of France and my time there. He said that he was proud of me.

"I never could understand that language," he said. "Beyond me." He spooned sugar into his coffee and stirred and then laid the spoon neatly on the paper towel near his elbow.

When my mother got up we ate scrambled eggs and toast and drank more coffee.

My mother gossiped. She said that Stella Armstrong was engaged to be married to Dale Fairfield, a rich rancher twenty years older with grown children. "I saw her at the Co-op the other day. She was glowing."

I felt a twinge of jealousy. "Good for her," I said.

My mother continued. "And Chester Dewey has cancer. He's not supposed to last till Christmas. The ranch is up for sale."

"What'll you do?" I asked.

"Get an apartment in town," my mother said. "Dad was offered work at the feedlot."

I looked at my father, who couldn't have been pleased with such a prospect, but he didn't register it.

I saw then, that once they moved from this house, my old life would pass away.

MY FATHER AND I RODE FENCE ONE MORNING. Normally my father would have taken the quad, but he suggested we ride. He saddled his palomino, I took my mother's blue roan mare. It was like the old days, only this time I was not tied to my father's belly, nor was I peeking out from the cracks of his coat, feeling the movement of his chest. The sky was vast and clear and blue. The smell of autumn blew in off the mountains. A red-tailed hawk sat a regal post, watched us approach, and then departed, dusting the grass with its wings.

Six miles on, at the border of the Granger stead, my father dismounted and took a wire stretcher from his saddlebag and spliced the top strand of broken fence. I sat the horse as he worked. His hands were gloved and quick. He worked without speaking. He might have been blind and still done the perfect splice. His hatted head was bowed and I saw the years of weather on his neck.

An hour later we stopped to water the horses at the bank of the Little Bow. I dismounted and went down on one knee and scooped the cool water to my mouth. I rose and wiped my hand on my jeans. We were near the place where Isobel and I had first lain naked together. The water flowed over the rocks and moved south and then east into Travers Reservoir and on to the Oldman River near Picture Butte and then into the Bow and the North Saskatchewan and finally into Hudson Bay. The stones at my feet.

I mounted again and we rode the river for a time and then turned west. My father asked me what my plans were.

I said that I didn't know. I might go to university in the fall.

"That's a good idea," he said.

"Don't count on it, though."

He said nothing. We rode on, side by side.

Then he said, "Bev's having a hard time. And your mother, she's a bit helpless. We all are."

I said that it was good Bev had Dorothy.

"She's a saint," he said. Then he said that Bev had always been a mean cuss. From the day he was born. "He was hard on you."

This surprised me. I hadn't known that my father saw such things.

He continued. "Guess you know by now that you're not your brother's keeper."

When he said this, he was looking straight ahead and his face registered no emotion, and so I couldn't make meaning of what he was saying, though there was certainly some meaning there.

Sometimes, in the afternoons, I took the pickup and drove through the countryside. The foothills and the snow-covered Rockies. Each person I passed waved at me. These were good people, so different from those in Paris, where I was ignored. I saw Sammy on the street. She was driving a pickup, her round face a star now slightly darkened. All seen in a glimpse, and then gone. My pickup broke down one afternoon on Highway 23. I rolled it to the shoulder and looked under the hood, fiddling with the spark plugs, checking for what I could not discover. I flagged down an old rancher who drove me back to Tomorrow. He knew who I was, who my brother was, and my parents as well.

I RODE UP WITH DOROTHY TO SEE BEV AT THE ALBERTA Hospital in Edmonton. Dorothy said that Bev was on heavy drugs and he didn't speak much and he might not recognize me. Physically, she was the same girl I'd left almost a year earlier, straight backed with long hair and a full face that was clean and healthy. I felt great affection for her, as well as pity.

I said, "You've got a lot on your plate."

She said that she could handle it. "I chose him," she said. "And he chose me."

"You wouldn't choose differently now? Knowing what you know?" I asked.

"Never in a million years."

That was Dorothy.

Upon entering the building I was reminded of Aniane and our visits with Rosalyn. A similar smell, the closed doors, the little locked windows, the stale air. Bev was sitting in a chair in his room, staring out the window. He was wearing a hospital gown and the first thing Dorothy did was strip him down and lead him to the shower and, after he'd bathed, dress him in clean underwear, jeans, a dress shirt, socks, and shoes. I helped her help him and I was deeply aware, as Bev stood naked before us, of the vulnerability of each of us at that moment. But Dorothy seemed oblivious. She talked as she worked.

"Arthur's here, Bev. He's back from France."

Bev mumbled something. I touched his shoulder and squeezed. He looked at me until I looked away.

"If I had my druthers," Dorothy said, "I'd steal him from this place and throw out all his pills and I'd drive him into the bush and live with him there and love him back to health. But they'd arrest me for that. So I make do with coming here twice a week and cleaning him up and dressing him and shaving him and talking. He likes that. Don't you, Bev?" She ran a hand through his hair and bent to kiss him. His eyes closed, and remained closed after she had kissed him. "He likes physical contact. Back rubs, foot rubs. Sex would be good, but I don't think he's up for it, and there's no privacy."

I didn't remember Dorothy being so free, especially about sex, and I wondered if I had missed something in our brief relationship.

We sat around for several hours, talking to each other and trying to talk to Bev, who fell asleep and later woke with a start. He was suddenly clear.

I played a game of checkers with him, and one time, after a careful move, he said, "How was France?"

"Very French," I said.

He said, "In Vietnam the French planted trees lining the roads. And they shipped in bread and built wide streets. In a strange place everyone wants to be reminded of home."

"I found nothing in Paris that resembled Alberta," I said. I wanted the conversation to be natural. I wanted not to care if Bev talked or didn't talk.

"I'm a little bonkers," he said. "She tell you?"

"She said a bit. Didn't say bonkers, though."

"Doctor says I can't help it. So he gives me pills. And the pills are slowly killing me. It's a fuckup."

"Don't," Dorothy whispered, and she took his hand and held it between her two hands, much like she used to with me.

When we finally left, it was late. Dorothy kissed Bev on the mouth and said we'd be back in the morning.

"You spending the night?" He looked at me.

"I guess we are."

"Stay away from her," he said. "She's a sweetheart."

"She is," I said.

We took a room at a hotel near the hospital. It had one bed and Dorothy said she had no problem sharing it, but I said that I'd make do with the armchair.

"That's ridiculous, Arthur. I trust you."

At supper earlier she had introduced the subject of girls. She said that when I was settled down she knew a girl I should meet, a girl who even liked books and had a big brain. She was attractive too, a real classic beauty, not too tall, not too short, with great wit.

"I'm doing fine," I said.

"You have a French girlfriend?"

"I don't."

"They're very sophisticated, I hear. And free."

"I don't know about that."

She was happy to be talking, and even happier to be away from the hospital. It had to be a burden.

I woke in the middle of the night with a sore back. In the darkness I heard Dorothy breathing. I reached over and snapped on a small lamp. The light fell across one of her bare legs that had slipped from under the covers. I loved being near her as she slept. I felt protected and warm. I reached out and covered her bare leg with the blanket.

Then, I read for a bit from a western. They still interested me. And I wanted to see if Mr. McMurtry got it right.

THE FOLLOWING WEEK I TOOK THE FAMILY PICKUP and drove up to Lethbridge and I sat an afternoon in a lawyer's anteroom, waiting for an appointment I had never made. The receptionist lifted her head at one point and finally said, "He will see you now." She stood and opened the oak-panelled door and I stepped into the lawyer's office.

His name was Mr. Lazarus and he was a man older than my own father. He sat in his chair as if he might just as easily have been sitting a horse. He wore jeans and a dark blue shirt tucked in all neat.

He rose and stepped around the desk and shook my hand and offered me a chair. I sat. He reclaimed his own chair on his side of the desk and said, "What can I do for you?" I said my name and I said the name of my brother and I explained that a year and a half ago my brother had been driving a car that hit and killed a Mr. Jed Armstrong from Tomorrow, Alberta. I said that people didn't know the whole truth. I said, "I told the police that I was driving the car. But I wasn't. It was my brother who was driving."

He nodded slowly. He crossed his legs carefully and watched me all the while. "Why now?" he asked. "Why are you revealing this?"

"Because I have to. I believe I did something wrong when I told that lie. That I betrayed my brother."

"Your brother knows about this, of course. That you're here."

"No, he doesn't." I said that I hadn't talked to my brother about it. "We've never really talked about it. He's in a mental hospital in Edmonton right now. He's unpredictable. He fought in Vietnam." I'm not sure why I said this, but perhaps I thought it might lend some credence to our taciturn ways, or to my brother's unpredictability, or to my own decision.

The lawyer picked up a pencil and held it in his fingers like a cigarette. I wondered if he was a smoker. He said then that he'd been in France during the war, with the infantry. "The countryside," he said. He shook his head and I had no idea what his thoughts were about the countryside, good or bad. I imagined that it must be bad, because it had been the war and his headshake was full of portent and meaning. Then he tilted his head inquisitively. "So, your predicament. Obviously your brother knew he was driving. Did anyone else know? Besides the two of you?"

"My father was talking the other day like he knew something. My mother's wilfully blind." I held my hands in front of my eyes, covering them up, as if words were not enough. I felt foolish as soon as I did this and pulled my hands away quickly. "So, just the two of us."

"Why would he let you take the blame?"

"I don't know. He'd been drinking. He was afraid. He kept talking about all that blood. And he was shaking. I don't think he knew what he was doing."

He was thoughtful. "You're still trying to help him."

"Am I?"

"It seems so. You want me to say that you should let it go. That your brother has suffered enough. That you're a good boy."

"Do I?"

"You're trying to be good. I admire that. The fact is, it

was an unfortunate accident and you claimed responsibility. It might not hold to redo what has already been done. I take it that the widow, Mrs. Armstrong, doesn't know about this."

"No, she doesn't. Well, she knows about me. I worked for her last year, on her ranch."

He lifted his eyebrows at this, but he didn't speak.

I said, "She thinks that I killed her husband."

"Those are strong words."

"They're true words."

"And she's forgiven you."

"Yes."

"That's a difficult and generous thing."

"I know."

"It seems you've got your wires crossed here, son. You're asking for forgiveness where it isn't due. Have you ever forgiven your brother?"

"For what?"

"For not speaking up. For not being a strong big brother."

I didn't say anything.

He sat up. Laid his pencil on the desk. He said, "As someone who has seen his share of cruelty and grief and behaviour that is selfish and wanton, I have to say that your situation is surprising. I don't usually get folks coming in here discussing morality. Mostly the other way around. My advice is to swallow your pride, for that is what it is, and face yourself and the choice you made, and let the widow get on with her life, and let your brother live the best life he can. Should you agree, after you walk out this door the conversation we just had will never be heard by anyone else. It will remain between you and me. That's my advice."

"You can do that?"

He said, "Were you raised on the Bible?"

"I was."

"You might know that story where Jesus talks to the prostitute like a real person and then says *go and sin no more*?"

"I do."

"That's pretty good advice."

I stood, hesitant. "What do I owe you?"

"Nothing."

We shook hands.

I went out through the vestibule and down the hall and out the door into the sunshine. It was late afternoon. I was sure hungry, and so I found myself a small restaurant and ordered a lunch of hamburger steak with fried mushrooms and gravy poured over top and french fries on the side. I washed everything down with a cold glass of milk. When I was done eating I realized that my heart was calm. That's about all you can ask for.

BEFORE I LEFT FRANCE, I HAD GONE WITH THE Godbout family to their summer place in Saint-Malo. On the train, riding towards the coast, I sat beside Christian and decided to read him a story. He loved this. I had found, over that last while, that Christian was an open vessel into which I could pour words. Even when the stories were poorly constructed, or when they were sentimental, or when they ended in a false way, he sucked up narrative with a surprising willingness.

I plucked the book from my bag. It was a slight volume, quite old, in English, with yellowed pages and the finest smell of "old book" that one could wish for. I opened the book in the middle and held it up to my nose. I breathed in. I asked him to do the same.

"What do you smell?" I asked.

He thought. "And you?" he asked.

"*Cannelle*. A little hint of dried leaves. Some foreign spice like black cardamom. Prairie grass. It reminds me of my childhood and the books I used to get from Mrs. Emery, the town librarian. The books were old and musty, but some smelled approachable." I said all of this slowly, seeking out words that he would understand, and he did understand, though I had to explain *musty* and *approachable*.

Christian nodded. He took the book once again and smelled. "Paper," he said.

This was a game we had played before, and each time it produced the same unimaginative answer from him. *Paper*.

I opened the book and asked if he was ready.

"Yes."

"The tale is called *The Most Valuable Thing*," I said. "'Once upon a time there was a mother who had three children,

Odette, Tristan, and Anatole. The mother, who ran a small inn, was guided by independence and by her own poverty, which was extreme, and this being so, when her children reached the age of seventeen, she sent them out into the world to seek the most valuable thing. When they had found this thing, they were to return home to their mother with this treasure. The children of course wanted to know what the most valuable thing was, what they would be looking for, but the mother simply said, 'You will know it when you find it.' The eldest, Odette, who was the only daughter, arrived at her seventeenth birthday, said goodbye to her mother and her brothers, and departed. Odette sailed by boat to a faraway land where she lived with a tribe of nomads who spent their entire life at sea. They were born on the ocean, they lived there, and they died there. The people of the tribe taught Odette to dive and hunt for fish and pearls and sea cucumbers, and to stay under water for sometimes up to five minutes, wearing only a loincloth and wielding a spear.

"'Her skin became dark like her people, and she grew strong and proud and beautiful. There was a young man named Subai, and it was with Subai that she spent much of her time. One day, diving with Subai, she uncovered the perfect pearl. She rose from the sea clutching the pearl, the water flowing from her hair. She thought that *this* might be the most valuable thing. And even though she thought of her mother, and the advice given that once she had found the most valuable thing she should return home, she did not go home. She fell in love with Subai, had children with him, grew old with him, and never saw her mother or brothers again.

"'Tristan, the middle child, was a fighter. He was quick and strong and muscular and he went to the king of the land and said that he wanted to be a soldier. He believed that war and the courage required in war would allow him to discover the most valuable thing. He trained. He fought. He was brilliant with every weapon imaginable. But he was most brilliant with his feet. He was a fast runner. He was known throughout the land as being the fastest. Even his enemies were fearful of his speed. He could chase down horses and slaughter the enemy in the saddle. His feet were like weapons. And then one day he was captured by the enemy and his feet were put in chains. His hands were free to do as they pleased. The captors were wily and understood the nature of their prisoner and the nature of freedom. They placed beside him a saw with a very sharp blade, and it was understood that if Tristan wanted to be free, he would have to cut off his own feet. For a year he was kept a prisoner and then one night, in despair, he picked up the saw and cut off his feet at the ankles. He was free. He crawled away from his prison. He managed to make his way home, where his mother gathered him up in her arms and nursed him back to health. Of course, it is a fact that the body is not just a collection of separate parts, and it was as if the loss of his feet affected Tristan's mind, for he slowly and methodically went mad from despair.

"'The youngest boy, Anatole, was not interested in pearls or grand exploits. He had heard of a woman, a queen in a far-away country, who had a vast library, and in that library there existed one book that could provide everlasting life. Now, no one had ever found this book. Many had died trying. They had grown old and wasted away. So it was that on the day that Anatole turned seventeen, he kissed his mother goodbye and set out. On a cold winter day he arrived at the queen's library. He was given free access to all the books, of which there were thousands. Anatole stayed for a year, seeking out the one book that might give him eternal life. During this time the queen died and was replaced by a striking daughter who would wander along the parapet above the library shelves and watch Anatole at work. She was quite taken with him. He, though, never had occasion to look up and see the young queen watching. If he had, he would certainly have fallen in love. He had set himself a goal of a year to find this one book, and knowing this, he began to steal certain books from the library and place them in a wooden trunk in his room. Finally, one night when everyone was sleeping, believing that he had that special book in his trunk, he took a horse from the young queen's stable and set out through the mountains to return home. The young queen, learning of his betrayal, sent out a posse to retrieve the books and the horse. About the young man called Anatole, she no longer cared. Anatole climbed high into the mountain pass and one night a storm descended, which lasted for four days. He huddled against the snow and wind. At some point he broke apart the trunk and used it to build a fire. That night the horse disappeared. When the wood from the trunk was all used up he began to burn the books. He fed the fire slowly, one book at a time. And then he ran out, save for one book, which he would not burn. He was found by the posse later that day, dead, holding the one book.

"'The soldiers buried Anatole on the mountain trail, piling rocks on his frozen body so that wolves and wild animals would not eat him. They returned to the queen and gave her the single recovered book. In it was a story, written by Anatole. It was a story of swashbuckling and adventure and romance, things that Anatole had never experienced. The young queen read the story and wept. She had numerous copies written out by her scribes, and she distributed these copies to her people and declared that everyone far and near should read the story. And so it was done. And Anatole became famous.

"'It so happened that a traveller from the young queen's land travelled to the town where the mother lived. He took a room at the inn. In his pack he carried the book that had made Anatole famous. One night after supper, the traveller pulled out the book and began to read to the mother and to Tristan. When the story was finished the mother wondered at the story and the adventure and darkness and marvel therein. And though she did not know that it was her son who had written the story, she understood that it was a valuable thing.'"

I stopped. This was the end. Christian's head lay on my shoulder. I looked down at him to see if he was sleeping. He wasn't. The story was a bit sentimental and corny, but he didn't seem to mind.

He said, "It's probably good that he didn't burn that book."

"Probably."

"If he had burned it, he might have lived a little longer. But maybe not long enough." He looked up at me. "Nobody lives forever." There again with that secular education. Then he said, "The mother must have been sad."

"Oh, yes."

"Odette was the happiest."

"Why do you say that?"

"She found love."

CARMINE SAID THAT CHRISTIAN ADORED ME AND would be very disappointed to see me leave. We were sitting by the pool on the terrace of her mother's villa, which sat high on a cliff in Saint-Malo, and our point of view gave onto the beach far below. We hovered in the rich air like gods. Christian played in the pool and called out for us to watch his various antics. We obeyed. Pierre had driven into town with the car to buy shellfish and so, once again, we were alone.

Carmine was wearing a pale yellow two-piece. I had noticed when she joined me, carrying two glasses of white wine, one for me, one for her, that she had faint marks across her stomach, and my heart leaped when I saw them, how vulnerable they made her seem. Her beauty, in the light of the ocean and the sun, was more pronounced. Her skin glowed, the humidity made her hair fuller and less manageable, so that now when she attempted to pull it up into her typical chignon, more strands fell loose, and there existed the possibility of chaos.

She had overheard my story on the train. She apologized for listening, but the words had just dripped into her ears. The story had been wonderful. She wanted to know who wrote it. I said it was by some obscure writer whose name I did not know. I had read it in my youth, when I was in traction, after my accident. I pointed at my scar.

"Yes, I see," she said. And she looked away.

I wanted her to touch the scar, because then, of course, I would fall into an epileptic fit and she would pity me. Instead, of all things, we talked about Stendhal. She said that she had studied *The Red and the Black* in school, and even then, as a young girl, she had not believed that a boy like Julien, from the provinces and ignorant and naive and much too young, would become the lover of Madame de Rênal.

"*Impossible*," she said in French, and I heard again the everlasting hope in that single word, the negation as a form of optimism. The forceful *no* that really means *yes*. I wanted to tell Carmine that I adored her and that I would miss her horribly. Instead I said Christian had been an excellent student. He was a fine boy.

"Do you think so? I worry about him. He has few friends. I fear that I have protected him too much. This is what Pierre says. I wanted another child, but Pierre said only one. A sister or brother for Christian would have made him braver."

"A brother can be scary. I have a brother."

"He shot your horse." She had great recall for what might have been a passing glance.

"That's the one."

"You are lonely since Isobel left."

It surprised me that she should notice what I had not. But then, this is what sensitive souls are capable of. She called me *delicate*. She said it in French and it is the same word in English, but there are various meanings, and I wasn't sure if she meant that I was weak, or that I was full of sensuous delight, or that I was modest and perceptive to propriety, or that I was full of feeling, or that I was soft and tender, or that I needed protection. Or perhaps she meant all of those things.

She said, "Sometimes you don't know what you want."

This too surprised me. It was the echo of that long-ago statement made by Renée: *It is important to know what you want.* The slight clack of *ce que*.

Carmine said, "When you know that, then you will know what others want. Otherwise, we run around trying to please." She said that I was falsely modest, and that I had a habit of making light of myself in order to make the listener feel sorry for me, but in the end the result was confusion, because what I was saying was not in fact true. It was a deception. "If you are proud of yourself, be proud. If you believe something, say it. Don't be false."

Christian appeared between us, all wet, shivering slightly, begging for a towel. Carmine rose and wrapped a white towel around his pale body. She placed him on a chair beside me and told him to wear his hat. "The sun is powerful," she said. She fetched him a glass of ice water and a whitish plate on which she had placed a slim piece of dark chocolate. She set these things before him as if he were a prince.

Christian asked if I could swim the length of the pool under water.

I studied the pool. It was not very big. "Four lengths," I said.

He laughed and said, "*Impossible.*" There again with that word.

"Certainly," I said, and I rose from my chair, walked to the deeper end of the pool, took a deep breath, and dove in. At some point, midway through my fourth length, Carmine and Christian stood at the edge of the pool. My eyes were open, I saw the dark lines on the bottom of the pool, and I saw the copper drain, and glancing sideways I saw Carmine and Christian clapping and cheering. They were two shimmering souls floating above me. Christian was jumping up and down. Carmine was crouched slightly, her legs bent, her hands clasped, and then unclasped, and then fluttering at her sides. The yellow strips of her bathing suit. Her mouth was opening and closing. She was talking. She was telling me that she adored me. That all would be fine.

I rose from the water, my arms raised in triumph. I leaped from the pool. I picked up Christian and hugged him, spraying water over his small white shoulders and his narrow face. He laughed and called out my name. I released him and took Carmine in my arms and hugged her and said that I loved her.

"I love you too, Arthur," she said.

She was a practical woman.

At dinner that night, a meal of octopus and scallops and crab salad and potatoes with rosemary, Christian described for his father my feat of swimming. His face was bright. His hands clamoured.

"And then Arthur leaped from the pool and he lifted me up and got me wet and then he hugged *maman* and said that he loved her." What joy.

Pierre raised his eyebrows and looked at me, and he said that everyone loved Carmine. "I sometimes think that she is so beautiful that I must lock her up, or she will be stolen. Not so?" And he winked at his son and smiled at me.

Carmine smiled as well, softly. Her eyes were pale green that evening, and shining. She was dressed in a gauzy top and matching gauzy trousers that were wide and flowing and hid her body.

It was my last night with the family. I would be leaving by train the following morning.

After dinner Pierre and I took a cigar down by the pool while Carmine put Christian to bed. We sat side by side, looking out over the edge of the patio that gave onto the abyss that was the cliff that held the chalet. Or citadel. Or castle. We smoked Maria Mancini cigars, of the type that Hans Castorp is so passionate about in *The Magic Mountain*, a novel I had read immediately after finishing *Death in Venice*. Pierre cut his cigar and lit it with great flair. I imitated him. He leaned back in his chair and extolled the virtues of the Maria Mancini. He called it dazzling. He talked of its flavour, *a medium mixture, quite spicy but light on the tongue*. He said that I should take notice of the second half, when my lips might burn, and when I might perceive a slightly sour and tangy flavour, with hints of nut. The ash was more grey than white, *she likes you to leave her ash long*, and to smoke it took about one hour, but it always proved to be a worthwhile hour. This is an approximation of what he said. In the dusk by the pool, sitting side by side, I could not see his mouth and so I may have missed some of the vocabulary and replaced his words with my own, words very much like those used by Thomas Mann, and so his murmurings have become mine, bent and borrowed from that fine book.

Pierre asked if I was pleased with my experience in France. I said that I was.

"You learned something about love?" He looked straight ahead as he spoke.

The verb *to learn* in French is very close to the verb *to take*, and my ear missed the prefix and so I became confused when Pierre asked the question. I thought at first that he had asked me if I had taken something of love. I asked him what he wanted to say.

"Well, you came here for life, for experience, not so? Did you find it?"

Ah. I said that I had found it. Certainly.

"So you are happy."

I agreed. I was happy.

In a letter to his mother Flaubert said that a writer *can depict wine, love, women and glory on the condition that you're not a drunkard, a lover, a husband or a private in the ranks. If you participate actively in life, you don't see it clearly: you suffer from it too much or enjoy it too much. The artist, to my way of thinking, is a monstrosity, something outside of nature.*

Pierre would have had none of that. He was too full with the here and now, with his Mancini cigar, fine food, and the women he visited in Africa. He had told me once, believing that he and I were cut from the same cloth, that the young women of Botswana were gorgeous and willing. This admission had floored me. I could not comprehend betraying Carmine. And so I had pretended to not understand, or perhaps Christian interrupted our conversation, or maybe I smiled and nodded and therefore entered into a terrible form of collusion that distressed me.

Pierre said now, "For every place one visits there are rules to live by, and I suppose that you are just learning the rules of France."

I said yes, though I did not know what that *yes* meant.

He asked what the rules were where I came from. Were they understandable?

I did not know the answer to his question, truly, and I did not have to respond, for Carmine appeared, holding a bottle of Calvados and three glasses. She placed the glasses and bottle on a small table and pulled up a chair and sat.

"May I join you?" she asked. This was her formality, for she had already joined us.

I admired her bare feet, and wondered if she lived in wilful ignorance.

We drank. For a long time no one spoke. Far below us came the sound of a car honking, and then it was quiet again.

"This is beautiful," I said.

"Always," Carmine said. She took Pierre's free hand and held it. "Christian was very happy tonight. He couldn't stop talking about you."

"I'll miss him."

"We will miss you. Won't we, Pierre?"

He agreed.

What I did not understand was that farewells are said, pledges are made to keep in touch, and then these fine people disappear from your life, never to be found again. Such is the manner of the world.

At that moment, though, the stars shone above us. My heart was full. To be an individual was of the essence. To make one's way, to shape and form oneself in a unique manner, to strive but to appear to not be striving too wilfully, to find one's ideas in the bedrock of civilization, to stand on the shoulders of great thinkers and then alter the thinking slightly so that one can shape a singular and novel greatness, to live forever, to love and be loved, to rise and then fall and then rise again.

I might have said all of this or none of this. Or parts of it. It would have been a jumble of two languages. I was talking, they were talking. Our conversation was elevated, that is certain.

Carmine asked about Isobel, who was dear to my heart, she could see that. I didn't disagree. Isobel was sowing her wild oats, and then she would come back and find me. I had my own oats to sow, here and there, and then to harvest. Before the silver cord was broken and the golden bowl was crushed, and so on and so forth. Not to be too grand. I was convinced that the world had room for me.

Acknowledgments

I would like to acknowledge the following works quoted in this novel:

Page 23: John Milton, *Paradise Lost*, 1.200–203.

Page 69: Gustave Flaubert, *Madame Bovary*, trans. Lydia Davis (New York: Viking, 2010).

Page 75: Gustave Flaubert, *La dernière heure*, my translation (Paris: Arvensa Editions, 2014).

Page 91: Rollo May, *Love and Will* (New York: W.W. Norton & Co., 1969).

Page 91: Stendhal, *The Red and the Black*, trans. Burton Raffel (New York: Modern Library, 2004).

Page 142: Søren Kierkegaard, quoted in Walter Lowrie, *A Short Life of Kierkegaard* (Princeton: Princeton University Press, 2013).

Page 156: Charles Baudelaire, *The Painter of Modern Life and Other Essays*, trans. Jonathan Mayne (London: Phaidon Press, 1995).

Pages 161–2: Wilder Penfield and Phanor Perot, "The Brain's Record of Auditory and Sensory Experience," *Brain* 86 (1963), 595–696. Originally presented as a lecture by Penfield at the University of McGill, Montreal.

Pages 163–4 and 165: Thomas Mann, *Death in Venice*, trans. H. T. Lowe-Porter (New York: Knopf, 1930).

Page 176: Gustave Flaubert, *The Letters of Gustave Flaubert*, trans. Francis Steegmuller (London: Picador, 2001).

Page 238: Gustave Flaubert, *The Letters of Gustave Flaubert*.

Page 243: Rainer Maria Rilke, *Letters to a Young Poet*, trans. M. D. Herter Norton (New York: W. W. Norton, 1993).

Page 270: Thomas Mann, *The Magic Mountain*, trans. John E. Woods (New York: Knopf, 1995).

Page 271: Gustave Flaubert, *The Letters of Gustave Flaubert*.